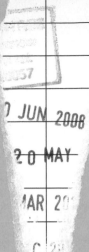

TILDY: POINTING WOMAN

In the autumn of 1822 Tildy has found employment as nurse to the mother of Charles Burke Bromley. Safe and sheltered with baby Davy, she nevertheless feels compelled to leave her haven after she turns down Bromley's offer of marriage.

Then her absent husband Tom Crawford erupts back into her life. Horrified, Tildy refuses to live with him again. But Crawford is a desperate man and will stop at nothing to force Tildy's hand—not even child-snatching... Searching for Davy, Tildy takes her stand against the might of law and order seemingly united against her as she determines to reclaim her child.

TILDY: POINTING WOMAN

Tildy:
Pointing Woman

by

Sara Fraser

Magna Large Print Books

Long Preston, North Yorkshire,
England.

British Library Cataloguing in Publication Data.

Fraser, Sara
    Tildy: Pointing woman.

    A catalogue record for this book is
    available from the British Library

    ISBN 0-7505-0726-8

First published in Great Britain by Macdonald & Co.
(Publishers) Ltd., 1988

Copyright © 1988 by Roy Clews

Published in Large Print February 1995 by arrangement with
Little, Brown & Co. UK Ltd.

Magna Large Print is an imprint of
Library Magna Books Ltd.
Printed and bound in Great Britain by
T.J. Press (Padstow) Ltd., Cornwall, PL28 8RW.

INTRODUCTION

In the England of 1822 a man's wife and his children were his property. His chattels to be treated in any way he wished. Even the law of the land supported him in this fact.

But when Tildy Crawford's brutal husband came back into her life, and tried to take her child from her, Tildy fought back...

CHAPTER 1

Portsmouth. September 1822

The woman stared at her reflection in the fly-spotted mirror and winced in pain as her fingertips explored the swollen mass of bruised flesh which imparted a grotesque lopsidedness to her face.

'That's it!' she ejaculated in sudden fury. 'That's the bloody finish!' Swinging round she glared at the sleeping man lying on the rumpled bed. 'I'll pay you out for this, Tom Crawford.' She hissed the words with a rabid hatred. 'And for all the other bleedin' hammerings youse gi' me, as well.' Snatching up a shawl to cover her bedraggled finery, she stormed from the sleazy room.

The resounding crash of the slammed door roused the sleeping man. He stirred and groaned softly as the throbbing pain exploded inside his skull. His bloodshot eyes opened reluctantly and moved blearily, seeking his bedmate.

'Must ha' gone to get me a drink,' he hoped, nauseatingly aware of the foul-tasting dryness of his mouth and throat.

'Jesus Christ.' He groaned again, and pressed his hands against his temples as if the pressure could ease the violent hammerings of his headache. 'It's no good, Tom,' he told himself mournfully. 'You'll ha' to cut down on the drink. It's causing you too much grief in the mornings.'

Vague recollections of the previous night's happenings came to him, and he lifted his hands before his eyes so that he could examine the bruised and cut knuckles.

'Goddam that bitch for a hard-head,' he cursed aggrievedly. 'I'll be breaking me hands on that thick skull one o' these days. Can't leave a man to take his drop o' drink in peace, but must always be nagging and whining until she drives me to shut her big mouth for her.' His sense of grievance deepened. 'She'll need to watch her manners,' he promised himself, 'or one o' these days I'll be flying off to another nest, be damned if I wun't.' The thought soothed him; he settled back onto the greasy pillows and closed his eyes to try and sleep once more.

He had barely drifted into oblivion when again the flimsy door crashed open to hit the wall and shake violently on its hinges.

'Get the bugger, lads,' the woman shrieked, and Tom Crawford came erect still half-fuddled by sleep and drink, but before he could make any move to defend himself the two cudgel-swinging men were upon him...

'Is he dead?' The woman's fearful question reached Tom Crawford as if from a mist-swathed distance. Barely conscious, he lay upon the floor drowning in a sea of blood-soaked pain.

'Don't fret, girl.' A harsh voice answered the question, and Crawford was brutally jerked into a sitting position. 'Now listen well, ponce.' The harsh voice grated loudly in his ear. 'I'm Betsy's man now. You got off light today, next time you wun't. So get you gone from Pompey, and don't you never come nigh here again...'

There was a brief pause, and then Tom Crawford shrieked and half-swooned in agony as an iron-shod boot crunched down upon his nose.

The two men lifted his writhing body and carried it down the stairs, along the narrow passage, and hurled it through the door into the stinking central gutter channel of the street.

'Gerron out o' Pompey, Crawford, and stay out.'

Tom Crawford tried to promise he would do so, but darkness overtook him and his lips moved but no sound came from them.

11

'D'ye hear me, mon? Can ye understand what I'm asking ye?'

Tom Crawford could hear, and he could understand, but he couldn't yet answer. He seemed to be rising, rising, rising through layers of varied colours, black, grey, dark blue, light blue, gold, red, gold, gold, yellow, yellow, yellow...

'Open your eyes, mon. Pay heed tae me!'

The yellow paled into white. White ceiling, white walls and then a solid mass of scarlet. Crawford blinked hard and his fuzzy sight clarified.

The scarlet-coated Corporal of Marines leaning over him grunted his satisfaction. 'Guid. Ye've wakened up.' His accent matched his sandy hair and red face.

'Scotch bastard!' Tom Crawford mouthed silently.

'D'ye ken wheer ye are?'

Crawford shook his head, and instantly regretted doing so as the movement caused white-hot agonies to lance through his skull. He tentatively lifted his hands to his face, and discovered to his horror that his head was swathed in bandages, with only small gaps for his mouth and eyes.

The corporal grinned. 'Aye, they've rightly spoiled your good looks for ye, whoever did this. Ye're in the sick bay at

12

Clarence Barracks. Ye've the honour to be a guest of the Royal Marines. Our patrol picked ye up some hours past from the sewer in Barracks Row, and being Johnny Raws, they thought you might be a seaman or even a marine in civil clothes.' The sandy head moved disparagingly from side to side. 'They're Johnny Raws all right, anybody wi' half an eye could ha' seen ye'd the stamp of a ponce. Anyways, we made a couple of enquiries about yer. Ye're Sheltie Betsy's fancy man. Or at least, ye was. She's got another ponce living off her earnings now. What was the trouble wi' you, mon? Have ye not got any balls left? Been all rotted away by the bloody syph, have they?'

Tom Crawford's gutter-devil was raging within him at the other's insulting manner, but even as his muscles tensed the sickening pain of his injuries caused him to subside helplessly, and he made no answer.

Visibly disappointed at the lack of reaction to his baiting the Scotsman got to his feet. 'Well, ye may lie stinking here for a wee whiles yet. The Provost Marshal 'ull be wanting a few words wi' ye, afore ye go. He'll likely be wanting you to give him information about a few things. If ye know what's good for ye, ye'll give it in full as well. We've had a few of our lads been hammered and robbed down by Barrack Row, and no doubt ye'll be able to tell us a little something about that.'

Left alone in the tiny cell-like room, Tom Crawford tried to collect his thoughts. The last person in the world he wanted to speak with was the town Provost Marshal. He had been involved in too many villanies himself for that, and tempting as the thought was of laying information against the men who had battered him, the sure knowledge that in their turn they could lay enough information against him to get him transported or even hung, was sufficient to ensure his silence.

His mind was clearing rapidly as he considered his plight. Obviously his time in Portsmouth was over, but where could he go? London? Jesus, no! The Bow Street Runners would love to lay him by the heels, not to mention certain members of the criminal fraternity who had their own grudges against him. No, London was definitely too risky for him. Plymouth, perhaps, or Bristol? Both wild roaring towns where a man with quick wits and a degree of gutter-devil could make some pickings. A few moments' reflection caused him to dismiss those possible destinations. He had no contacts there, no local knowledge, and no money with which to support himself while he rectified those lacks. He cursed viciously as he tenderly explored the extent of the bandagings upon his head. While he was like this he'd not find any woman prepared to keep him for the sake of his handsome face and virile body.

'Better those bastards had broke both me legs rather than done me face in,' he muttered bitterly, and lay racking his brains in what seemed an increasingly hopeless quest for a way out of this present predicament.

Then an idea occurred which at first he was inclined to dismiss out of hand, but which persisted until he began to consider it seriously as a possible solution to his problems.

'Tildy! I could go back home and look Tildy up. She's bound to have found herself a man, she might even have married agen, thinking that I'd gone for good. Either way, if she wants to stay with whoever she might ha' found, she'd pay to keep me from queering her pitch for her, that's certain sure... And if she's on her own? Well then, she's still me lawful wedded wife, and she can't refuse me her bed.' A sudden acute memory of his wife's face and body caused him to experience a surge of sexual excitement despite his injuries. 'Jesus! This has got to be the best notion I'se had in months,' he told himself with enthusiasm, 'the sooner I put it into

15

action, the better. And now I'd best start looking for the back way out o' this bloody hole, afore the bloody Provost Marshal gets here...'

CHAPTER 2

Redditch, Parish of Tardebigge,
  Worcestershire.
September 1822

'She does you credit, Crawford. 'Pon my soul, she does.' Doctor Hugh Taylor smiled at the young woman standing facing him across the wide four-poster bed. The subject of his praise leaned back comfortably amongst the pillows, her toothless jaws champing vigorously upon the savoury onion porridge which she spooned voraciously from the steaming wooden bowl upon her lap.

Matilda Crawford coloured slightly with satisfaction at the praise and her luminous brown eyes were gentle as they dwelt on the bent-bodied, withered old crone, who in her turn was oblivious to anything other than the clamourings of her appetite. The doctor, a very handsome young dandy in his violet coloured swallowtail coat and pantaloons, sky-blue satin waistcoat and white froths of lacy linen at neck and cuffs, kept his own gaze fixed on Matilda Crawford, experiencing powerful frissons of sexual desire as he savoured the sight of her glossy dark hair, the flawless skin of face and throat, and the outlines of her shapely body and full breasts beneath the simple dark grey woollen gown she wore.

Hugh Taylor swallowed hard as his vivid imagination pictured what the young woman's body would look like divested of the gown, and then became uncomfortably aware that her luminous brown eyes were regarding him levelly, with a considerable degree of ironic amusement lurking in their depths. He coughed hard to cover his momentary confusion, before nodding curtly.

'I'll bid you good day, Crawford. Take care that you follow most strictly my regimen of diet and medicine with your mistress here,' he instructed pompously, and left the room, annoyed with himself for being so easily discomfited by that young woman.

Left alone with the old lady, Tildy allowed the smile of amusement to curve her full lips. Over the years she had become accustomed to being the object of men's sexual fantasies, and by now had some considerable understanding of the peculiar power it gave her. But she was realistic and sensible enough to realize the limitations of that power, and of its dangers if misused, and consequently did not make a practice of acting the coquette with men to gain her own ends. In fact despite her beauty, or perhaps because of it, Tildy's experiences with men had not been particularly happy ones, and had only served to strengthen her natural inclinations to make her own way in the world independent of men's help.

The vigorous scrapings of the pewter spoon against the bottom of the empty bowl signalled the ending of the old lady's mealtime, and Tildy gently took the utensils from the clawlike hands that clutched them so grimly.

'That's it, my dear,' she said. 'It's all gone. Let me sponge your face now and get you settled comfortable again.' Her voice was soft with an overlay of rustic burr.

Downstairs, Charles Burke Bromley, Tildy's employer and the only son of the bed-ridden old crone, stood in the front of his shop and listened with barely concealed distress to what the doctor had to tell him.

'Regretfully, Bromley, your mother's intellect has deserted her, and there is naught to be done about it, I fear.

Quite simply, her brain has run its course. She is a greatly-aged, worn-out body, and there is nothing that can be prescribed in medicine to restore her mind. You have the consolation that she is being accorded all the care and kindly treatment that can be procured and I will state quite positively that despite my earlier forebodings, the Crawford woman has proved to be a most excellent nurse. Without doubt your mother is content enough with her lot, and of course she will not live to see many more winters upon this earth...' Even as Hugh Taylor's tongue was uttering these condolences his mind was making scathing comments on the man before him. 'By God, but you're a poor example of manhood, Bromley. What a damned milksop you are! Look at you now, trembling like a whipped cur because you will not much longer have a mammy to wipe the snot from your nose, and you a grown man of more than thirty years...'

In all truth, Charles Burke Bromley was a woefully unprepossessing physical specimen. A tall, slender, weak-bodied man, invariably swathed from his hooked chin to his spindly ankles in a long white apron, his thin face badly pitted with the blue scars of childhood smallpox, and the few oiled strands of hair brushed across the shiny pink scalp emphasising his premature baldness. Add to this watery red-rimmed eyes that blinked continuously behind thick-lensed spectacles balanced on an over-long nose, and Charles Burke Bromley could only be described as an ugly man.

But beneath the physical façade Charles Burke Bromley had much to offer: a good brain, a gentle heart, and a natural kindliness and generosity. He was possessed of a multitude of skills and attainments to which the jumbled contents of his shop bore mute testimony, resembling as it did an Aladdin's cave of goods and articles pertaining to his many and varied business interests. He was a printer, stationer, bookseller, druggist, medicine vendor, book-binder, music seller, grocer and dealer in sundries. He was also an inveterate dreamer, a fact which prevented him from achieving any real success as a merchant. So despite his undoubted abilities and accomplishments, Charles Burke Bromley endured successive financial crises, aggravated by his practice of giving credit to almost anyone who asked it of him.

'You are certain that nothing more can be done to aid my mother, Dr Taylor?' he ventured nervously, and visibly flinched when the other man snapped curtly, 'God dammee, Bromley, what have I just been telling you, man?' The handsome features twisted in a petulant frown. 'Of course, if you so wish then you are free to obtain another professional opinion.' He looked spitefully at the other's shabby clothing. 'That is if you can afford to do so, of course.'

Bromley's thin face coloured deeply, and he flustered in acute embarrassment. 'Indeed, Sir, I was not doubting your competence, I do assure you of that. I ask your pardon if I have inadvertently caused you any offence.'

'No matter!' Taylor waved away the proffered apology. 'I must go, Bromley, I've other patients to attend. I'll call again within the week. Good day to you, Sir.'

'Good day to you, Sir,' Bromley muttered, and stared miserably after the doctor's retreating figure, as he thought over what he had been told. Immersed in his reverie he was unaware that Matilda Crawford had come into the shop until she touched his arm. Startled, he jumped and turned to her, then smiled, displaying his one good physical attribute. A set of perfectly proportioned white teeth, incongruously beautiful in his plain face.

'Is it good news?' she questioned eagerly, and his smile died as he shook his head.

'I fear not, Tildy,' he told her sadly. 'The doctor has informed me that my

21

poor mother is not long for this world.' He sighed heavily, and tears brimmed in his red-rimmed eyes.

Tildy was touched by his distress and to comfort him took his hands and pressed warmly. 'There now, Mr Bromley, do not grieve yourself so. Your mother has been blessed with a long and happy life, and twice blessed by having such a son as you to care for her in her old age.'

He tried to smile. 'You are a great comfort to me, Tildy. Knowing that you will be here at my side after my mother has gone strengthens and uplifts me more than words can express. Together we will endure and triumph over any adversity that is sent to afflict us.'

A sense of unease invaded Tildy. She owed this man a great debt of gratitude. When it had seemed that the whole world was ranged against her, he had given her and her child shelter and protection. Food, warmth, work and a home in the truest sense of the word. During her time in his house, in his employ, never once had he treated her otherwise than with respect and kindness. But Tildy knew that she did not want to spend the rest of her life in this house, and she increasingly feared that Bromley was going to ask her to do just that. To stay with him forever as wife or mistress.

To her relief the bell above the shop door jangled as a customer entered, and she was able to break contact without hurting Charles Bromley's feelings. For she truly liked and respected him as a friend, even though the thought of being his lover filled her with a faint physical revulsion.

Tildy went through the house and into the gravelled yard at the rear where a long line of fresh-washed clothing and bed linen hung drying in the warm sunlight.

A tiny boy was marching solemnly around the edges of the yard, drawing behind him on a length of string a wooden box in which stood a wooden soldier, a gaily uniformed hussar some eight inches high with fierce black eyes and mustachios, and a busby and pelisse made from real cloth and fur.

Tildy stood silently, feasting her eyes on her son's sturdy body, his thick mop of black hair, the sun-kissed bare arms and legs and the rosy-cheeked face. Little Davy, two years and three months old, and the only source of unflawed happiness she had known in her bleak twenty-one years of existence.

Now, as always, she marvelled that this constant source of joy should have come from her violent loveless marriage to a man she had never even liked or wanted, but had been forced to marry by circumstances beyond her control. Briefly the memory of Tom Crawford's swarthily handsome face passed before her mind's eye. He had run off and abandoned her and her baby almost a year and a half before; Tildy blessed the day that he had done so and prayed fervently that he would never reappear in her life. A faint frown line marred the smoothness of her forehead as she stared at her son's face, unable to stop herself searching for some resemblance to his father in his features and expression. Thankfully, she again found none, apart from the colour of his hair, black instead of her own velvet brown.

Little Davy became aware of her standing in the doorway and shouted delightedly, 'See Mammy, Sergeant Hawk is having a ride in his cart.'

Tildy crouched low, her arms held wide in invitation, and the child came running to her. She enfolded him in a loving embrace, her lips tasting the silky tenderness of his cheeks as she straightened and lifted him. 'Come now, honey-lamb, it's time for your bread and milk.'

'Sergeant Hawk is hungry too, Mammy,' the child informed her seriously, and Tildy smiled.

'Then he shall come with us and eat his own bread and milk.' Moving with a lissom grace she retrieved the wooden soldier and the three of them entered the house in happy companionship.

When the customer had made his purchase and departed Charles Bromley tried to busy himself in rearranging his stocks in a vain attempt to take his mind from what Dr Taylor had told him. Very quickly he realized the futility of the attempt and experienced a sudden need to escape from the confining atmosphere of his home. Removing his apron to disclose a rusty-black, threadbare coat and trousers, he called to Tildy.

'I'm closing the shop for a while, Tildy. I feel the need to take the air. I'll not be long.'

She came to the connecting door to answer him, her eyes mirroring her concern. 'Do you feel all right, Mr Bromley?'

He smiled reassuringly. 'Indeed I feel very well, Tildy. But I crave for some fresh air.'

Outside in the street he breathed deeply, gulping the sun-warmed air into his lungs before starting out to walk through the town that he knew and loved so well, which boasted the peculiar distinction of being the world centre for the manufacture of needles, fish-hooks and tackle. It was

25

built across sprawling hillsides which fell away to the west, north and east into broad many-streamed valleys, but to the south the land rose sharply in a long ridgeway which narrowed, then widened then narrowed again. The central part of Redditch was a flat plateau and the northern section of this plateau was a triangular common edged by rows of cottages, forges, inns, workshops and houses. From this common the dirt road plunged down a steep hill, known as the Fish Hill, and ran north towards the city of Birmingham, some fifteen miles distant. At the south-western corner of the common was the main crossroads of the town, overlooked by the squat cupola'd Chapel of St Stephen, the Anglican place of worship, its railed burial yard shaded by fine elm trees.

Bromley's shop stood some three hundred yards along the main thoroughfare of the town which ran south from the Fish Hill across the crossroads, to the base of the Front Hill, the commencement of the rising ridgeway.

For some moments he stood, undecided whether to turn up the hill, or towards the Chapel Green. The decision was made for him.

'Hullo Charles, we're well met. I could do with some company.' The speaker was a tall strong-bodied young man, wearing travel-stained dark brown riding clothes and a curly-brimmed white top hat. His face was ruddy from wind and weather, his hair close-cropped and unpowdered.

Charles Bromley returned his greeting with evident pleasure. 'We are well met indeed, Rob. I did not expect to see you for some weeks yet.'

Robert Stafford was a commercial traveller for the needle trade and spent the majority of his days roaming the country from end to end to obtain orders for the needle masters of the district. Now he grinned happily. 'I'm back early for a reason, Charles, but come, let us walk together. Don't invite me into your house because I've been riding non-stop and my arse is too damned sore to plonk it on a chair just yet awhile.'

Together the pair began the ascent to the Front Hill, and as they walked Robert Stafford talked excitedly. 'For how long have you been saying that the greatest evil engendered by the manufacture of needles is the "pointer's rot"?'

'Nearly all my life, my friend,' Bromley rejoined solemnly. 'Too many times have I followed the coffins of men cut down in the prime of life by it; and too many times have I seen the wives and children they left behind rendered half dead with distress before the parish will relieve them.'

Stafford's grin was irrepressible. 'I can assure you now, Charles, that within scant months the "rot" can become nothing more than an evil memory in this district. But mind, you must not breathe a word of what I am saying to anyone.'

'If that could but be true!' Charles Bromley's watery red eyes blinked furiously. 'If only the "rot" could be banished, then think of the effects it would have on the operatives in this district. It would do more than any other thing that could be done to raise them from their vile-brutish ways... My God, my friend, when I think of the sufferings I have seen engendered by the "rot" in this town...' He lapsed into silence as his memories ranged back across the years. It was bad enough that many of the processes in the making of needles were ideally suited to the delicate fingers of small children, and that for as long as he could remember children of seven, six, five, even four years of age had been forced into long hours of labour in the workshops and mills of the town. But there was another process that he considered the most abhorrent of all: the needle pointing itself. This deadly task involved dry-grinding the points of both needles and fish-hooks.

On average two hundred men would be employed throughout the district as needle pointers at any given time. On average their ages would range from twenty to twenty-eight years. On average every one of them would lie in his grave before he reached thirty years of age.

Their working hours were spent sitting with straddled legs, heads bent over spinning grindstones, the slivers of steel rolling between flattened palms against the grindstones' surfaces and the clouds of steel and stone dust thus created being sucked down into their lungs despite the protective rags wrapped around their mouths and nostrils. The deadly dust would ravage the minute capillaries of their lungs, puncturing and tearing the soft tissues hour after hour, day after day, week after week, month after month. After scant years at the trade the pointer would develop a racking cough, he would suffer a constant difficulty in drawing breath, he would begin to spit up blood. His flesh would waste from his bones and his strength would slowly desert him, until finally his lungs would collapse in bloody ruin and he would drown in his own blood.

Charles Bromley shook his head in wonderment. A wonderment that men would deliberately choose to do such work. Admittedly the wages of a pointer were very high. A farm labourer would toil for more than a week to earn what a pointer lad could gain in a day. And Bromley could also accept that a certain glamour attached itself to the pointers, with their reputation as tough roaring blades, who feared neither man nor God, and who drank, gambled and brawled their short lives away seemingly without a care for what the morrow might bring.

'Why is it that I concern myself about the pointers? They do not ask me to do so, or offer me any thanks for it,' Bromley smiled wryly to himself. 'Certainly I've not courage enough to ever want to be a pointer lad myself. To do what they do, to take my chances and live life to the full, then pay the price for doing so with a brave heart...'

'Charles, you're not listening to me,' his friend complained indignantly, and Bromley hastened to apologize and to give his full attention to the other's words. 'I go to Sheffield a great deal these days. You know what it's like in Sheffield, Charles. The grinders there are much the same as our pointer lads, and die the same type of miserable death, but the poor devils can't earn the same high wages as our bold buckos here. Anyway, an acquaintance of mine, a man named Abraham, has invented a device which I feel sure can be adapted for use in our pointing shops. It's a type of magnetic muzzle which draws the steel particles from the grinding dust. He assures me that this device renders complete protection against the "rot". He says that the steel dust, being the harder of the two substances, is the one which causes the major part of the damage to the lungs. What do you think, Charles? Could this device stop the "rot"?'

After pondering briefly, Bromley nodded his head. 'If this device does indeed remove the steel particles from the atmosphere, then I would think it to be a preventative to some extent, at least.'

Robert Stafford appeared to be a trifle piqued by his friend's apparent lack of enthusiasm. 'God dammee Charles, I thought you'd welcome my news a sight more warmly than this.'

Bromley displayed a touch of impatience. 'I've much weighing upon my mind at present, Robert. Forgive me, but I feel the need to be alone with my own thoughts.'

With that he walked away, leaving his friend staring moodily after him.

It was dusk when Charles Burke Bromley returned to his home. Tildy was in the lamplit parlour at the rear of the shop, engrossed in a book. She would have risen as he entered, but he gestured to her to remain seated. On the table his supper was laid out ready for him. Cold boiled beef, onions and cheese, and a small wicker basket of brown bread. He drew a flagon of cider from the small keg in the corner of the room and seated himself at the table.

'My mother, and the boy?' he queried.

'Both soundly sleeping,' Tildy answered. He nodded, then closed his eyes and clasped his hands together, voicing a brief prayer of thanksgiving for the food before him. Bromley was a deeply religious man, and a prominent member of the local Methodist persuasion. His prayer finished, he toyed listlessly with the food, but after only a few mouthfuls he laid down his knife and turned towards the young woman.

'Tildy?' His quick shallow breathing betrayed his nervousness. 'Tildy, I wish to talk of our future.'

She closed the book on her lap and gazed at him with calm eyes, which belied the stirrings of agitation his words aroused in her.

'We both know that my mother is fast declining, and with God's help I must face the fact that she is not destined to be long with me. When she has gone, then your situation here becomes a difficult one. A young woman living beneath the roof of a bachelor, and no other person present.' He flushed with embarrassment, and a slight stutter crept into his voice. 'P-p-people have c-cruel tongues, Tildy. There are th-th-those who would try t-t-to blacken your character because of it.' He halted and drew long breaths in an effort to calm his speech. When she would have spoken he held up his hand to silence her. 'No, pray hear me out, Tildy. Please listen to what I must tell you.' Calmer now, he went on unhurriedly, 'It is nigh on two years by your own account since your husband abandoned you and the boy, is it not? He might well be dead, or gone abroad never to return. What I propose is to have enquiries set afoot to trace him. If it should be discovered that he has indeed died, then you will be free to remarry, Tildy.' He paused, and drew a long noisy breath as if gathering all his courage, then said hastily, 'If he is indeed dead, Tildy, then I want you to become my wife. I love you, Tildy, and I would cherish and protect you, and prove to be a most tender and loving parent towards Davy.'

Tildy's hands entwined upon her lap, and she bent her head. This was the moment that she had dreaded, for she knew that she must wound this man who had shown her and her child only kindness. While she desperately searched for the gentlest way of refusing him, he went on speaking.

'...even if Crawford is found alive, then you could still live with me as my wife, Tildy. He could sell you to me. It is a custom that is accepted hereabouts, and has known common usage for many centuries. Some of my Chapel Brethren might frown upon it, but we should demonstrate by our mode of life and behaviour that we are true Christians, and I'm sure that even the most obdurate of the Brethren would eventually give their blessings to our union.'

'Dear God!' Tildy exclaimed inwardly with dismay. 'Why must he now close any way left to me of refusing him without hurt to his pride.' Steeling herself, she lifted her head and spoke out gently but firmly. 'Mr Bromley, it matters not if my husband be dead or alive, I will never marry again, or live with any man as his wife. I've no desire to enter into that state again. I like you as a true friend, Mr Bromley, and respect you above all other men, but I can never act as a wife towards you.' A momentary irritation mounted in her at the way he had forced her to react, and sharply she accused, 'You have forced me to answer you bluntly, Mr Bromley. So I will make it plain, that on this matter my mind is firm and set. I shall never change. Please excuse me now, I must go to my child.'

The man sat with bowed head and

listened to her clogs clatter up the wooden staircase and along the passage to the bedroom she shared with her son. He heard the door of that room close firmly; then there was silence. A wave of utter desolation swept over him as a harsh sob tore from deep in his chest.

For long hours sleep eluded Tildy. She lay on her narrow bed, listening to the peaceful breathing of her child in his cot beside her, and stared into the darkness while memories passed like a panorama before her mind's eye.

By any standards Tildy's life had been a harsh one. Orphaned before she was three, raised by a paternal aunt and her religious maniac husband, treated by them as an unwanted drudge, forced to marry a man she despised at eighteen years. A man who had treated her brutally and dragged her into the very depths of poverty. For the last year and a half Tildy had struggled alone to support herself and her child, knowing the shame of the poorhouse and the pauper's badge, enduring hunger and want, but despite all obstacles finding within herself reserves of courage and determination which had enabled her to survive and to keep her child with her, without surrendering to the degradation that some would have forced upon her.

Still only twenty-one years of age, Tildy

Crawford had achieved a degree of maturity far in advance of her years, and also a determination to be her own woman, and to make a way in the world for herself and her child independently of others. Tildy was a sensual woman, with all the needs of a woman, and because of her physical beauty many men made approaches to her. Some of them she felt attracted to in return, but she would not allow herself to surrender to her own desires, if by doing so she would again place herself under a man's domination. In an age when women were men's chattels, regarded as inferiors, she had chosen to follow a hard path, and at times it seemed that the whole world had determined that she should not be allowed to.

Now she briefly dwelt on what had occurred between Charles Bromley and herself that evening. A brief sadness assailed her. 'I've been content in this house,' she realized, 'and my Davy has thrived here. But now I don't feel that I can remain here any longer. It would not be fair to Mr Bromley.' A pang of deep regret caused her to catch her lower lip between her white teeth. 'I hope I've not caused him too much distress by refusing his offer. He is a truly good man, and God knows, I've no wish ever to hurt him.'

She took mental stock of her assets. 'I

can read well now, and scribe a fair hand, as well as do my sums accurately. I've learned a lot about keeping house, and treating sickness, and I can bake and cook with any woman. I'm strong and healthy, and my Davy is bonny and thriving. I've only a few shillings and a couple of gowns and shifts, but no matter. The trade has improved lately, and there's work to be had in the needles. And I can always get a room again with Mother Readman, until I can find a place for me and Davy to have for our own.'

Her full moist lips quirked in sardonic self-mockery. 'There now, Tildy, it didn't take long for you to make up your mind to leave here, did it.' At this realization a tremor of apprehension passed through her. 'You'll be leaving a safe haven, girl. You're comfortable here, and secure. You dwell in peace and cleanliness. What awaits you if you leave?'

The image of Mother Readman's filthy lodging house with its dirty, thieving, raucous, drunken, brawling denizens presented itself vividly to her but she fought back the fear that accompanied it. 'I've survived it before, and worse than it, and I can survive it again,' she told herself determinedly. 'But Davy? What of Davy?' A sharper fear attacked her, and for a few moments she wavered. 'He could have a good life if I stayed here with Charles Bromley,' she was forced to admit. 'And I'm sure that Mr Bromley would prove a benevolent guardian to him... But could I face sharing the bed and life of a man I do not love for the rest of my own life? I tried that once, and it proved a hell on earth for me. Oh, I know that Charles Bromley is kind and good and gentle, not like Tom Crawford. But still he is a man, and he would want what all men want from their wives. And could I stand to have him use my body as and when he chose to? To feel his hands and lips upon me, and his manhood inside me in the night?'

Tildy knew with a complete certainty that with the best will in the world, she still could not endure the intimacy of such a relationship with Charles Bromley. 'No! It's hopeless even to consider it. Inevitably I would eventually reject him physically, and he in turn would come to hate me because of that, and through me, mayhap, grow to hate my Davy.' Her resolve solidified, though sadly and reluctantly. 'I must leave here, and hope that even though I do so, yet Mr Bromley and I can remain as friends...'

A remembrance that tomorrow's date, September the twenty-eighth, 1822, was also her birthday caused Tildy to smile wryly. 'So I'll be starting my twenty-third year of life with yet another change of the roof above my head. Ah well, so be it...' She drifted into unquiet sleep that was troubled by strange dreams.

CHAPTER 3

'Well, I'll go t'Hanover, Tildy! I'm buggered if I can understand you, me wench,' Mother Readman exclaimed incredulously, and her great scarred, moon-like face was a study in disbelief. 'Youse upped and left a snug berth like that 'un was, to come back here, and to tell me that youm agoing to work at the bloody needles. To be a bleedin' soft worker?'

The two women were seated in the kitchen of Mother Readman's lodging house. A large, low-beamed, smoke-blackened room reeking of stale cooking and the odours of countless transient bodies. A great wooden table, its top ingrained with stains and dirt, stood in the centre of the floor and rough wooden benches lined the walls. In the huge inglenook hearth near where they sat, a gigantic iron cauldron hung on a massive chain above the smoking fire, its greasy contents seething and bubbling noisily. Mother Readman's famous penny-a-bowl-stew.

The proprietress was a fearsome figure. Massive bodied, hugely fat, swathed in thick layers of shawls, ruling her domain and its rough, tough inhabitants with her tongue and fists, ready and willing to toe the line with any man, woman, or beast. Shrewd and hard, yet without viciousness, and possessed of a natural kindliness, in the past she had proven a good friend to Tildy, and in return Tildy greatly liked and respected the older woman, and admired the way she could hold her own in a merciless environment.

'I'd have thought you would ha' bin set for life wi' Charlie Bromley,' the fat woman went on now. 'He's got the shop, and a nice big house, and he's a good-hearted soul, for all that's he's a mealy-mouthed, methody pisspot. He'd have made you a good husband, girl. You'd never ha' gone short o' vittles or clothes on your back wi' him, and he wouldn't have served you like most of the other bastards serves their women, giving you knuckle sandwich and boot pie when he'd got drink in him. Why, I'd wager he'd never ha' raised his voice to you, ne'er mind his fists.'

Tildy smiled and answered quietly, 'I know what you say is right, Mother Readman.' She shrugged her shapely shoulders. 'But I could never have lived with him in the way he wanted me to. And he is such a good man, it wouldn't have been fair to him if I had led him on to hope for something that could never have been.'

'Ah well, happen youm right, girl. And o' course youm welcome to stop here as long as you please. But in all truth, it arn't the healthiest place in the world for your nipper to grow up in!'

Tildy was forced to accept the truth of that statement. The lodging house was situated in the Silver Square, one of the worst slums in the town, where three out of four children born in its fetid atmosphere died before their fifth birthday.

'Mind you, kids sickens and dies no matter wheer they be, Tildy,' the older woman said, offering an ambiguous comfort. 'When God wants 'um, He takes 'um be it from palace or pigsty. The little cratur 'ull come to manhood if he's meant to no matter where he's living, and that's all there is to it. We all takes our chances in this life, girl.'

Again Tildy silently accepted the truth of the words, but in the same instant sent fervent mental prayers to the unknown arbiter of life and death that He would not take her beloved child from her.

'Now then, about your work,' Mother

Readman's mouth pursed judiciously. 'The trade's picked up a bit of late. I reckon I can easy put you in the way of a bit of "soft work". But think about it, girl. The wages am terrible short and the hours be terrible long. It's a pity your babby arn't a couple of years older, he could do summat in that line wi' you then and earn a couple of bob. But he's still too small to be of use.' She suddenly sighed gustily. 'By the Christ, Tildy! I can't help but think that youse jumped from the frying pan into the bloody fire.'

Not for the first time, Tildy's own doubts assailed her. She could have stopped on as housekeeper and nurse to Bromley and his mother. When she had told him of her decision to leave his employ the man had almost wept as he begged her to stay on, on any terms she cared to name. The temptation to agree had been all but overwhelming. But Tildy's personal morality ruled her with an iron rod. If she conceived a course of action to be wrong, then no matter what the world's opinion of it was, or what expediency dictated, she would not take that course of action. Many times throughout her life she had cursed what she conceived to be her own mulelike stubbornness in acting the way she did, but she could no more disobey its dictates than she could alter the movements of the planets in their courses. No matter what the consequences to herself might be, when she had set herself on a course, then nothing would deter her from attempting to complete it.

Now she fought down her misgivings, and told her friend. 'Well, if I'm in the fire, then I must make shift to climb quick out of it, before it burns me to a cinder. Who do you know, who might give me work?'

Silver Street was the long narrow alley of tumbledown terraced cottages that led from Silver Square out under an archway at the side of the Red Lion Inn into the thoroughfare that bore the inn's name. It was into the Red Lion's taproom that Mother Readman led Tildy. Even at this hour of the morning the room was crowded with pipe-smoking, ale-swilling men, many of them wearing the distinctive rig of the feared needle pointers: square, low-crowned hat fashioned from heavy brown paper, sleeveless leather waistcoats worn over red flannel shirts with kerchiefs tied loosely around the throat, knee breeches, ribbed woollen stockings and heavy iron-shod wooden clogs on their feet.

Tildy was not surprised at the full room. It was Monday after all, and many working men treated Monday as an extra holiday, making up for the time lost from their work by toiling for up to eighteen hours at a stretch during the remaining weekdays. The air, thick with a fug of tobacco smoke and beer-fumed breath, resounded with laughter and loud oaths. Tildy kept her shawl drawn over her head and close about her face, but still the sight of her moving gracefully behind the bulk of Mother Readman brought lewd comments and invitations from all sides of the room.

Mother Readman pushed through the close-packed bodies to grasp the shoulder of a thick-set pointer sitting with a group of card-players. 'I wants a minute wi' you, John Pinfield,' she stated, and the man grinned up at her with yellowed teeth.

'Then youse come at a good time for it, me duck. Because this fucking hand Ise drawn is fit only to chuck onto the bloody midden.'

He rose and followed the two women outside into the road, accompanied by a chorus of jeers and catcalls.

'You greedy bastard, Pinfield, keeping them two to yourself.'

'Ahr, let's have seconds arter youse done wi' 'um.'

'If it's the young 'un, I don't mind having thirds.'

'Or bloody fourths.'

'I'll take tens!'

'Now then, my old duck, what's amiss?' Pinfield asked Mother Readman, but his eyes flickered appreciatively across Tildy's face and figure. 'And who's this toothsome little wench?'

'Her name is Tildy Crawford. Her's a very good friend o' mine.' Mother Readman's tone held a note of warning. 'And a good-living wench, as well. So be clear on that, John Pinfield.'

'More's the pity.' His pleasant features assumed an exaggerated expression of disappointment, then he laughed easily. 'Don't fret yoursen, Mother, I'll not offer insult to her.'

'Be you still wanting another hand in your shop?' the woman wanted to know.

He paused, and then asked Tildy directly, 'Is it you that's wanting work, then?'

She nodded. 'Yes, Master Pinfield. I'm wanting work.'

He paused for another few seconds, then told her, 'Right then, be at me shop at crack o' light tomorrow. Me missus 'ull show you what's needful. And now I'll get back to me game.' He reached out and briefly stroked Tildy's cheek with his fingertips. 'Theer now, that'll bring me good luck wi' the cards. Touching a pretty wench always does that for me. Tarra Mother, Tarra, pretty wench.' Turning on

45

his heel he re-entered the inn.

'That's you settled then, girl,' Mother Readman said with evident satisfaction. 'John Pinfield pays straight and fair, even though he's a bit too quick wi' his fists when in drink. I'll direct you wheer to go tomorrow. We'll goo back home now, and have us a dish o' tay... Now you'n going to be a soft worker.'

There were many stages in the manufacture of needles, and those processes which could be carried out by hand tool bore the collective title of 'soft work'. Although every needle master employed some soft workers directly in the mill or factory, the major portion of this type of work was given out as a form of sub-contract. The soft workers would collect packets of steel wire already tempered, cut to length and pointed, from the mills and bring them back to one or other of the myriads of domestic workshops spread throughout the district.

In these workshops the wire lengths would be fashioned into needles by hand. A couple of experienced soft workers acting in concert could make about five thousand needles a day, earning between them perhaps five shillings. But to earn this amount entailed long hours of unremitting, eye-straining, tedious labour, and also depended on the quality of the steel wire. If it was of poor quality and flawed, then it would splinter under the eye-punch, and become only scrap metal.

Earnings for the independent soft worker were therefore uncertain and in times of sudden trade fluctuation, extremely irregular. Yet still the majority of the local people preferred the comparative freedom of the out-worker before the rigid time-keeping and work discipline of the in-workers of the mills and factories. During times of good trade the out-workers who had large families of children were envied, for even a child of four or five years could be trained to use a small hammer and punch, or handle a guttering file, or wrap needles into packets. And so successive generations knew very little of the reputed joyous freedoms of childhood, but all too much of the sadnesses of adult life's restrictions.

CHAPTER 4

'And who be you?' The woman's voice matched her sour, tallowy-complexioned face.

A chill easterly wind was blowing; Tildy shivered slightly in the grey dawn, and pulled her shawl tighter about her shoulders as she stood outside the front door of the isolated house. 'My name is Matilda Crawford. Are you Missis Pinfield?' she asked in return, and the woman nodded and answered shortly, 'To my sorrow.'

'Your husband told me to come here this morn. He said that there was work for me here.'

'Work is it?' the woman sniffed. 'Oh, there's work all right. More than enough. Goo on round the back theer. You'll see the shop.'

A trifle disconcerted by such a welcome Tildy did as she was bade. Built onto the rear of the house was a long, narrow, single-storied lean-to with an almost continuous row of windows penetrating its outer wall. A loud clamorous metallic clinking and tapping sounded from inside it. The low-lintelled door in the side wall opened and Mrs Pinfield beckoned Tildy to enter. As she did so she was met by a dozen turned heads and pairs of staring eyes, which dutifully swung away as Mrs Pinfield shouted.

'Gerron wi' your bloody work, 'ull you.'

Tildy gazed around with interest. Along the outer wall beneath the window line and stretching the length of the lean-to was a thick, solid workbench, and sitting on benches in front of it a close-packed row of women and children of all ages. Before each of them was a pile of steel slivers and their hands were moving with a dazzling speed and dexterity as with small hammers and punches, files and tongs, each performed their part in the operations which produced the needles.

From the house beyond the lean-to a high-pitched wailing cry issued, and Mrs Pinfield clucked her tongue impatiently.

'God blast that bleeding kid. Wait here,' she ordered Tildy, 'I'll set you to a task in a minute.'

She disappeared through the inner doorway into the house, and as she did so all eyes again swung onto Tildy.

'Wheer you from, duck?' the thin, haggard-faced, poorly clad woman nearest to Tildy whispered.

'From Redditch,' Tildy felt constrained to whisper in her turn.

The woman grinned, displaying greenish-black stubs of teeth. 'I means whereabouts in Redditch. Who's your kin?'

'I've no kin, at least, only my little son. I'm living at Mother Readman's in the Silver Square.'

Surprise showed on her questioner's face as her eyes studied Tildy's appearance, but before she could say anything more, Mrs Pinfield was back.

'God strike me dead, Aggie Southall!' she shouted. 'No sooner me back's turned than you stops work to bleedin' natter.'

Surreptitiously the thin woman put out her tongue, and the small boy next to her began to giggle. Next instant his giggle transformed itself into a bellow of pain as Mrs Pinfield slashed him across his ear with the small file that miraculously appeared in her hand. The other women on the benches immediately rounded on her furiously.

'Theer's no call for that!'

'You nasty, bad-tempered bitch!'

' 'Tis not the nipper's fault that you and your old man had been rowing agen.'

'Don't take your bloody spite out on the childer, you cow!'

'No, take it out on that drunken bugger you calls husband!'

Mrs Pinfield's eyes screwed tight, her face seemed to crumple and bursting into noisy tears she once more disappeared through the inner door. Tildy stared after her with open-mouthed amazement, fearing for a brief moment that she had unwittingly wandered into a type of lunatic asylum. Then Aggie Southall tugged at her arm.

'Set you down here by me, what's your name?'

'My name's Tildy, Tildy Crawford.'

'Set down here then, Tildy Crawford, and start earning your bit o' grub. I'll show you what you mun do.'

Everyone moved until a space had been created at the workbench, and Tildy obediently seated herself. Aggie Southall pointed to the small iron anvil, measuring only inches across and tapered to sit firmly in the tapering hole in the thick solid bench.

'Your task is to do the flatting.' Aggie took up a small hammer and demonstrated the work. In her left hand she lifted four pointed slivers from the pile in front of Tildy, spreading them between her fingers and thumb with the pointed ends against her palm. Laying the blunt ends against the anvil's face she brought the hammer in her right hand sharply down on each of the ends in turn, to flatten them. 'That's all you has to do, my duck, and then chuck 'um onto my pile. Here,' she handed the hammer to Tildy. 'Get stuck into it, Tildy Crawford.'

Nothing loth, Tildy obeyed and very soon fell into a rapid, mindless rhythm. Lift, spread, lay, tap, tap, tap, tap, pass on. Lift, spread, lay, tap, tap, tap, tap, pass on. Lift, spread, lay, tap...time ceased to exist and her world shrank to a tiny area encompassing only steel slivers, wooden bench, iron anvil and hammer...

CHAPTER 5

The Fox and Goose Inn stood on the southern side of the Chapel Green, and was the favourite meeting place of those who considered themselves to be of a higher social stratum than the common herd. It was here that the needle masters, merchants and minor gentry of the district gathered to drink their clarets and brandies, take snuff and smoke their pipes. Fat Tommy Fowkes the landlord kept his ears and eyes open, but his mouth tightly closed, and knowing this his clientele discussed openly the trials, tribulations and triumphs of their various businesses.

Robert Stafford's mother was the landlord's favourite sister, and apart from this family connection the young man was also personally liked by Tommy Fowkes, and had many times profited from the discreetly imparted morsels of information vouchsafed to him by the fat man. Today he waited in the bar parlour until he could catch Fowkes' eye, and then requested,

'A private word, uncle?'

The round, pink-shaven head bobbed, and the young man went upstairs to the private parlour and waited. A few minutes later Tommy Fowkes joined him.

'You'll needs be brief, nephew. It's busy downstairs.'

The young man wasted no time. 'I've obtained the assurances we wanted, uncle. At the prices I've quoted we can dispose of all the needles we can lay our hands on. Even the oldest customers would be ready to cut existing connections and buy from us. So whenever you give the word I can see about setting up the workshop and go to it. See, here are the revised figures.' From his pocket Stafford took a sheaf of closely annotated papers.

The fat man's protruding eyes scanned the sheets expertly.

'The only way we can make these prices is by cutting the rate for the pointing,' he observed, and the doubt was noticeable in his tone. 'I still can't see how youm going to get the buggers to point your needles at these rates youse quoted for.'

'Have I not told you already about Abraham's new invention?' Stafford answered impatiently. 'The magnetic muzzle renders the process so much safer that the pointers will be only too happy to take a cut in their wages. My God, uncle, we'll be able to meet those prices I've quoted, and mayhap even drop them further.'

'But what's to stop the rest o' the masters

using these bloody muzzles and being able to drop their own prices?' Tommy Fowkes objected. 'Does you really think that the Milwards, or the Chillingworths, or the Smallwoods for example, be thick in the yed? Does you really think that they'd not catch on to a dodge like this afore you could say Jack Robinson? Don't be a bloody fool, boy. They'm sharp buggers. Too bloody sharp be far to let a snot-nosed young sod like you steal a march on 'um.'

Robert Stafford was unabashed by the other man's apparent contemptuous dismissal of his capabilities. 'Give me some credit for being sharp myself, uncle. Do you not think that I've already considered that possibility, and have taken the necessary steps to secure our interests?'

'What steps?' The older man's attitude made it plain that he would need a great deal of convincing.

His nephew smiled confidently. 'Over the last months I've made it my concern to spend time with Abraham in Sheffield. I think I can state most positively that I have the man's complete confidence. I have also come to know a great deal about his personal affairs. Like most of his type he is a hopeless man of business. I know for a fact that he is in dire financial straits, and faces the prospect of being committed for debt. He has a wife and a large family, and naturally is desperately worried as to what might befall them if he is sent to the debtors' prison.'

'How the hell does that profit us?' his uncle broke in impatiently.

'I would have thought that to be perfectly obvious,' Stafford stated smilingly. 'Because of his financial difficulties I have managed to persuade him to sell the patent rights of the magnetic muzzle to me. I am to have complete control of it. No one will be able to make use of it without my permission. I shall have a monopoly.'

'And how much is that complete monopoly going to cost?' His uncle went straight to the main point.

'Why, a few hundreds only,' his nephew told him airily. 'It's a cheap price to pay for what it will mean to us.'

'A few hundreds only?' Tommy Fowkes was notoriously mean. 'Tell me, pray, exactly how much is a few hundreds?'

'Between two and three.' Robert Stafford denigrated the amount with a casual wave of the hand. 'That's nothing compared to what we shall eventually gain through it.'

'Be damned to that!' The fat man threw the sheaf of papers down onto the table and pointed his finger at the columns of figures covering them. 'On those damned prices youse put down theer, all we could afford to pay for the patent, and still get a reasonable return on our money within a couple of years, 'ud have to be a hundred at most. And that's assuming that the trade stays good. You knows better nor I that it jumps up and down like a bloody Jack i' the Box. We takes sufficient chance of losing all our investment as it is, wi'out adding two or three hundreds o' pounds on top of it.'

'But without the magnetic muzzle we'll not stand a chance of success anyway,' Robert Stafford counter-attacked. 'It is having that in our sole control that makes the whole idea feasible.' Afraid of provoking his relative into a complete rejection of his plans, he abruptly softened his tone. 'Suppose I could bring Abraham's price down, mayhap to a hundred and fifty, would you agree to pay that?'

The fat man fell silent, and for a while remained deep in thought, periodically turning over the papers on the table as he checked and rechecked the figures. Finally he grudgingly acquiesced, 'Ahr, maybe so. But not a penny more. Not one single penny. Is that understood?'

With a smile of relief Robert Stafford

gathered up the sheaf of papers.

'It shall be as you say, uncle. I'll leave for Sheffield within the week. Will you give me the money so that the sight of it spread before him may serve to still his doubts?'

Again the fat man gave a grudging acquiescence. 'Come here tomorrow afternoon. I'll have it ready for you then.'

'That is capital, uncle.' The young man's ruddy features glowed with delight. 'And never fear, we'll make our fortunes.'

'Just you remember, boy, I want no word of my involvement with this to get out. Not a bloody whisper. It 'ud ruin me trade here if my customers knew that I was setting up in opposition to 'um, and worse than that if they found out that we'd already poached some o' their best customers. So keep a still tongue in your head.'

The young man winked happily, and drew his forefinger across his throat in silent mime.

'How about the premises? Is that settled?' his uncle added.

Stafford nodded. 'That is all being taken care of, uncle. Let me worry about that.'

'I worries about everything when it's my money that is backing it, boy,' his uncle told him grimly. 'So you just watch that you don't make any mistakes.'

CHAPTER 6

In the gathering dusk the women and
children wearily filed out of the lean-to
door. Tildy's head ached and her ears still
rang from the constant metallic assault they
had been subjected to for so many long
hours. Her body was stiff and cramped
from remaining seated at the bench and
she thankfully gulped in the cool air to rid
her throat, mouth and nostrils of the stench
of rank body odours and foul breath that
in the close confinement of the workshop
had saturated her senses like a miasma.

'Youse done well, Tildy,' Aggie Southall
praised. 'Most newcomes takes a week or
more to get the speed up. Truth to tell at
fust sight of you I thought you looked a bit
too soft and gentle for our sort o' work.'

Tildy smiled wryly, remembering the
gruelling months of muscle-straining toil
she had endured at the nail forge, with
her husband brutally driving her to greater
and greater efforts as if she were a dumb
beast of burden.

'I've worked hard all my life, Aggie,' she
replied quietly. 'I'm well used to it.'

Pinfield's house was some two miles to

the west of Redditch on the road that led towards Bromsgrove, and Tildy knew the area well. 'My way home lies along the Salters Way,' she told her companion, referring to the ancient trackway along which the packhorse trains had carried the sacks of salt from the beds of Droitwich to the Abbey of Bordesley at mediaeval Redditch.

'So does mine,' Aggie Southall informed her. 'I lives nigh to the Unicorn, not so far from the Silver Square.'

Together the two women made their way along the ancient sunken track through the deepening gloom, and coming out from enclosing woodland saw the faint glimmers of lighted windows from the town across the broad shallow valley.

'Who cares for your kid when youm at work?' Aggie Southall wanted to know.

'Mother Readman keeps an eye on him for me, and she's giving him his vittles,' Tildy told her.

'He'll do well enough then. Her's a good sort, no matter what some folks might say about her and what goes on in her lodging house.'

'Do you have children?' Tildy asked in return.

'Ahr, too bleddin' many o' the little sods.' Aggie Southall sounded bitter. 'Nine I've birthed, and five be still alive. I has

59

to keep me eldest at home to look arter the little 'uns while I'm working. Her's a sensible little wench though, so I arn't got any worries about leaving 'um for the day.'

'How old is she?'

'Nigh on ten years now.'

Tildy half-turned in surprise, and crimsoned with embarrassment when the other woman perceived her sense of shock, and said bitterly, 'I'm only twenty-six, my wench, for all I looks nearer bleedin' fifty. Iffen you'd had my life, you'd not be looking so bonny yoursen.'

Tildy had sufficient sense not to gush meaningless words in a futile attempt to soothe her companion's ruffled feelings. Instead she merely said, 'Women have a hard time in this life. Some more so than others.'

'Amen to that,' Aggie Southall intoned fervently, then enquired, 'And wheer's your man, Tildy?'

'God only knows. I've not seen hide nor hair of him for close on two years. He left me and my baby, and to tell you the truth, I blessed the day he did so.'

'I reckon we could all feel like that about our men at times,' Aggie Southall agreed. 'But my bloke arn't too bad, as men go. "Bonny" they nicknames him, and true enough he's a bonny bugger to look at all right. He's a pointer lad though, so I doubt he'll be bonny looking much longer. Bin at the pointing for seven years almost, and he's begun to cough a bit o' blood now, and make the bedclothes wringing wet wi' the night-sweats. That's always the fust sign that the rot is taking a hold, that is. Still, wi' any luck he'll last a few years yet, and by then most on our kids 'ull be growed enough to work, so we'll survive all right wi'out him.'

Tildy was not shocked by the apparent casual acceptance her companion displayed. Death was an ever-present companion to rich and poor alike, and any woman who married a pointer knew that if he remained at his trade for more than a few short years, then his early death was an inescapable fact.

'Let's hope that you gain more years with him than you expect,' she wished aloud, and the other woman suddenly cackled with laughter.

'Let's hope so, Tildy, because I does like me bit o' the other, of a night, and that's a fact, that is. Even though he only has to put his hand on me cuckoo's nest and I gets pregnant... Tell me now, how does you go on for it wi' your man being gone?'

Her question was only half-joking, but Tildy giggled with a genuine amusement.

61

'Not very well, or very often, I'm afraid, Aggie.'

Loud, rough-sounding voices came from the lane ahead of them, and as they rounded a sharp bend they saw a group of men coming up the slope. Despite the deepening gloom Tildy could see the men clearly, and a twinge of unease struck her as she took in their broad-brimmed hats, heavy rough-cut clothing, and saw the bundles and the tools strapped upon their bodies.

'They're navigators,' she whispered to Aggie Southall.

Travelling gangs of navvies were objects of dread in the country districts. Wild, lawless men, they worked on the canal constructions and the various public building projects, and at times created virtual reigns of terror in the areas they passed through.

'Never you mind them bastards,' Aggie Southall spoke out loudly, so that the approaching men could not help but hear her. 'Navvies they might be, but they knows better than to offer insult to pointers' womenfolk. They should know what happened to the last lot o' bleedin' navvies who come through this town, and iffen they tries to act up wi' us, then they'll not be long in finding out for themselves what did happen, and that's a fact.'

'Please, Aggie, lower your voice,' Tildy pleaded. 'God knows what they might do to us if you provoke them so.'

'They'll do fuckin' naught.' Aggie's face was rabid with aggression, and Tildy was baffled by her companion's attitude, which in all fairness to them these particular navvies had done nothing to deserve.

'Now then, my lass, what's amiss with thee?' A tall, powerful-bodied man in the lead of the navvy group grinned at Aggie Southall, and came to a standstill before her.

'Theer's fuck-all amiss wi' me, navvy,' she spat the words at him. 'But there 'ull be plenty amiss with you, if you don't stand aside and let us pass.'

The big man's white teeth gleamed in his darkly sun-bronzed features, and his eyes noted Tildy's worried frown and tense body. 'Don't fret thy'sen, pretty 'un,' he told her. 'We'll not offer harm to either of you, even though your butty here is offering us insult for no reason.'

His easy manner quietened Tildy's nervousness, and she was able to relax somewhat. 'We'll bid you good night, then, master,' she told him, and taking Aggie Southall's arm in a firm grip, she went to move on.

'Hold for a tick, pretty 'un.' The big man held up his hand but made no attempt to touch her. 'Wilt at least do me the favour of directing me to Tarbick Cut?'

For a moment Tildy frowned puzzledly, then her face cleared. 'Why, you mean the Tardebigge Canal,' she told him, 'but the canal is finished. It was all dug out years since. Why do you seek it?'

'We're contracted to dig some more wharf basins, Missy. So happen we'll be here for some time. Mayhap you'll be seeing more on us than you've a liking to.' He grinned broadly and winked at her so cheekily, that despite her natural reserve with men, particularly strangers, Tildy could not help but smile back at him.

'Carry on to the end of this lane, then bear to your right hand,' she instructed. 'The canal lies about a mile and a half along the road towards Bromsgrove.'

'That'll do me,' he answered, 'and I'll bid you good night and sweet dreams, pretty 'un, but mayhap I'll be visiting you in your dreams and paying court to you, so watch out for me.'

His mates laughed uproariously at this sally, and blushing furiously Tildy took an even firmer grip on Aggie's arm and hurried on towards Redditch.

They had nearly reached the outer buildings of the town when Aggie Southall broke her extended silence. 'Does you know why I hates them fucking navvies so, Tildy?' She immediately answered her own question. 'Because a few years back, when the canal was fust being dug at Tardebigge, three bastard navvies got a hold o' me one night when I was collecting kindling in the Brockhill wood. They served me real badly. It warn't enough for them just to shag me. No, they had to knock me about as well, the rotten bastards! That was afore I was married, I warn't no more than a kid. I was too scared to tell anyone what had happened to me for bloody years. I hates the bloody sight o' navvies now, and always will do.'

Tildy nodded sympathetically. 'Well I can understand you feeling like that, Aggie. I've known other girls who've had something of the sort happen to them, and been too afraid to tell of it.'

'Who can you tell?' the other woman demanded bitterly. 'The bloody magistrates and constables be all men themselves, and if another man tells 'um that the girl is lying, why then, ninety-nine times out on a hundred they believes the bugger, and calls the girl a lying whore.'

They continued in silence, and when they reached the hill that led up into the centre of the town, Aggie Southall left Tildy. 'I'll be seeing you tomorrow, my wench.'

'Surely you will.' Tildy went on alone up the hill and over the crossroads, past the Chapel and the Fox and Goose, and the castellated town lock-up with its massive gothic-arched doorway. She entered Red Lion Street, which was dark and quiet except for the Red Lion Inn where lights shone from windows, and the sounds of fiddles playing and voices raised in song and laughter echoed from its rooms.

'The pointer lads must be holding holiday on Tuesday as well this week,' she thought, and momentarily envied those who could afford to spend so freely on making merry. Then she remembered the price they paid to do so, and her envy left her. She turned under the high archway at the side of the inn and picked her way along the deep-rutted, filth-strewn Silver Street and into the equally filthy Silver Square.

The lodging house kitchen was surprisingly quiet; only a couple of trampers were seated on a bench picking over the rags and oddments they had collected that day. Tildy, happy to find it so peaceful, felt that she could not have borne the normal packed, raucous hubbub after the peace and tranquility she had known for the past months in the house of Charles Bromley.

Mother Readman was enthroned in her

vast chair by the inglenook, and she greeted Tildy warmly. 'The babby's upstairs sound asleep, my wench. He's ate full to busting, and played 'til he couldn't keep his eyes open.'

'Has he been any trouble to you?' Tildy enquired anxiously.

'Bless him, no. He's a good little cratur, so he is. He's bin afollowing Apollonia round the house most on the day. She loves his bones, so she does.'

Apollonia was Mother Readman's maid of all work, and general deputy. A fourteen-year-old parish bastard that Mother Readman had taken in and treated with a rough kindliness, and who in turn was fiercely loyal towards her only friend and protector. The girl came into the room now, a stunted, normally skinny-bodied, birdlike creature, but not now. Her pregnant belly bulged hugely in incongruous contrast to her matchstick arms and legs.

'Apollonia must be near her time,' Tildy remarked.

'Any day now,' the old woman cursed angrily. 'The silly little cow. Getting copped for a bastard, and her not yet fifteen.'

'Who is the father?' Even as she asked the question Tildy realized its futility. She knew that Apollonia sold her body to men and had been doing so for years, and that the father of her unborn child could be any one of a score of nameless transients.

Mother Readman cackled mirthlessly. 'That's a riddle we'll ne'er know the answer to, Tildy. The little cow has bin a tanner whore for bleeding years, and no matter how I belted her for it, it ne'er made a wink o' difference. She was up wi' her skirts and down on her back the minute I took my eyes off her. Still, Ise told her straight, that this 'un will be the only bastard of her'n that I'll give shelter to. I'll care for this 'un, but if she cops for another, then that 'un 'ull be birthed in the bloody poor'us, and spend its days theer.' The brown stubs of teeth bared in rueful laughter. 'But then, having said that, I reckon the only way I'll be able to stop the little cow opening her legs for every Tom, Dick and Harry, is to nail her bloody thighs together, and sew her up. And if I does that, then I don't doubt that she'll get the blacksmith to draw the sodding nails and cut the stitches.' She stared keenly at Tildy, and asked at a tangent. 'Be you feeling as clemmed as you looks, girl? Go on, take a bowl of stew. You can have it on the house.'

Tildy was indeed voraciously hungry, having eaten nothing all day, and although the stew tasted of tainted meat, still she was glad to gulp down the steaming bowlful, and soothe the gnawing ache of hunger. Once replete, a wave of tiredness swept over her, and she was thankful to make her farewells and climb wearily up the rickety staircase to the tiny attic beneath the gable roof that she shared with little Davy. She gently kissed her sleeping child, and lay down on her own narrow cot, intending to rest for a few minutes before fetching water to wash in. But no sooner had her head touched the pillow than her bodily exhaustion overcame her, and she fell into a deep sleep.

The first palings of dawn were gleaming along the eastern horizon when she woke, with a vision of the night still vivid in her mind. The big navvy she had met on the Salters Way had indeed come into her dreams, but try as she might she could not remember what had occurred between them, except that she had awoken with a feeling of happy well-being.

Little Davy was awake also, lying quietly sucking his thumb and cuddling his beloved Sergeant Hawk. 'Where are you going, Mammy?' he asked, as Tildy rose.

'I'm going to my work, honey! You be a good boy and go back to sleep now, until Mother Readman calls you to get up.'

'I want to come with you, Mammy,' he beseeched.

She shook her head regretfully. 'I can't

take you with me, my pet. Mammy must work hard to earn some pennies for us, and I wouldn't be able to stop and play with you at all. It's best that you wait here for me.'

'And you must bring some pennies for Sergeant Hawk, Mammy,' he urged forcefully. 'He wants some pennies as well.'

'All right then, honey, I promise I'll bring some pennies for Sergeant Hawk as well.' She chuckled softly and bent to smother the solemn, delicate little face with kisses. She tickled the small body and the child laughed and gurgled with delight, wriggling furiously to escape her questing fingers. After a couple of moments she stopped tickling him, and hugged him tenderly. 'I'll needs get ready for work, my honey.' Reluctantly she released him and he contentedly snuggled down in his bed once more with his wooden soldier clasped tightly to him, and even as Tildy lifted her towel and toilette bag from the hooks on the door his eyes were again closed in sleep.

Downstairs Tildy threaded her way through the sleepers lying sprawled across the benches, table and floor of the kitchen, and went into the walled rear yard with its reeking midden heap. She worked the pump-handle vigorously, sluicing her head

70

and arms beneath the gouts of icy-cold water, and dried herself on the coarse towel. She brushed her teeth using the powder of wood-ash and salt she kept in a small stone jar in her bag, and then went back upstairs brushing her hair. Replacing the towel and bag on the door hooks she checked that the child slept, then wrapping her shawl around her shoulders set off for work.

Even though it was not yet five o'clock there was a lot of movement on the streets and lamps were lit in some of the shops. On the still air the clanging bells of the mills and factories carried faintly across the red-tiled gabled rooftops around the Chapel Green, summoning the in-workers to their daily toil, and from the scattered huddles of buildings the in-workers were spilling in answer to that summons. Mostly unwashed and frowsty from stale-smelling, over-crowded rooms, tousle-headed and sleepy-eyed men, women and children of all shapes and ages clumped in their iron-shod clogs over the rutted roadways.

Tildy called at a small shop and bought a lump of cheese and a small penny-loaf for her midday meal. On her route she passed the needle mill and pin factory of Ben Holyoake, where outside its gates a pedlar sold hot coffee, buns and baked potatoes from his canvas-roofed, wheeled handcart with its massive brass urns and cast-iron baking oven. Tildy joined the throng around the cart and for a halfpenny received a pannikin of the hot, harsh-tasting liquid, and a sugared bun, upon which she made a hasty breakfast. Then, returning the empty pannikin to the pedlar, she began the two miles' walk to the Pinfield's workshop.

CHAPTER 7

Robert Stafford had also risen early from his bed, but his breakfast was a more leisured process than a hasty sup of coffee, and he lingered over the thick slices of fatty bacon, the eggs fried in bacon fat, and the crusty bread, still warm from the baker's oven, spread thick with fresh salty butter. His mother and two teenaged sisters hovered about him trying to anticipate his every desire, for since his father's death Robert had been the Master of the house, and its sole breadwinner.

'Another dish of tea, Robert?' his mother urged. 'Shall I brew a fresh pot for you?'

'No Mama, this will serve well enough, I thank you.' The young man was invariably kind and considerate to his females and greatly enjoyed being fussed over by them as he was.

'Why have you risen so early, Brother Robert, you are surely not going away today? You've been back such a short time.'

'No, Helena, I'm not going away today. But I shall have to return to the North Country within the week, I fear. Today, however, I have business nearer home to attend to.'

'Will you be back in time to accompany us to Mrs Boulton's tea-party, brother?' his other sister, Dorothea asked.

Robert smiled at the pair of them, so alike in their rosy-cheeked prettiness, frizz-curled ringlets and beribboned dresses, that they irresistibly reminded him of a pair of China dolls he had once seen in a toyshop window. 'Yes, sister, I shall doubtless be back in time to accompany you there.'

They glanced at each other archly, and giggled in concert.

'And who else is to be there?' he asked, to indulge them.

Again they tittered in concert, holding their hands up in front of their faces.

'Let me see if I can guess.' He pretended to cogitate intently, then clapped his hands sharply. 'Of course, I have it now. Your dear friend Hetty Milward. She will be there, will she not?'

'You know well that she will be so, Brother Robert. And you know well that you will flirt with her quite shamelessly, and make great eyes at her, and try to dazzle her with your worldly experience.'

Both girls giggled hysterically, and Robert smiled fondly at them. For despite their silly childish ways he loved them dearly.

His mother sniffed loudly. 'Hetty Milward is a deal too fast for my taste.' She frowned. 'She a sly minx, that one. A forward young hussy, and over-indulged shamelessly by her parents.'

'Now Mama, do not be so unkind and unjust towards Miss Milward,' Robert reproved her jokingly. 'She's is a most accomplished young lady, and a damned pretty one as well. There is no real harm in her, only a natural high-spirited mischievousness!'

'A natural waywardness, more likely.' His mother was a puritan of the old school, and greatly disapproved of the free-mannered forwardness and flighty behaviour of the modern girls. 'If I had behaved so freely in front of young men when I was a girl, then my father would have taken a stick to my back in very quick order, I'll lay to that.'

'Very well, Mama. I shall most certainly thrash her frequently when she is my wife,'

Robert teased, and laughed aloud at his parent's aggrieved expression. He drained the last of his tea and rose from the table. 'And now I must be off.'

In a froth of skirts and petticoats his sisters accompanied him to the front door of the house, which was situated on the eastern edge of the Chapel Green towards the top of the Fish Hill. They watched with admiring eyes as he adjusted his cravat, his coat and white top hat, and drew on his riding gloves. Then they stood in the open doorway waving as he strode across the Green in the direction of his uncle's inn, where he kept his horse stabled.

Fat Tommy Fowkes was bustling about the inn yard when his nephew reached it, and while the ostler saddled the horse, uncle and nephew shared a flagon of hot mulled ale in the tap room.

'Wheer be you off to, so early?' Tommy Fowkes wanted to know.

'Now uncle, you know what curiosity did for the cat?' his nephew cautioned him teasingly.

The fat man swore violently, and Robert Stafford shouted with laughter. 'Calm yourself do, uncle, before you break a blood vessel. If you must insist on knowing, then I'll tell you... I'm off to have a look at our future premises.'

'John Pinfield's place, I'll wager.' Tommy

Fowkes' eyes, almost buried in balls of fat, gleamed with grudging admiration. 'Youse worked the oracle well theer, boy, I'll gi' you credit for that,' he conceded. 'How much does he owe you now?'

'A bit more than his workshop and tools can cover,' the young man told him.

'Mind now, don't press on him too harsh,' Tommy Fowkes warned. 'No need to mek more enemies than you needs to.'

'Don't worry, uncle, I learned long since that a spoonful of honey catches more flies than a gallon of vinegar.'

Tildy was nearing the top of the Salters Way when she heard the thumping of horses' hooves coming at a rapid pace behind her. She moved to the side of the narrow track and glanced up at the horseman as he passed, recognizing him as a friend of Charles Bromley's who had often been at the shop. He recognized her in return, and reined in.

'Why Tildy, what bring you abroad at this hour?'

'I'm on my way to work, Master Stafford.'

'Work?' He was puzzled. 'But are you no longer working for Charlie Bromley?'

'No,' she told him. 'I left his employ some time past.'

'H'mmm, did you now.' He digested the

information, but made no other comment. Inwardly however he was wondering if his friend had made some advances towards this very desirable young woman which had caused her to leave the house. He had realized long since that Charles Bromley nursed a secret infatuation for the girl. 'And who could blame him?' Robert Stafford thought now. 'She's a tasty piece. I'd not be hasty to kick her from my bed, and that's a fact.' Aloud he asked, 'Where is it you work then, Tildy?'

'At John Pinfield's shop,' she told him. 'At the soft work.'

'Then I can give you a ride to your work, Tildy. I'm on my way to the very place... Come.' He held his hand down to her, slipping his foot from the stirrup so that she could use it to mount behind him.

Tildy hesitated and the young man grinned. 'Come on, girl. No one will think any harm if they see you having a lift from me.'

She accepted the invitation and the next instant was perched side-saddle behind him. The horse moved at a trot and as they travelled Robert Stafford became pleasantly aware of the feel of the young woman's soft arms about his waist, and the pressure of full, firm breasts against his back. He was a hot-blooded man, and he could not help but indulge himself with fanciful images in which the girl behind him figured prominently. He also savoured the fact that if all went as he planned he would become the girl's employer himself in a short space of time. He dwelt upon that prospect with some considerable satisfaction. That a lot of needle masters indulged themselves sexually with their female workers and servants was an open secret in the town, and if he was to become a master himself, then Robert Stafford acknowledged that he would more than probably enter into such liaisons himself. And who better to have such a liaison with than this succulent example of woman-flesh riding behind him.

'Tell me, Tildy, you read and write well, do you not?'

'Yes, Master Stafford.'

'And your numbers? Can you add, subtract, multiply and divide accurately?'

'Yes, Master Stafford.' Tildy was wondering why he should ask her such questions. But she did not ask him for his reason. She was sufficiently a woman of the age to accept the right of her social superiors to quiz her without offering any explanations.

'Do you enjoy the soft work?' he wanted to know next, and she smiled ruefully.

'Soft work is there to be done, Master Stafford, not to be enjoyed.'

He found her soft voice pleasant to listen to, and was surprised that her diction and accents were those more suited to a woman of a higher social station in life. 'You are well-spoken, Tildy,' he remarked idly. 'You do not sound like a factory wench.'

She made no reply, but inwardly felt a sense of resentment at the implications behind his words. 'So, he thinks I do not sound like a factory wench. Would my life have been any easier for me if I did? Why must people like him only ever see the poor as illiterate brute beasts? Why should we always be expected to conform to their low opinions of us?'

They were now in sight of the Pinfield house, and Tildy told him, 'I'll get down and walk from here, Master Stafford. I've no wish to be teased by my workmates.'

He appreciated her sensitivity and reined in to let her slip from the horse's back.

'My thanks for the ride, master.'

On impulse he bent towards her from the saddle, and said, 'Learn as much as you can about the soft work, Tildy Crawford. Mayhap in a few weeks you will have a chance of bettering yourself.' With that he kicked his mount into a trot, leaving Tildy walking and wondering about the import of what he had said.

Her workmates were waiting at the

locked lean-to door, and Aggie Southall greeted her.

'Hello, my duck. Be you as eager to get stuck in as the rest on us be?'

Tildy laughed and shook her head. 'I think not, Aggie. But I fear that I'll still have to get stuck in, come what may.'

'The missus is taking her time about opening this bloody door,' Aggie grumbled and shiveringly pulled her threadbare shawl closer about her as a gust of night-chilled wind swirled the women's skirts and caused the ill-fitting casements of the lean-to to shake and rattle. 'By the christ, but this bleedin' wind is uncommon cold for the time o' year.'

'Ahr, youm right theer, Aggie,' another woman put in. 'Weem agoing to have a hard winter, I reckon.'

'When as the likes of us ever had an easy 'un, Molly, tell me that?' Aggie Southall's haggard features were bitter. 'For us it's always bin a cold blow.'

The others murmured their agreement with her sentiments, but the mood was broken by the sound of a key in the lock, and the women cheered with ironic plaudits as the door was flung open and Mrs Pinfield beckoned them inside. 'Come on, blast you! Don't keep me a'waiting all bleedin' day. There's work to be done.'

Tildy glanced at the woman and saw

80

that one of her eyes was badly swollen and discoloured. Aggie Southall saw it also, and winked surreptitiously at the other women, before asking with false sympathy,

'Did you and your man come to blows agen, Amanda?'

Mrs Pinfield seemed near to tears. 'The bugger was drunk out on his brain agen, Aggie. I ne'er said a word to him, when he ups and lays into me. I'm fair sick to death on him, so I am. I works all the bleedin' hours God sends to try and help him, and all the bugger does is knock me about every time he gets the bleedin' drink in him.'

She turned and disappeared through the connecting door into the house, and Aggie Southall dropped her voice as she told Tildy,

'John Pinfield is good-hearted enough when he's sober, but he's a real devil when he's in drink. The trouble is, he's a terrible man for the gambling, and bloody unlucky wi' it, too. He earns good money at the pointing when he's a mind to graft, and gets good money from this shop, as well. But what he don't piss up the wall, he loses on the cards and the fighting cocks and the bloody dogs. O' course, Amanda Pinfield nags him for it, and then he loses his rag and blacks her eyes for her. Regular as clockwork, so it is. No wonder the poor cow is always so sour-faced. Her's got more reason than most on us to be miserable, and that's a fact.'

Tildy listened without comment, remembering her own violent marriage. A man's right to beat his wife, his children, his servants, or his animals, was unchallenged, and consequently among the male sex there were many who all too frequently exercised that right, with or without provocation. She sighed, and inwardly renewed her vows to herself that never again would she allow any man to exercise that right over her.

Without further delay the women and children seated themselves at the workbench and commenced their gruelling, soul-destroying labours.

In the house John Pinfield and Robert Stafford faced each other across the parlour table. Sick and grey-faced from his protracted debauch, the pointer's hands shook uncontrollably as he fumbled to fill his broken-stemmed clay-pipe with the rank-smelling black tobacco he favoured.

Robert Stafford was talking in low-pitched, sympathetic tones. 'You've had terrible luck, John. There's no doubt about it, terrible luck. How did it go at the cards yesterday?'

The pointer hawked and spat disgustedly

into the cold ashes of the fireplace. 'Fucking terrible! That's how it went. Fucking terrible! I arn't held a winning hand since Saturday morning. Not one fucker!'

The younger man nodded commiseratingly. 'How much did Jonas Crowther win from you?'

'Nigh on thirty guineas in coin and scrip. God rot him! He's got the Devil's own luck has that evil bastard. It's cleaned me out, Rob, and worse nor that, the bugger's took notes from me for another fifty guineas, and I've not got it to give him.'

Again Stafford made commiserating noises, and then remarked, 'He's a bad bugger to owe money to as well, John. If a man don't pay up to time, then Crowther sets his rippling boys against him.'

'I arn't afeared to fight any o' them bastards,' the pointer asserted doggedly.

'Oh, I know that well enough, John. And there's no doubt but that you'll prove to be the master of any one of them if it came to blows. But the rippling boys don't work that way against a fighting man like yourself, do they? No, against someone of your mettle it's the broken windows in the night, and the fireball thrown inside. The horse getting its throat cut in the paddock and the pigs and dogs being poisoned. They're a bad crew, and Jonas Crowther makes a terrible enemy.'

There was a brief silence, then the older man burst out desperately, 'It's a bad time for me, I'll tell you, Robert. Thank God you arn't pressing me for what I owes you.'

Robert Stafford's ruddy features were sorrowful as he answered with evident regret, 'Well, as to that, John, I'm afraid that the reasons I came here this morn was to ask you if you could see your way to paying me something on account of what you owe me.' He shook his head sadly. 'I've taken a hammering myself just lately, John, and I'm in sore need of the readies.' He held up his hand as if to forestall any protest from his companion. 'But don't you fret, John. I'm not a man to kick a fellow when he's down. I've given the matter a lot of thought, and I consider that I can make you a proposition which will solve both our problems.'

'Will it get Jonas Crowther off me back?' The pointer grinned mirthlessly. 'Because I reckon that's about me wustest problem.'

Robert Stafford nodded slowly. 'Yes, John. It's my opinion that if you should agree to what I'm going to suggest to you, then we can do something about keeping Jonas Crowther and his gang happy, as well...'

An hour later Robert Stafford rode away from the Pinfield house humming merrily to himself. He now had premises, tools and a labour force, and had achieved this without making an enemy of John Pinfield. In fact, the pointer had been more than grateful.

'I think I've handled it very well,' Robert Stafford congratulated himself.

His uncle, after due consideration, also congratulated his nephew. 'Yes, Rob, to my way o' thinking youse done it right. Now go and see Lawyer Browning and get the contract drawn up legal.'

'I've already done that, uncle, and Pinfield's name is signed to it.'

'Then don't sit here wasting my time and your own, boy. Get away to the North Country and seal the bargain with Abraham.' The fat man handed a small soft leather pouch to his nephew. 'Here's the money. Now get across that horse.'

Nothing loth, the young man took the bag and his leave, and within the hour, despite the disappointed wails of his sisters, was spurring his horse northwards.

During the day Tommy Fowkes was his usual affable self, greeting his needle master patrons with jokes and laughter.

The more he thought of how his nephew had handled John Pinfield, the more he appreciated the young man's shrewdness. His nephew had not tried to force the pointer to sign over his workshop and tools. Instead, under a solemn pact of secrecy, he had agreed to let the man's debts to him be counted as rent on the premises. Pinfield remained the owner, but for the next four years Robert Stafford, and through him, Tommy Fowkes, would be the tenants of the workshop and the controllers of the labour force. Tommy Fowkes grinned happily to himself.

There was yet another advantage to the bargain, perhaps the most valuable of all. The agreement was to include that part of the ground floor of Pinfield's house which had originally been a pointing mill, and the old horse-powered gin with its mighty cogged wheels was still in place, and with some renovation could quickly be made operational once more.

'By the Christ!' The fat man's pink face glowed with satisfaction. 'By the Christ! Weem practically set up as needle masters. We can make a mint o' money, and it wun't ha' cost me above three hundred sovereigns to do it.' Then he frowned disgruntledly. 'Oh bollocks! I was forgetting the fifty bloody guineas for that sod, Jonas Crowther...'

CHAPTER 8

The news that a gang of navigators were once again at the Tardebigge Canal spread swiftly through the town and provoked diverse reactions. The local prize-fighters, whores and beer-house keepers welcomed the news. For each of them in their separate ways could see a ready profit to be made from the newcomers. The more respectable inhabitants of the district, however, greeted the news with distaste.

'Have we not sufficient of our own drunken brawlers, thieves and God-forsaken sinners already, without these damned navigators coming to swell the numbers?' was among the mildest comments voiced.

The subject of the navvy gang was brought up at the Saturday afternoon meeting of the select vestry, the local governing body of the Tardebigge Parish, which met in the vestry room at St Stephen's Chapel, Redditch. The greater part of the town lay within the parish boundaries and it was the major settlement and concentration of population for the parish.

There were four vestrymen present: the

newly appointed chairman, the Reverend John Clayton, a youngish, attractively ugly-faced and exceptionally well-built man, whose muscular body strained against the seams of his clerical-black clothing, and plain white linen; the previous chairman, William Smallwood, needle master and factor to the trade; George Holyoake, farmer, and Josiah Cutler, the district's largest dealer in coals, whose lean features were as dark-grimed and louring as his stock in trade.

The vestry had sent for the Parish Constable, Joseph Cashmore, and when he arrived, bearing his long staff with its crown top, the Reverend Clayton wasted no time.

'It is in the matter of these newcome navigators we wish to speak with you about, Master Cashmore. What do you intend to do concerning them?'

The burly constable frowned sullenly. 'I don't rightly see what I can do about 'um, parson. Theym contracted for by the Canal Company, and they arn't making any applications for Parish Relief to my knowledge. So I can't use the Law o' Settlement to kick 'um out of the parish, can I?'

'Weem not asking you to kick 'um out o' the parish, Joseph,' William Smallwood interjected. 'But weem agreed that it 'ud be no bad thing iffen you was to goo up theer and have a word wi' 'um. Tell the buggers straight and plain, that if they kicks up any randies, then weem agoing to run 'um clean out o' the county! Ne'er mind the bloody parish!' The needle master was a self-made man, and his expensive broadcloth coat, and fine laced linen did nothing to soften his manners or modes of speech.

'Now Master Smallwood, I think it wiser if a more diplomatic approach was to be made,' John Clayton suggested, and the needle master showed his big yellowed teeth in a savage grin.

' 'Tis no use spouting fine phrases to talk wi' bloody mad dogs, Parson Clayton. The only thing them buggers understands is a good smack in the chops when they talks out o' turn. I arn't forgot the last time we had the navigators in this district. Eight or nine years ago, that was, afore you come here, Parson. The trouble we had wi' 'um was nobody's business, I'll tell you. It was like bloody Waterloo every weekend.'

'I've heard it said that our own pointer lads were more than eager to instigate those battles,' Clayton remarked dryly. 'And that you yourself, Master Smallwood, were not averse to the occasional bout of fisticuffs with the navvy champions.'

'That was afore I'd reached my present

position in life, parson,' the needle master stated pompously. 'Times has changed. I've a business to think about now, and I can't afford to have my workpeople spending their time arandying around wi' bloody navigators.'

'Then it's you that'll have to stop 'um adoing so, Will Smallwood,' Cashmore asserted forcefully. 'And not expect me to do it for you. Ise got problems enough keeping the peace in this town as it is, wi'out looking for more to add to 'um.'

'What about my livestock?' George Holyoake, still erect and strong-bodied despite his sixty years, challenged the constable. 'What be you agoing to do about protecting my livestock from being stole and ate by these navigators? I arn't the only farmer hereabouts who'll be asking you that, Joe Cashmore. My land arn't far from the Tarbick Cut, and I lost more nor a few lambs last time the navigators was here... Ahr, and a bloody fine bullock as well.'

'Gentlemen! Gentlemen!' John Clayton rapped his chairman's gavel upon the table as he called for order. 'Let us not squabble among ourselves, I beg you. You know well, Master Holyoake, that the Constable can do little or nothing to protect the livestock in the vicinity of the navigators' encampment. It would take a regiment of soldiers to guard against such accomplished thieves. You must simply do what you can with your farm servants and labourers to maintain a watch. I, for one, am fully confident that Master Cashmore will continue to uphold the law in this parish despite the advent of these navigators adding to his present arduous duties, and let us be thankful that they are not here in large numbers. How many are here, do you think, Master Cashmore?'

'Not above forty on 'um, by all accounts, parson.'

'That's forty too many of the sods.' This was Josiah Cutler's first contribution to the subject under review.

John Clayton realized the futility of maintaining this discussion any longer. 'What I suggest, gentlemen, is that we charge Master Cashmore to monitor the situation and report his findings back to us at the next vestry meeting. If these navigators are found to be creating any undue disturbances in the parish, or committing any depredations against our people, then we will apply to the magistrates for their assistance in dealing with the problem. However, until such offences are proven against the navvies, then let us allow them the benefit of doubt. After all, gentlemen, we do not wish to stand accused of giving dogs bad names and hanging them simply because of that, do we?'

The expressions of his fellow vestrymen appeared doubtful about the point he was making, but they voiced grudging acceptance of his suggestion, and Joseph Cashmore was duly instructed to maintain a close surveillance of the navigators, and permitted to depart. After some further business had been dealt with, the meeting closed and the vestrymen dispersed.

The hour was nearly six o'clock; John Clayton remained standing on the chapel steps looking at the scene around him. Since it was Saturday the mills and factories had closed at five o'clock and the in-workers had flooded into the town centre where the Saturday market was in full swing. The stalls were erected in two lines on the southern boundary of the Chapel Green, and stretched from the crossroads to the lock-up. It was mainly women and children who thronged about them, the men for the most part being already inside the inns and alehouses celebrating their release from the week's bondage in their normal hard-drinking manner.

The scene in the market place was animated and lively as the stall-holders bellowed their wares and engaged in light-hearted chaff and badinage with the crowds. Acquaintances greeted each other and stopped to exchange news and gossip. At one end of the market a group of youths sky-larked and flirted with some young girls, who blushed and coquetted and gloried in these snatched moments of romance. Smaller children played hide and seek among the skirts and stalls and ran shrieking with excitement in games of tag, and follow my leader. Their mothers, laden with wicker baskets, mob-capped and white-aproned and beshawled, haggled prices and purchased their families' needs with many anxious looks at their scant, fast-diminishing stocks of coins.

John Clayton's eyes grew wistful as he viewed the easy camaraderie of the elders, the entwined hands of the young lovers, and the rough and ready confidence that one and all seemed to possess in abundance, finding it so different from the stilted exchanges demanded by the formal manners of his own stratum of society. There were times, such as now, when he wished he could be truly a part of the crowd, and move among them as one of their own. Then he thought of the other aspects of their lives. The grinding poverty, the cramped, overcrowded housing, the fetid unhealthiness of their streets and alleys, the drudgery of their work, the illiteracy, the ignorance, the casual brutality of the daily life of the poor, and admitted to himself that after all he would prefer to live as he did.

A young woman walking hand in hand with a small child caught his eye. He recognized the uncovered glossy hair, the smooth pale skin of face and throat, the graceful sensuousness of the body beneath the shabby dark dress and neat clean white apron. Matilda Crawford. He had come into contact with her on several occasions, and viewed her now with very mixed feelings. He considered her to be a deal too independent in her ways, and sadly lacking in the proper degree of respect for her betters. Indeed, her attitude at times towards those of a superior station in life to herself could be termed positively insolent. If she were a man she would undoubtedly have been a Luddite, a radical, a revolutionary, if not worse. And yet, mingling with his condemnation there was a grudging respect. She kept herself and her child clean and presentable. She bore herself with modesty, and did not sport with men in the alehouses, but lived respectably despite being surrounded by so much immorality and loose-living. She had spoken out far too freely at times, but when she did so there had been considerable truth and justice in what she said.

John Clayton was forced now to concede that although he had personally heard her bitterly decry the church and its ordained ministers, and its faithful flock, yet she appeared, on the surface at least, to lead what could be termed a Christian life—even though to his knowledge she never stepped across the threshold of any religious house of worship.

He was also forced to admit to himself that he found her physically beautiful to look upon. 'God protect me from carnal thoughts,' he muttered half humorously, as he watched her until she was lost to his sight among the crowded stalls, experiencing a distinct sensation of deprivation as she went from view.

Tildy was enjoying her walk amid the bustle and high spirits of the market place. Little Davy was enjoying it also as he sucked greedily on a long stick of garishly coloured rock candy, and gazed with huge eyes at these exciting events taking place all around him. Tildy looked down fondly and so intent was she upon her son that she failed to see the man stepping across her path until she cannoned bodily into his tall figure.

'Now then, pretty 'un! I'd hoped we'd meet again, but not that you 'ud near knock me flying.' It was the big navvy that she had spoken with on the Salters Way. 'My name is Israel Lee. What's your name?'

'Matilda Crawford, but most people just call me Tildy.' She found him physically attractive, his thick brown hair bleached by sun, his body tall and powerfully built. Today he wore an expensive velvet-collared dark green frock-coat, white shirt-front with a high stock and pearl-silk cravat. Black trousers tucked into polished riding boots and a wide-brimmed, low-crowned beaver hat.

He grinned as he noted her eyes evaluating his present dress. 'I'm no mere navvy, Tildy Crawford, but a contractor in my own right.'

Outwardly, she appeared unimpressed by this information, and slightly piqued by this he went on, 'The name of Israel Lee is known and respected in bigger towns than this one.'

'I don't doubt that, Master Lee, but you should know that in this town all navigators carry a bad name, whether they are mere navvies, or contractors who are known and respected in bigger towns than this one.'

White teeth glistened as he enjoyed her mischievous humour. 'Navigators carry a bad name wherever they go, my lass, but it's not always deserved. My lads are rough and ready, but they're not bad-hearted on the whole. They don't go round terrorizing the countryside. I won't tolerate that sort of behaviour in my work-gangs. No, the name of Israel Lee is held up as the example of how to control navvies, and that's a fact.'

'Well, I'm pleased to hear that, Master Lee.' Tildy smiled inwardly at his artless boastings. It was a boyish trait which in this man she found appealing.

'And now, Tildy Crawford, do you know where Mrs Barnet's shop is?'

'Do you mean the pastry cook?' she queried.

'Yes, I mean the pastry cook.'

'The shop lies along the Evesham Street.' She jerked her shapely chin in the direction of the road leading southwards from the crossroads, at the far end of which was also situated the shop of her late employer.

'I'm told Mrs Barnet keeps eating-rooms, is that right?'

'She does.'

'And that her cakes and pastries are marvellously good.'

'So people say.'

'Then, Tildy Crawford, will you and your fine son do me the honour of accompanying me to Mrs Barnet's shop and sharing a few platters of whatever you'd fancy, with me?'

Tildy's immediate reaction was to shake her head in refusal, but Israel Lee was not deterred by this. 'Come now, Tildy Crawford, I'm inviting you to a most respectable establishment. I'm sure your boy would love to eat a fruit tart, and drink a glass of ginger ale.'

'I'm a married woman, Master Lee, even though living separate from my husband. It wouldn't be decent to be seen keeping company with a stranger.'

'But I'm no stranger to you now, Tildy,' he cajoled. 'And let me assure you that I'm a very respectable man. I'm not married, and I've no mistress or kids hid away anywhere. And if you're living separate from your husband, then where is the sin in keeping me company to eat a pastry? Besides, you'll have this fine young grenadier with you to serve as a chaperon.

'Come now, please keep me company for a little while. I get very lonely for the company of decent women, Tildy. The wenches who follow the navvy gangs are as rough as the men. I need sometimes to talk with women like yourself, if only to remind me to watch my manners. Surely you'll not deny me that pleasure, and deny your boy the pleasure of some fancy cakes and ginger ale?

'No offence to you, my lass, but I've

a notion that you've not much to spare for fripperies, so a little bit of a tea party will do you and the child a power o' good.'

He had found the weak point in Tildy's defences when he spoke of her child, and eventually she smiled in agreement.

'Very well then, Master Lee. My Davy and me accept your kind invitation. But let us be very clear on one point. I am only going to keep you company in the pastry shop. Me and Davy will be going home by ourselves.'

He removed his hat with a flourish, and half-bowed. 'You have made your point very clearly, Mistress Crawford, and I accept that condition.'

As the trio made their way towards the pastry cook shop several pairs of eyes noted them. They made a striking couple, and there were men among the onlookers who envied Israel Lee his beautiful companion, as well as women who envied Tildy her handsome escort. One woman did not envy her however. Aggie Southall, her runny-nosed, rickety brood clinging to her skirts, recognized Tildy's escort, and an unreasoning anger filled her. 'Jesus Christ, Tildy Crawford! I'd n'er ha' thought that you'd become a navvy's whore? Wait 'til I tells the rest o' the girls about this... Just wait!'

CHAPTER 9

When Tildy awoke on Sunday morning her first recollection of the previous day was the hours spent with Israel Lee in the eating room of the pastry cook.

'What a feast we had!' She blushed as she remembered just how many of the delicious pastries she had sampled. 'Dear God, what must he have thought of me, gorging myself so?' But then she consoled herself with the recollection that it was her companion who had virtually forced those delicacies upon her, refusing to accept her own refusals.

She smiled down at her sleeping child, remembering how he had enjoyed himself. For both of them it had been a rare treat, such as they had never known before, and in all likelihood would never know again. 'So, we ate like pigs. What if we did?' She snapped her fingers in a gay mood of defiance. 'A fig for anybody's opinion of our gluttony. It was a once in a lifetime treat for us, so be damned to it. I'll not spoil it by feeling any guilt about it now.'

She stretched luxuriously in the bed,

planning how to spend this precious day of freedom. 'I must get up now, and wash our clothes and bedding, and then mayhap I'll take Davy to the meadows, and we'll fish for minnows. He'll love to have his own pet fish in a jar.'

She rose from the narrow bed, and dressed by pulling the gown over her head to cover her night-shift, then rolled her white cotton stockings up her shapely smooth-skinned legs, and slipped her small feet into the wooden clogs. Taking her towel and toilette bag she hurried downstairs.

A dreadful shock awaited her in the kitchen of the lodging house. Seated on a bench talking to Mother Readman was her husband, and the father of her child, Thomas Crawford.

'Dear God! Is it really you, Tom?' she gasped, and a sudden onset of faintness caused her to sway visibly.

Crawford's head turned, and she saw the fresh livid scars, the broken, misshapen nose and cheekbone, and the still swollen discoloured flesh. He rose to his feet and came towards her, his hand outstretched.

'Now then, Tildy, arn't you got a welcome kiss for your lawful wedded husband?' He grinned, disclosing teeth also broken by the cudgels of his attackers.

Tildy's heart was pounding furiously,

101

and her breath came in shortened gasps as waves of nausea broke over her, causing her face to blanch and cold, clammy sweat to start from her pores. He reached for her, and she drew back, shaking her head.

'Don't you put a finger on me, Tom Crawford. Not one finger.'

'What's this you're saying?' His black eyes filled with the heat of anger, and for a moment the old sickeningly familiar fear of his violence assailed Tildy, but she refused to surrender to that fear, and screwed her courage to the sticking point.

'I'm saying that you keep your hands off me, Tom Crawford.' She fought to firm her shaking voice and to steady her trembling body. 'It's only the shock of seeing him that's making me like this,' she told herself desperately. 'It's just the shock, that's all. I'm not afraid of him any more.'

She swallowed hard to ease the painful stricture of her dry throat and mouth. 'What do you want here? How did you find me?'

A calculating expression overlayed the fury in his eyes, and he stepped backwards a pace, studying her closely. 'Fuck me, but she's looking good,' he told himself, and the lust he had always felt for her surged powerfully in him. 'I'd best play this a bit careful-like. Treat her gently,' he decided, and aloud said, 'Now don't upset yourself, Tildy. I'm not here to bring you any harm.' His mind was racing as he spoke, examining and rejecting stories to tell her. 'Look, I'll not offer to come nigh you, let alone put a hand on you.' He stepped back another couple of paces. 'See, I'm not offering you any harm, am I? I just wants to talk wi' you, that's all. Just to talk wi' you.'

By now the first shattering impact of his appearance was wearing off, and Tildy was reasserting control over her badly shaken nerves.

'Does you want him gone from here, Tildy?' For the first time Mother Readman intervened between man and wife. 'Because if you does, then say the word, and I'll have him run out of here this instant.'

Tom Crawford was too cunning to challenge Mother Readman. Instead he turned to her and said quietly, 'If you wants me to leave your house, Missus, then I'll go right now wi'out any argument. But I swear to you that I never come here to cause Tildy or anybody else any upset. I only come wi' the hopes of having a quiet talk wi' her—arter all, she's me lawful wedded wife, and she's got my son.'

The old woman ignored him, and kept her gaze on Tildy. 'Well girl, does you want him in or out? Say the word.'

Tildy's breathing was shallow and rapid, her mind a maelstrom of indecision. Then she looked squarely at her husband, and all the bitter memories of their time together came flooding back. 'You'd best go from here, Tom,' she told him. 'I can't talk to you now. Perhaps later, when the shock of you coming back has eased a bit, but not now. You'd best leave me be for now.'

Vicious fury sparked in the black eyes, but his lips smiled, and his voice was apologetic and full of understanding. 'Of course I'll go now, Tildy, if that's what you wants. I'd no notion o' causing you any shock or upset. I arn't the man I used to be, Tildy. I'se grown older and gentler now. If you don't want our son to know his own father, then fair enough. I know I gave you sufficient cause to hate me in the past.'

He turned to Mother Readman. 'I'll bid you good day, Missus, and say thanks for letting me see my wife in your house. And don't you moither about Tildy here, I means no harm to her.'

He moved towards the door, and Tildy could not stop herself from shrinking back as he passed her.

'There's no call for you to cringe away from me, my wench,' he told her softly. 'I means no harm, nor wishes you none. Mayhap I'll call agen in a day or so. You'll no doubt be a bit easier in your own mind by then. Let's hope so anyway, because we needs to talk, Tildy. If not about us, then about our son. He needs a father, girl. Every boy needs a father...'

When he had gone, Tildy slumped down upon a bench, feeling sick and spent with all the happiness of the morning drained from her, leaving in its stead a sensation of hopeless despair. 'How did he find me here?' she asked the other woman.

Mother Readman chuckled grimly. 'It's easy enough to find anybody in this town, Tildy, the way everybody noses into others' business. You ought to know that by now. 'Tis a pity you rose so early afore I could come and warn you he was here. He was talking so soft and sweet about you I couldn't hardly believe he was the same bugger that you described to me. Said he'd made enquiries for you in Bromsgrove, and they'd told him you'd bin removed to here under the Settlement Laws. Well, all he needed to do then was to find the constable, Joe Cashmore, warn't it. And o' course, that miserable sod was only too ready to tell a husband wheer his missus was at.

'But you listen to me, girl. There's no need for you to be afeared of the bugger, not while youm under my roof, at any rate. There's a few of the rough 'uns in this town as owes me favours. I can soon get Crawford's yed broke for him, if needful. Come to that, I'll break the bugger's yed meself if he comes here offering you harm. He'll not be the fust man to come a cropper wi' me, not by a long chalk he wun't.'

'I'm truly grateful to you, Mother Readman.' Tildy tried to smile, but an acute anxiety had begun to gnaw at her. 'But to tell truth, it's not the thought of him trying to harm me bodily that worries me. It's what he said about every boy needing a father. Needing his own father.'

'Bollocks to that!' the older woman exploded. 'What sort of a feyther has he ever bin to that babby? Youse bin feyther and mother both to the little cratur.'

'Yes, but what would happen if he applied to the magistrates to gain the boy?' Tildy caught her full lower lip between her teeth.

Mother Readman's great tallowy face became sombre. 'Ahr, youse got a point theer, Tildy. The magistrates 'ud be bound to give him the babby. Arter all, him being the lawful father, they couldn't gainsay him, could they. Is Tom Crawford registered as the feyther?'

Tildy nodded miserably. 'Yes, I got the birth registered in the Tardebigge church ledger myself, naming Tom Crawford as the lawful father. But what else could I have done?' she pleaded for understanding. 'If I hadn't got it entered so, then Davy would have been numbered as a parish bastard, and have to bear that stigma all his life. Plus whatever else the overseers wanted to do with him. And indeed, there is no denying that Tom Crawford is my lawful wedded husband, and Davy's lawful father.' Tears brimmed in her eyes. 'Dear God, what am I to do? What am I to do if Tom Crawford goes to the magistrates and demands the child be given him?'

'Now just stop that bloody shrawking, my wench,' Mother Readman scolded angrily. 'It arn't like you to skrike like some soft-raised maid. Youse faced troubles afore, arn't you. And you knows as well as I does that tears and moans don't alter nothing. So dry your eyes and gather your courage, girl, because I reckon youm agoing to need it. But you arn't alone in facing trouble this time, because I'm wi' you, so let's have no more bloody skrawking, or by the Christ, I'll take a bloody strap to your back.'

The rough, but well-meant admonitions were exactly what Tildy needed to stiffen her faltering resolve; and now she wiped her eyes and quite deliberately began to fuel a savage anger against her husband, which enabled her to steady herself and summon the courage to face boldly up to whatever he might try to do to harm her. She blew her nose hard and loud in a strip of clean rag, and forced a smile.

'I'm all right now, Mother Readman,' she said haltingly, but with a grim determination. 'I'll not give way to tears again.'

'That's the way, my wench,' the older woman applauded. 'Instead of you shedding tears, you start thinking how you can make that bloody husband o' yourn shed a few tears if need be...'

But for all the bold face she showed to the world, Tildy's anxiety about her husband's return clouded her every waking moment. She did not take her child to the meadows that day, but instead kept him close to her in the lodging house. That night her fears drove her to push her cot against the door of her room to bar it, despite the realization that she was behaving irrationally.

But even with this barricade sleep still eluded her, and long before dawn she was astir. Not able to bear the thought of leaving Davy in the lodging house where his father might gain access to him, she decided to take him with her to her work.

Davy, still wanting to sleep and made peevish by being taken from his warm bed and out into the chill morning air murky with drizzling rain, cried and complained continuously as Tildy carried him in her arms over the rutted, pot-holed muddy tracks, her clogs slipping and sliding and causing her to stumble at frequent intervals.

'Be quiet, damn you!' she shouted suddenly, driven almost to distraction by her own weariness and his constant wailings, and then remorse struck deep into her as she saw the uncomprehending fright in his wide eyes at this untoward display of anger from his usually all-loving mother. She hugged him fiercely to her, and kissed the rain-damp skin of his temples and cheeks. 'There now, don't be fritted, my honey. Mammy didn't mean to shout. But you must try to be a very good boy today, and not whine so. I know it's cold and damp, honey, but we'll soon be in a nice warm place, you'll see.' She kissed him again. 'Be good now, sweetheart. Be good.'

Her arms and back were aching agonisingly from his weight by the time she arrived at the lean-to door, where the customary crowd of sleep-sodden women and children waited in weary, dulled apathy. Tildy saw Aggie Southall staring curiously at her child, and smiled at the haggard-featured woman.

'I hope Mrs Pinfield won't mind me bringing my boy with me, only I...' Tildy stopped abruptly as she saw the other woman's hostile expression, then asked, 'Why Aggie, what's amiss?'

'Naught's amiss wi' me!' the woman snapped curtly. 'But then, why should there be? I arn't bin playing fast and loose wi' damned navvies.'

Tildy's mouth opened slightly in shocked puzzlement. 'What do you mean by that?' she questioned, and Aggie Southall hawked and spat on the ground at Tildy's feet, then answered,

'You knows well enough what I means. I don't know how youse got the gall to come and work wi' decent folk arter the company youse bin keeping.' She swung to the avidly listening group of women around the door. 'What does you say, girls? Can you credit the hard neck this bleedin' navvies' whore has got?'

Little Davy had fallen into a fitful slumber, his head lolling in the cradle of Tildy's neck and shoulder, and she had no wish to wake him. Realizing now that the news of her tea party with Israel Lee must have spread to many ears, she merely replied, 'Look Aggie, I don't really understand why you should behave like this towards me, but I've no wish to row with you.'

'Jesus Christ! Butter 'uddn't melt in her mouth, 'ud it girls!' Aggie Southall jeered.

A couple of her cronies nodded and voiced their agreement, but most of the women only looked on silently, with some tittering and surreptitious nudging, while the children were unconcerned by yet another adult dispute, and only hunched their under-nourished, ill-clad bodies against the drizzling rain in the dank cold dawn.

Aggie Southall swung to confront Tildy once more, and spat out accusingly, 'I saw you wi' me own eyes a'walking out wi' that navvy. The one who bloody insulted me that day in the Salters Way when you was wi' me. I saw you wi' him, as bold as brass, looking for all the world as if you thought you was Lord and Lady Muck taking the bloody air. Well, my fine tart, you might think you was Lady Muck wi' your bloody fancy man beside you, but to any decent 'ooman in the town, you was nothing more than a tanner-slut. A bloody navvies' whore!'

Tildy's fiery spirit rose in rebellion at these unjustified insults, and bright spots of angry colour flared in the pale smoothness of her cheeks. Hot words came to her lips, but aware of her sleeping child, she bit them back. Instead, exerting all her

111

control, she explained in a low voice, 'Master Lee bought Davy and me some pastries. He was a perfect gentleman, and I see no harm in what I did. I'm no whore, no slut, and never have been. So don't you ever becall me again, Aggie Southall, for I've done nothing I need be ashamed of, and apart from that, what I do in my own time is no concern of yours, or of anybody else in this town. So keep your nose out of my affairs in future, and look to your own matters instead.'

Eyes glittering feverishly in the skull-like sockets, her mouth opening and closing soundlessly, Aggie Southall raised her thin arms high and seemed about to hurl herself at Tildy. Then the door of the lean-to crashed open and the sour expression of Amanda Pinfield loured out at the group.

'Come on, let's be having you. There's work to be done, so don't stand theer gawping like a load o' bloody mawkins. If you arn't ready to work, then you can bugger off right now.'

Relieved that the threatened violence had been averted, Tildy spoke to her employer. 'Mrs Pinfield, I had to bring my child with me today, I couldn't leave him at the lodgings. But he'll cause no distraction, I promise you that.'

The sour expression did not alter as the woman stared at the sleeping child. 'If he does, then youm out of a job, my wench.' She grunted, and jerked her head. 'Come on, for God's sakes, let's get some bloody work out on you. What does you reckon we pays you for, you shiftless load o' sods? Get in here and get stuck in...'

CHAPTER 10

The murky drizzling rain of early morning had become a continuous driving downpour by midday, and looked set to last for many more hours to come. At the New Wharf of the Tardebigge Canal Company, Israel Lee stared moodily up at the leaden skies, then down into the great pit where his navvies floundered in an ever-deepening morass of mud, swearing lustily as they struggled to wrench their boots and legs from the glutinous embrace that sucked them further and further down. Their clothing was saturated with clay and wet, and the sacks they wore over their shoulders and heads gave little or no protection from the onslaught of the weather.

Narrow runways of planks had been built for the barrowmen to push the massive triangular-bodied barrows up from the bottom of the pit to the spoil carts waiting on top, but the rain turned the spilled clay into an ice-slick mess on the planking and made the footing treacherous. Even as Israel Lee looked down a young navvy, heaving and straining to push his heavy barrow up the steepest part of the incline, slipped on the muddy planking and bellowed with fright as he toppled into the pit below, his barrow landing on top of him with a sickening thud. His mates' rough laughter at his mishap changed to concern as he lay still and bloodied beneath the barrow, and dropping their shovels and picks they went to his aid, cursing as they struggled to wrench their boots from the mud, falling over as feet came free with an unexpected suddenness.

Israel Lee watched in silence as the men reached their workmate, to claw the pile of clay from his body and hurl the barrow aside. With a rough tenderness they lifted him high, and moving with a painful slowness battled their way through the knee-deep mud and up the runway.

When they reached the top, Israel Lee told them, 'Take him straight up to the pub, we'll have a look at him there, in the dry.' Then he shouted to the rest of the men in the pit, 'Come on out of it, lads.'

Nothing loth the rest of the gang shouldered their tools and hastened to obey him.

There were two separate wharves and barge basins, each with its own workshops and cottages and store-sheds at the hamlet of Tardebigge to serve the newly completed Worcester to Birmingham Canal. These wharves were divided by a hill beneath which a tunnel a full half-mile long had been driven to carry the canal. At the southern end of this tunnel stood the New Wharf; on the hillside above the tunnel mouth was the Plymouth Arms inn, which catered to the needs of the wharf's permanent and transient population of artisans, canal workers, bargees, leggers, as well as the local agricultural labourers and their families.

George Archer, the landlord of the Plymouth Arms had been a local prize-fighter of some repute in his youth and was the ideal man to keep his house orderly, despite the roughness of the majority of his customers.

'What's this then?' he demanded, as led by Israel Lee the navvies bore their limp, bloody, moaning burden into his freshly cleaned tap room.

'One of my lads came off a runway, and he's sore hurt,' Lee explained, as his men laid their workmate gently upon the table nearest the window, and started to strip the mud-caked clothing from his inert body.

George Archer's practised eyes scanned

the inert form on the table, and he said gruffly.

'Don't bother undressing him. He's past any mortal help.'

Even as he spoke a belching moan came from the young navvy, his head flopped to one side and a thin stream of dark blood ran from his mouth onto the scrubbed surface of the table top, where it formed a small puddle.

A concerted groaning sigh gusted through the men in the room, and George Archer said with a gentleness that belied the battered brutality of his features. 'You'd best take the poor lad out to the back and put him in the end stable. It's empty, and there's a trough in it agen the far wall that's long enough to lay him in. There's a bucket by the yard pump, so you can draw water to wash him, and ask the woman in the kitchen for some clean rags to use for flannels and for plugging him up. He'll do well enough there, until you decides about his funeral.'

'Many thanks to you,' Israel Lee said, as the navvies also voiced their appreciation. 'And I'll make sure you'll not lose by it.'

As the corpse was again lifted and carried outside the landlord shouted to his barmaid, 'Mary, get in here wi' a pan of hot water, and sluice this table down!' Then he turned to Israel Lee. 'And what's

116

your pleasure, Master Lee, the usual is it?' He knew the contractor's tastes well, because Lee had rented his best room from him, and was living at the inn while the contract was being worked.

Lee nodded. 'I'll take a glass, Master Archer, and you'd best start drawing some ale for my lads. No doubt they'll all be up here in a few moments.'

As if his words had been a cue, the rest of the gang began arriving at the inn, and within a few minutes the room was heavy with tobacco smoke, pungent with the scents of snuff, noisy with talk and laughter.

Israel Lee stood in the corner leaning against the bar counter, sipping his potent dark rum and watching his men. During his years on the canals as navvy, gangerman, and now contractor, he had seen more grievous accidents and more sudden deaths than he cared to remember. He knew the necessity after a bad or fatal accident occurred on the workings to let his men drink and make merry for the remainder of the working day. It was their way of saying farewell to the victims, since it took their minds from the immediate horror of the event, and the probability of themselves encountering a similar tragedy.

The landlord, red-faced and sweaty with the effort of serving his clamorous customers, took a moment's respite himself and came to stand by Israel Lee while his barmaids continued serving.

'Did you know the young cove well?' he wanted to know.

The contractor shrugged. 'Hardly at all, Master Archer, he'd only been with my gang from the start of this contract. He'd not been long at the navvy-trade either, that's why he was a barrow-man. He'd not got the strength for pick and shovel work.'

'That's not so bad then,' George Archer offered as morbid comfort. ' 'Tisn't like you'd lost an old mate, or a valuable hand, is it.' He could not hide a slight grin of satisfaction as he looked over the voracious trade his house was doing.

Israel Lee noted the grin, and smiled sardonically. 'Still, Master Archer, it's an ill wind, as they say.'

The landlord's grin broadened. 'There's truth in that, Master Lee, truth indeed. What about the burial?' he went on to ask, and again Lee shrugged.

'I'll try to find out if he's got any kin who'll want him. If I can't trace any, then I'll have to pay to have him buried here in this parish. It's not our way to leave one of our own to be shovelled into a pauper's grave like some tramper found on the roadside.'

'Well you needn't worry about keeping him here for a while,' the landlord assured. 'I never uses that stable these days, so I'll padlock the door. I've got plenty o' rock salt to cover him with, an wi' that and a good big onion in his mouth he'll not cause any stink.'

'I'm grateful to you,' Lee told the man again, 'and I'll see you all right for doing me this favour.'

George Archer waved his hand in airy dismissal. 'There's no need, Master Lee. The rock salt only costs me a few pence, and a bloody onion comes for nothing from the field next door. No, there's no need.' Again his eyes roved over the crowded room. 'I'm well enough paid for whatever I does, already.'

'Right then.' Lee drained his glass. 'I'll be off to see the constable down in Redditch and make a report on this.'

'It might be as well if you can find him down there, to have a word wi' the parson as well. He's the chairman of the select vestry this year, and it pays to keep the vestry well informed as to what happens in the parish,' the landlord advised. 'You'll find John Clayton a good enough bloke, for a bloody parson, that is.'

'I'll do that,' Lee answered. 'And give my lads whatever they want while I'm gone. I'll settle the reckoning with you later.'

'You'd best take my pony and trap, Master Lee. It's shutting down outside, and the trap's got a good tarpaulin over it. Better to keep dry than get bloody soaked. Tell young Joe to put the pony in the traces. Tell him I said so.'

'By God, Master Archer, you're doing me some good turns today, and I'm grateful for them.' Israel Lee meant what he said, and smiled as the other winked broadly, and told him,

'We all has to help each other when we can, don't us, Master Lee. Mayhap I'll be looking for favours from you, one o' these days.'

'And you'll find them,' the contractor assured him warmly. 'That's a certainty.'

The hours passed with a grinding slowness for Tildy and she experienced a deepening sense of lonely alienation. Taking their lead from Aggie Southall the rest of the women ignored her completely. Tildy could with equanimity have endured this treatment of herself; what she could not tolerate was the way they rebuffed little Davy, when in his childish innocence he tried to make friends with them.

'They can send me to Coventry, and welcome,' Tildy thought angrily. 'But why must they take out their spite on a child, a mere baby?' She soon realized the futility of reacting visibly to this type of baiting, and instead made Davy sit on some clean sacking at her side, until eventually he fell asleep.

Although mentally she had little or nothing in common with her workmates, still Tildy was hurt by their behaviour. She had years since known that she did not fit easily into coteries, and she had always felt an inner isolation from her fellows, but she had learned to accept that fact. It was not that she considered herself to be in any way superior to her peers, she merely felt that she was different. Although at times, particularly when younger, this had caused her considerable heartache, now, with more maturity, she was able to accept the fact of her difference—and the consequent loneliness—with equanimity. But today, to be deliberately and hostilely excluded from their companionship without any just cause had brought back to her the old feelings of utter apartness, and at times during the long weary hours she felt perilously near to tears. Each time this happened, however, she angrily upbraided herself for indulging in self-pity. 'Just so long as I can love and care for my Davy, then that is sufficient. That is all I want, or could ever need from my life.'

Still the onset of an early dusk engendered by the louring darkness of the rain and clouds brought to her a sensation of intense relief.

'Soon be time to go, thank God,' she told herself thankfully, and when finally Amanda Pinfield laid down her tools and announced the finish of the working day, Tildy hastened to lift her sleeping child wrapped in his bedding of sacks, and make her escape from the workshop. Even as she did so she heard Aggie Southall jeering loudly.

'Look theer, girls, her can't wait to get out to meet her bloody fancy man. I'm buggered if I'd run arter a stinking navvy like that. But then, Ise got some pride in meself. I was raised respectable and decent. I warn't raised to be a shameless slut!'

Tildy's face burned, and her own fiery temper threatened to explode. She was no coward, and was quite prepared to face any physical threat. But her child's welfare was her prime consideration in life, and she would swallow almost any insult to avoid having him frightened by seeing her in violent confrontation with others. So, bending her shawled head against the gusting wind, she hurried on in the murk towards the Salters Way. She turned into the lane and the rain worsened. Davy began to whimper loudly, so she tried to cover him better with the sacks.

'We'll soon be home, my honey,' she comforted. 'Mammy will walk very fast and we'll soon be home.'

Returning from Redditch, Israel Lee was allowing the sturdy pony to walk up the steeper parts of the lane, when he recognized Tildy's slender figure. He watched her nearing him and his heart filled with a mingling of emotions, tenderness and pity dominating.

'The poor little wench, having to maul her nipper around with her in weather like this.'

Not wishing to startle or frighten her he called out her name while she was still some distance from him.

Tildy's head lifted, and to her own surprise an acute sensation of pleasure at seeing him filled her. He brought the pony to a halt and climbed out of the small covered trap.

'Come on, Tildy Crawford, get in here out o' this rain. No! No buts about it! Do as I say.'

With a glad relief she surrendered the child to his arms while she climbed into the trap. He handed the child back to her then took the pony's head and led it to turn the trap in the direction of Redditch once more before resuming his seat.

'It's a blessing I met you, Tildy,' he said

as he pointed his finger at the underside of the barrel-hooped roof. The pouring rain was throbbing drumlike upon the tautly-stretched canvas. 'You and the nipper would have been drownded afore you'd reached your lodgings.'

Tildy thankfully allowed herself to relax, cradling Davy on her lap and luxuriating in the easement of her tired body. Israel Lee kept the pony to a walk, not wishing to end too quickly this close proximity with a young woman that he was already half in love with.

'Why did you bring the little 'un to work wi' you?' He nodded at the drowsy child who, thumb in mouth, was once more near to sleep.

'Because I was nervous about leaving him out of my sight.' Despite the shadowed gloom beneath the tarpaulin roof she saw clearly the puzzlement on Israel Lee's face, and on impulse began to unburden herself to him. From the very moment she began to speak it seemed to her as if a great oppressing weight was slowly lifting from her spirits. 'You see, Master Lee, I daren't leave the baby because my husband, Tom Crawford, has come back...' Once started, she held nothing back, driven by the overpowering need to tell someone who would perhaps understand and sympathize with her in this bleak period of her hard

124

life. '...and when I went downstairs, there he was, with a girl of twelve years, and her the daughter of his own brother.' Her story drew to its end. 'So, it's nigh on two years since he left me, and now he's come back, and I'm sore afraid. Not so much of what he might try to do to me with kicks and blows. But what he might do if he thought of it, and that is to take Davy from me. If he went to the magistrates they might well support him in doing that.' She fell silent, marvelling at how relaxed and eased she felt now that she had told this man beside her about her troubles.

It was some moments before he replied, and then he coughed nervously, and said tentatively, 'Now don't you take offence at anything I might say, Tildy, because I've no talent for pretty speeches or fancy talk. I can only say what I think plain and open.'

He paused, as if waiting for her assurances, and she felt obliged to say aloud, 'No, Master Lee, I'll not take offence at whatever you might say. I can promise you that.'

'Well, that's all right then,' he continued with a more confident tone. 'From what you tell me, this husband of yourn is a piece of bad money, and to my mind such men as he are better dead. I think you're quite right to be worried, because from the sounds of him there's no telling what devilment the bugger might get up to. So what I'm offering is this. That you and your babby come and live wi' me, and travel on wi' me when this contract is done with.'

'Live with you? Travel with you? But I hardly know you, and you hardly know me. What sort of a woman would I be if I accepted? A married woman living with another man. I'd be counted a whore.' She was half-angry, that he should think she would jump to accept his offer, yet at the same time, pleased that he had made it. She recognized the illogicality of her two differing, simultaneous reactions, but could not have put into words the reasons for them.

'Listen well to me, Tildy,' he spoke slowly and gravely. 'You would be like a wife to me, and I'd raise the nipper as my son. I'd prove a good and faithful husband to you, and a loving man. You'd want for nothing, and as my woman you'd be treated with respect by the world. I'd make sure of that. There's no one who'd call you whore in my presence, or behind my back.'

Tildy gave a slight shake of her head. Men always seemed to be offering her their protection, but in reality they wanted only to possess her. She had sufficient vanity to be well aware of her good looks and sensuous body, and admitted that she enjoyed the admiration these attributes brought her from men. But she did not want to be any man's possession, no matter how prized. Of course she wanted someday to fall in love with a man, and to be loved by him in return; to share the rest of her life with him, care for him and bear his children. But she wanted that relationship to be one of equals, a true partnership.

Again she shook her head. No man had ever offered to be her true partner in life. No matter how gilded or luxuriant it might be, the cage was where they wanted her.

'I know that I'm probably a fool to myself,' she accepted the thought. 'But no matter what any man can offer me, for now at least, hard though life is, I want to be my own woman. Free to live and think as I choose. To make my own decisions, and if needs be, to pay the price for my own mistakes.' Her lips quirked in a bitter smile. 'God knows, I've made sufficient of those, and God knows also, I've paid a heavy price for them...'

'Well, Tildy, what do you say?' Israel Lee broke into her train of thought. 'Will you come and be my woman? If you do, then you'll not need to worry that pretty yed of yourn about your husband ever again. I'll guarantee that. And I can make you happy, Tildy, if only you'll let me.'

She remained silent, not wishing to perhaps anger him by her refusal, and he went on persuasively, 'I know that we've only just met, Tildy, and I know there's not been time for us to come to know each other proper, or for me to pay court to you like a lover should. But I'm a man who believes in fate, and the moment I clapped eyes on you, it was as if something was telling me, "Here she is, Israel. Here's the girl you've bin fated to take for wife. That's why none of the others ever suited you before, because this is the one who you had to wait for. This is the girl who was destined for you..." '

'Please, Master Lee, say no more,' Tildy begged him. 'Because even if what you say were to be true, still at this moment in my life, it cannot be. I can't come to live with you, or be your woman.'

The contractor was a man with considerable experience of women, and he recognized that she really meant what she now said. That this refusal was not any coquetry. However, he was also an extremely determined man.

'All right Tildy, that's straight spoken,

and fair enough, and I'll accept what you say without any more argument.' He masked his disappointment with a bluff smile. 'But don't forbid me to come courting you, will you. Because I can always hope that you'll maybe change your mind about my offer, somedays. Meanwhiles, I'm going to make you another offer, but this 'un is without any strings attached.' He paused for a moment, studying her mood, and encouraged by what he sensed, went on. 'This offer concerns your husband. I want you to let me deal with him, if he should prove too much for you to handle by yourself.' He paused to let the words sink into her mind, before asking, 'Do you accept that offer, my lass? And let me say again, there's no strings attached to it. I'd only be acting as a true friend.'

She smiled with real gratitude. 'Then if that's the case, I'll accept, Master Lee, and gladly.'

He nodded. 'That's a struck bargain then.' And well content that he had thrown a bridge out towards this girl that might eventually help him claim her for his own, he hummed contentedly as the pony plodded on through the pouring rain towards the dimly flickering lights of the town.

CHAPTER 11

Tom Crawford had very unhappy memories of Redditch. The last time he had been here was on his wedding day, and he had spent some of that day sitting padlocked in the stocks, being bombarded with rotten fruit and vegetables, human and animal excreta, dead animals and brickbats. His mind vividly recalled the sickening terror and pain he had suffered during those hours, and a sullen rage of hatred smouldered within him.

'That cow brought that upon me. That fuckin' missus o' mine. I hadn't a care in the world until I married that bitch. But by Christ, she'll pay now all right. She'll pay for everything I've suffered because of her.'

He was sitting in a sleazy beer shop in a fetid alley close to the Chapel Green, half-drunk and morose as he fingered the few coins left in his pockets. Before the cudgel beating he had been a handsome man, swarthy complexioned with short black hair and long sideboards which he kept twisted up below the cheekbones in carefully clipped vanity curls. Tall and strong-bodied, with a glib tongue and surface charm, women had always fallen easily to him. His puffy lips twisted petulantly. 'Tildy hadn't fallen easy though. Not that little bitch!'

Tom Crawford had been the manservant and footman to the Reverend Phillip Wren, Rector of the neighbouring parish of Ipsley, which environed some eastern parts of Redditch Town.

'That was a prime job, that was. Until I met that whore!'

Memories passed through his mind in panoramic review... The Michaelmas hiring fair of 1819 at Redditch, to which he had accompanied his master. Tildy had been standing in the lines of maidservants, and the Reverend Wren, taken by her clean fresh appearance, and touched by her artless naïvety, had engaged her.

Tom Crawford himself had later in the day gone in search of this new maidservant, and when he had found her had flattered and flirted with her, and taken her round the fair. In her ignorant innocence she had trusted him as a fellow servant, and he had taken full advantage of that trust to ply her with unaccustomed drink until she was helpless, then lead her to a sleazy ale house where he rented a room for the night.

Even now Crawford's mouth dried with

lust at the memory of how Tildy's naked body had looked in the soft light of the candle. 'I should ha' been content wi' that one night,' he told himself now. 'Arter all, she never told anybody how I'd raped her when she was senseless wi' drink. But no, I had to be greedy didn't I, and want more o' the same. I was too fucking decent about it, that was my trouble. When old Wren asked me if I was the father o' the kid, I said yes, straight away, didn't I, and told the old bastard that I was ready to marry her. Even though the little bitch had gi' me nothing but hating looks since the fair night.'

Under immense pressure from the clergyman, the heavily pregnant Tildy had agreed to marry her rapist. Then, immediately the marriage ceremony had been performed the Reverend Phillip Wren had paid the newly-weds off, and dismissed them from his service.

'God rot that fucking hypocrite's eyes!' Tom Crawford swore sibilantly. 'He shouldn't ha' done that. He could ha' kept us iffen he'd a mind to, and chance what his bloody missus was saying. But ne'er mind that now, it was that little bitch's fault in the fust place for agreeing to the wedding, and I'll make her pay now for all the bad luck she's brought me. I'll make her pay all right. But I'll need to box clever wi' it. Spy out the land. I don't want to go getting meself into any more trouble because of her. But how does I survive in the meantime, while I'm seeing how the land lays?'

The beer shop was merely the front downstairs room of a small terraced cottage, and its only furnishings were a trestled table, a bench, and a few broken-backed chairs and rickety stools. A turf fire smouldering in the rusty grate gave off more smoke than heat, and the atmosphere was pervaded by a damp sour smell.

Crawford scowled at his surroundings. 'Fucking pigsty! I deserve better.'

The proprietress of the beer shop came into the room. A woman in her late forties, her body bloated by child-bearing, her face ravaged by drink and disease, she presented an unappetizing spectacle in her dirty, greasy clothing, her lank greying hair hanging unwashed about her face. She stared speculatively at her solitary customer. He was a bit of a mystery man, who had vouchsafed nothing about himself ever since he had come to her house the previous day. Last night she had let him sleep on the floor before the turf fire. Tonight, if she felt so inclined, she might well invite him into her own bed in the room above the shop. Her last paramour had died some three weeks previously, and she was looking for a suitable replacement. Despite the injuries to his face, she found the stranger a personable man.

Tom Crawford was well aware of the woman's interest in him, and recognized that if he made the effort to charm her, his immediate needs for food, drink and shelter could be catered for. 'She's a pig, right enough, and this fucking pigsty is the right place for her, but Ise got to be realistic about my situation, arn't I? It's needs must when the Devil drives.'

He grinned cheerily at the woman, and lifted the battered leather drinking jug in his hand. 'It's a raw day out theer, my duck, so I'll thank you to draw another pot o' this to warm me insides. And perhaps you'll do me the honour o' joining me in a glass o' something.'

The woman disclosed her stained, gapped teeth in a broad smile. 'Yes, he'll do,' she decided. 'He'll do very well.'

CHAPTER 12

The last week in October caused much excited speculation among the women at Pinfield's workshop. Firstly a huge carrier's waggon drawn by eight massive horses had groaned to a halt outside the house, and unloaded round grindstones, their wooden cradles and saddles, as well as pulleys and leather belting, mysteriously shaped baulks of timbers, poles, cog-wheels, bars and straps of iron, boxes of bolts, sacks of nails and screws.

Then the women had been conscripted to clear the Pinfield's furniture from the ground floor to the rooms above; while they toiled all Amanda Pinfield had done was to crouch in various corners of the rapidly emptying rooms with her apron flung over her head, and wail and sob ceaselessly while from its cradle her child howled in concert with his mother.

A team of millwrights and their helpers arrived, and within scant days the great horse-driven gin mill at the side of the house was completely refurnished and made operational again. The axles, the pulleys, the cogs, the wheels, the seemingly endless rolls of leather belting were fitted together, and once again a pointing shop, with its row of low-cradled grindstones and pointer's saddles stood where Amanda Pinfield's cherished Welsh Dresser had been. Another carrier's waggon arrived, but this time only a set of rag-wrapped packages were unloaded and left in the pointing shop with strict instructions that they were not to be touched or tampered with in any way.

Tildy was also curious as to what these alterations might mean. Remembering what Robert Stafford had said to her, she wondered if it might involve him, but the matter was of only secondary interest to her. She had other, more pressing matters to engage her mind. Tom Crawford had not returned to the lodging house, and had made no attempt to see her, but she knew that he was still in the town.

Mother Readman had a network of informants, through whom she was kept abreast of most events taking place in the district. Tildy knew that her husband was staying at a beer shop in Clarke's Yard, close to the Chapel Green, and only a few score yards from Silver Square. His relationship to Peggy Green, who kept the beer shop, was assumed by everyone to be one of intimacy, even though the couple had met only a short time before. Tildy, knowing her husband's sexual propensities, considered it a safe assumption to make. Tom Crawford was a man with extremely strong sexual hungers, and was not at all fastidious as to the women he satisfied those hungers upon.

Tildy still carried her child to and from her work, and kept him in her sight at all times. However one aspect of life had improved. Although the women were sending her to Coventry, they were

136

feminine enough to have relaxed their strictures against Davy, and now treated the child pleasantly enough. Even Aggie Southall sometimes tousled his curls and called him 'honey' on occasion. Tildy was grateful for this, and felt it easier to bear her own isolation from her fellow workers because of it. Fortunately Davy was too young to realize what the relationship between his mother and the other women was, and he spent his days happily enough amid the noise, the smells, the oily dirt and steel filings of the squalid workshop.

Tildy was desperately poor. Her wages barely exceeded six shillings a week, and were sometimes less, and out of that she had to pay two shillings for the rent of her tiny attic room. In order to ensure that Davy had sufficient fresh milk, cheese, eggs and good bread, and the rare treat of a sugar stick or bag of ginger snaps, Tildy ate only the plainest of foods herself, and barely sufficient of them. For the most part she lived on Mother Readman's penny bowls of watery tainted stew, which although unappetizing to the taste, at least kept her belly filled. She blessed the fact that her two grey gowns, and her under-shifts, were not yet too threadbare, and her shawl was thick and warm. Her clogs also were almost new, and should last for some time.

She desperately desired that as soon as possible Davy should begin his schooling. There were several dame's schools in the town where, for a few pence weekly, tiny children could try to learn their alphabet, and the first elements of writing and arithmetic. There were other schools as well for older children, but Tildy refused to let herself think that far ahead.

The one blessing that she counted above all else was that both she and Davy were healthy. She secretly feared that if either of them were to suffer illness, then she would be very hard pressed to cope with her situation.

She constantly sought in her mind for ways in which she could increase her income. Certain Rabeleisian ideas always re-occurred, which at least afforded her a chance to chuckle at her own wayward thoughts, but given the long hours she spent at the Pinfield's workshop, and her lack of any formal training, not to mention the fact that she was a female, and thus barred from all but the most menial of callings, Tildy could only concede that for the present at least she was trapped in the relentless morass of poverty. Of course, she had had the opportunity of raising her standard of living by becoming a mistress to some man or another, and allowing him to support her, but Tildy had already dismissed that alternative. Only the extremest desperation would ever force her to consider such a course.

So, the only faint hope that she might find some way of bettering her position and income was that engendered by the brief encounter with Robert Stafford, when he had urged her to learn all she could about the soft work, because then she might be offered a chance to better herself.

During the days when the pointing shop was being re-constructed, Tildy increasingly wondered if indeed Robert Stafford had something to do with the reconstruction, and if indeed she might be offered such an opportunity by that young gentleman.

Amanda Pinfield, despite the eager questions and badgering of the women, grimly refused to answer anything but only reiterated over and over again, 'I knows naught about bloody naught: So let me be, 'ull you. I knows bloody naught!'

Of John Pinfield himself they saw little or nothing, but that was the normal state of things anyway, and on the one occasion he did appear in the workshop he seemed cheerful enough, and inevitably was half-drunk, reeking of gin and tobacco. When Aggie Southall demanded to be told what was the reason for the alterations, he only laughed and tried to kiss her. Aggie pushed him away, and he staggered off singing lustily to himself, while Amanda Pinfield threw her apron up over her head and howled in misery; and so the month of November 1822 dawned with none of the women any wiser as to what was to happen.

CHAPTER 13

The Milward family possessed numerous branches, whose progeny could be found in every station of life. Miss Hetty Milward's father, Henry, counted himself to be of a very high station in the life of the district. He was a needle master, manufacturer of fishhooks, factor and merchant, a chapel warden of St Stephen's Chapel, an overseer to the poor, and a select vestryman of the Redditch Liberty in the Half-Shire Hundred of Worcestershire. He was also a loyal monarchist, and a stalwart patriot. During the war he had been among the first to enlist in the local Redditch Volunteers, ready to fight to the death against the daily expected onslaught of the French upon the Tardebigge parish.

These days, when in his cups, he boasted of his military service, and lamented his absence from the battlefields of the Peninsula, Flanders, the West Indies, the Americas. The fact that by deliberately choosing to enlist in a local volunteer corps he had made sure he would not be balloted for the militia, or pressed into the navy with the consequent possibility of finding himself on active service, he conveniently forgot. When those local roughs who had stood in the ranks at Waterloo, Salamanca or Vittoria, and had run out the cannons of frigates, cruisers and line of battle ships, jeered at his vaunted military prowess, he chose to ignore their gibes as being beneath his contempt, contenting himself with the knowledge that only he really knew what a lion's heart beat within his portly breast.

He ruled his workpeople with a rod of iron, but in turn was ruled himself by his formidable wife, Millicent.

'And I'm atelling you, Mister Milward, that you mun spake to that daughter o' yourn, and spake firm and plain.' Millicent Milward's diction and accents were those of the soft worker she had once been. 'God knows Ise tried to make her practise that bloody pianner, but her just farts about at it. Three bloody years, and her carn't manage her bloody scales yet! When I thinks on the money wese spent on her education, and all the bloody use it's served for, I could bloody well weep, so

I could. Bloody well weep!'

Henry Milward sighed heavily, and stared unhappily out of the window of his parlour towards his needle mill. He watched the ancient, decrepit blind horse plodding round in its endless circle harnessed in its wooden frame which was bolted to the huge horizontal wooden wheel above the horse's drooping head. As the beast moved in its laborious, straining progress, so the great wheel, creaking and groaning turned with it, and in its turn powered smaller belt, wheel and cog systems which in their turn powered the grindstones of the pointing shop and spun the revolving barrels of the drying shop, and sent the great blocks of the scouring and polishing shops trundling backwards and forwards, backwards and forwards.

As Henry Milward watched, he saw the horse stumble and come to a standstill, and the small urchin who was the animal's driver start to belabour the wretched beast with a thick stick to force it onwards again.

'I'll needs think about getting another nag for the gin,' he murmured aloud. 'That bugger's about ready for the knacker's yard.'

His wife screeched indignantly. 'What's that youm saying, Mister Milward? Be you apaying attention to me, or what?'

142

'I'm paying attention, Mrs Milward,' he answered with laboured politeness. 'But surely to God Hetty is your task. I've the business to run. I can't be worriten me yed about our daughter day in and day out. Youm the mistress of the house, and it's up to you to take her in hand, if needs be.' He remained staring out of the window, frowning as he saw the blind horse stagger again, and then slump slowly down, held from collapsing completely by the harness which held it in its wooden frame.

'God damn and blast the sod!' he cursed angrily, and his wife rose to come and stare over his shoulder. She saw the collapsed horse, and the urchin belabouring it in a fruitless attempt to make it rise.

'Theer, I might ha' knowed it,' she snorted contemptuously. 'That's four bloody horses ha' died in five weeks. Why the bloody hell you don't convert to the steam, I'll never know. Youm practising false economies, Master, like I'm always a telling you. Youm penny wise and pound foolish.'

Inwardly Henry Milward sourly conceded that his wife did occasionally make a shrewd point. But he refused to give her the satisfaction of his agreement, and instead ranted blusteringly, 'Convert to the steam, her says! Does you know how much that u'd cost me, woman? There 'ud be no bloody pianners in the parlour, and no fancy-talking nancy boy dancing master for Miss Hetty, and no bloody carriage and pair for you to flaunt yourself about the town in, if I converted to the steam to power me works. Anyway, there's naught wrong wi' horse power.'

His wife was more than eager to meet his attack. 'No, there's naught wrong wi' horse power, not if you gets good horseflesh to drive the gin. But you, being tighter nor a duck's arse, all you ever gets is bloody knacker's meat. Theym always ready to be turned into glue and dogs' meat by the time they arrives here; and how much does it cost you when the pointing stones stop turning, and the scouring stops, and the drying stops?

'You knows, as well as I does, that you can forget about getting any more work today from the bloody pointers. They'll be off on the drink now, and God knows when the buggers 'ull turn to again. By the Christ, Mister Milward! There's times you makes me want to throw up, youm so bloody thick-yedded and stubborn. I'm giving you good advice, master, when I tells you to convert to steam, or failing that, then at least go out and buy a couple of good young shire-horses that'll do the job proper for you.'

144

'And what does you think a couple of good shires 'ull cost, woman? A small bloody fortune, that's what. And then, if there's two on 'um, that means that one 'ull forever be standing idle, ateing its yed off at my expense. No, Ise got a better idea nor that. Instead of me buying more horses, why don't I just use them bloody carriage-mares o' yourn to drive the gin? What does you think to that idea, Mrs Milward?'

'You'll take them over my dead body, master,' she hissed. 'Ise worked hard all me days, and still does, and it's thanks to me that youse got any bloody mills at all. Don't you be forgetting that, Mr Milward. Ise well-earned my mares and carriage, and I'll not give 'em up for you nor twenty buggers like you.'

Secretly afraid of her rabid fury, Henry Milward looked away from her and out of the window again. By now the tiny urchin had stopped hitting the fallen animal, and from the mill the overlookers were coming to see what the trouble was. Henry Milward was quick to snatch at this chance to escape the threatening storm.

'I'll needs get out there,' he grunted. 'Afore the whole bloody boiling of 'um lays aside their tools.'

Before his wife could move to stop him, he was gone, leaving her fuming in frustration behind him.

Hetty Milward stood in front of the full-length mirror in her bedroom, regarding her reflection with considerable satisfaction. She was undeniably a pretty girl, with her fair hair dressed in piled curls upon her head, her skin glowing with youth, high-breasted, slim-waisted, her bare shoulders softly dimpled, her throat invitingly rounded.

She had dressed for her dancing class in a high-waisted, low-cut blue gown, fashionably short to display her shapely silken-stockinged calves, trim ankles and dainty-slippered feet. She lacked the height to assume the 'Grecian stoop,' that exaggerated, slope-shouldered posture of the ultra-ton of her sex. But Hetty did not allow her lack of height to worry her. Instead she preferred an erect, straight-backed posture, which brought into prominence her full firm breasts. Now she leaned forwards slightly evaluating the effect created by rounded smooth whiteness and deep cleavage.

'Bugger the Grecian stoop!' she giggled to herself. 'What man faced by these would care a hang for the Grecian stoop?'

'Hetty? Be you ready yet, our Hetty?' Her mother's voice sounded from below, and the young girl took a final lingering look at her appearance before slipping a

146

loose cloak over her bare shoulders, and hurrying to join her parent.

'Where is Pa?' she enquired, and her mother snorted indignantly.

'He's over at the gin. The bloody horse dropped dead again.'

Hetty's mischievous sense of humour sparkled. 'How many times has that horse died now, Mama?' she asked sweetly. 'Will he resurrect again, I wonder.'

Her mother scowled at her. 'Be you trying to make mock o' me, girl?'

'Why of course I'm not, Mama. How could you think such a thing.' Hetty's eyes were wide pools of innocence. 'Only you said that the horse had died again, and naturally I was wondering how many times exactly this particular horse had dropped dead.'

'And I'm wondering how I ever did come to gi' birth to such a saucy little cow as you be?' Millicent Milward had been born in the Silver Street, and unlike many of her contemporaries among the more successful of the townspeople, she was unashamed of her lowly origins. 'You hark to me, girl. Iffen I'd ha' spoken to me Mam and Pa like you speaks to yourn, I'd have got their fists in me gob, and bloody quick too. So you just take care, me wench, because I'm a believer in what's good for one is better for another.'

'Oh yes, Mama, but you are forgetting that you were the daughter of a needle pointer, but I am the daughter of a needle master. I am born a gentlelady,' Hetty teased.

Millicent Milward grimly shook her head. 'No, my wench, youse got it all wrong. Youm the daughter of a soft worker. Namely me. I arn't like some of the silly mares in this town who forgets wheer they was birthed. Not me! I was birthed in bloody Silver Street, and Ise had to slave night and day to gct what Ise got now. I'm not shamed to remember where Ise come from, or that Ise got kin still living in Silver Street and Silver Square. No, and I'm not shamed to own to my kin when I meets 'um on the street neither, and if there's any stuck-up bugger who cares to look down their bloody nose at me, for being what I am, then they can do as they bloody well pleases, for I don't give a tinker's fart for any one on 'um. I am what I am, girl, born plain Milly Brough, and no amount o' fancy frills and lace is agoing to change me. So stick that in your bloody pipe and smoke it.'

Hetty's assumed air of innocence dis-appeared in a noisy splutter of laughter, and running to her mother she threw her slender arms about the older woman's stout waist and hugged hard. 'Oh Ma, I do love you,' she laughed fondly. 'And I'd not change a hair of you.'

The girl truly meant what she said. Hetty Milward was something of a rebel in her own way, and possessing a lively intelligence coupled with innate shrewdness, could recognize the false airs and graces of certain of the local gentry, and perceive the weaknesses of character that those assumed fine manners camouflaged. Although her mother's blunt speech and coarseness had at times embarrassed her when younger, as she grew older Hetty increasingly appreciated the honesty and openness of her mother, and secretly admired the older woman's courage and self-confidence.

Millicent Milward's manner softened, and she chuckled throatily as in turn she reciprocated her daughter's embrace. 'That's me, my lamb,' she said. 'A real sow's ear from Silver Street, if ever there was one. Come on now, Amelia Boulton 'ull be afluttering and aflustering all over the bloody shop if youm late again. You know how her hates to keep that fancy man of hers waiting round for you lot to put in an appearance...'

CHAPTER 14

Mrs Amelia Boulton regarded herself as the torch-bearer of culture in Redditch, and the doyen of whatever artistic society it possessed. Music, art, literature, poetry, the dance: she firmly believed it her God-ordained mission to lay them all before the benighted inhabitants of this notoriously uncultured district. A very wealthy widow, middle-aged, over-weight, over-rouged and at times over-powering, she nevertheless possessed a kind heart and a generous nature.

That kind heart was troubled now as she sat in what she termed her 'salon', the largest room in her large house, and talked to the willowy young gentleman sitting by her side on her chaise-longue.

'But my dear Augustus, I'm quite sure your Papa is not being intentionally cruel to you. He merely lacks understanding of your true nature.'

Augustus Bartleet was a poetic-looking young man with a great mass of flowing blond locks falling about his ears and onto the big floppy collar of his laced shirt, which he wore over the velvet collar of his lavender shooting jacket, and opened at the front to the top button of his silken-brocaded waistcoat. A large gaudy silk kerchief was loosely tied around his long slender neck, and his long slender legs were tightly encased in yellow knee-breeches and stockings. On his long slender feet were a dainty pair of lavender dancing pumps. He lifted both hands, long and slender like the rest of him, and declaimed sonorously in a deep bass voice, which sounded curiously incongruous coming from such a slender, delicately featured face,

'But my dear Mrs Boulton, how can a man engaged in sordid trade possibly know when he is behaving cruelly? He lacks any perception of how sensitive, artistic souls such as you and I would wish to spend our days.'

Amelia Boulton fluttered her eyelashes over her myopic belladonnaed eyes frantically. She adored being described as a sensitive and artistic soul. She laid her plump, white-enamelled hands over the soft white hands of the young man and brought both pairs firmly onto her cushiony thighs.

'Do try to remember, my dear boy, that your father has many matters of worldly business to attend to. I happen to know that his trade is not thriving at this time.'

The Bartleets were another old town family with numerous branches, and Augustus's father, William Bartleet, was a needle master in a small way of business.

'That is as maybe, Mrs Boulton, but how can my entering into his manufactury assist his business? I am no ink-stained clerk, Mrs Boulton, born to spend his days on a stool in a counting-house entering dreary columns of figures into dreary ledgers. I am an artist, Mrs Boulton. A free spirit, striving to soar free, and I must have liberty to pursue my artistic muse wheresoever I might search to find her. If I have not that, Mrs Boulton, then my life is worthless to me, and I would as soon sink into my grave.'

His throbbing voice made Amelia Boulton's body throb and tingle as she thrilled to her very marrow to be witness to this tragic artist's torment. She felt that she was an enormously privileged spectator of some magnificent soul's battle against sordid Mammon.

Tenderly she smoothed the tumbled blond locks back from the noble brows, while with her other hand gently squeezing his long slender fingers, and with a smile of heart-wrenching gratitude, Augustus Bartleet told her, 'I cannot fully express what your friendship, and your concern, and your understanding mean to me,

Mrs Boulton. Amid these dark-souled Philistines that surround us you appear to me as a veritable angel of light.'

Again the myopic eyes fluttered frantically, and the widowed heart beat faster. She gloried in these moments, relishing every soulful, tremulous sigh that issued from his lips, every gleam of moisture in his big cowlike brown eyes, every quiver of his long luxuriant lashes as he gazed down at their clasped hands. And Amelia Boulton experienced a distinct thrill of annoyance when her maid came in, without so much as a tap on the door, to announce the arrival of the young ladies of the dancing class.

They entered in a froth of coloured silks, and a cloud of sweet scents. Laughter hovered on their lips, and brightness sparkled in their eyes. They were the daughters of needle masters, merchants, successful shopkeepers and farmers. There were the three Misses Chillingworth, Emily, Anna and Agatha; the Stafford sisters, Helena and Dorothea; Hetty Milward and Emily Cutler; Rebecca Merry and Jane Holyoak and Samantha Melen.

Unlike their parents they had some pretensions to gentility of speech and manners, and unlike their parents they had never known the poverty and drudgery of life.

'Girls, girls! Pray do not shout so, you

are positively making my head to ring like a bell.' For a moment or two Amelia Boulton was petulant at having her delicious tête à tête so rudely interrupted, but very quickly her customary good humour reasserted itself, and she was joining in the girlish jokes and laughter.

'Ladies?' Augustus Bartleet had metamorphosed from tortured poet to tyrannical maestro. 'If Mrs Boulton will do me the honour of taking her seat at the pianoforte, then I am ready to begin today's lesson. We shall commence with the quadrille.'

His announcement was met with moues of disappointment, and he smiled. 'We shall concentrate on figure three, *"la poule"*. When we have mastered that, and only then...' He paused, relishing the bated breaths and the expressions of excited anticipation. 'And only then,' he repeated, 'shall we move on to *"la valse"*.'

A chorus of delighted exclamations greeted this last announcement.

'La valse', the Waltz, was considered to be the most daring and modern of dances, almost sinful in its intimate entwinings of arms and close-pressed proximity of bodies. The girls glowed with pleasure, and satisfied that he had asserted his mastery over the class, Augustus Bartleet nodded to Amelia Boulton and clapped his hands smartly together.

'Come now, ladies, let us take our positions for the third figure of the quadrille, *'la poule!*" '

While the pianoforte tinkled and the girls dipped and swayed and moved with differing degrees of grace through the intricate steps of the dance, another type of dance was being executed in the yard behind the sleazy beer shop of Peg Green. Two young men, stripped to the waist, were moving round each other, fists weaving, bare feet sliding through the filth.

Other men were ranged around the yard urging on the two combatants with jeers and oaths. Most of these spectators wore the needle pointers' rig, and all of them bore on their faces the scars of past brawls and the marks of hardship and dissipation.

The two in the centre, as if losing patience with their dance, rushed at each other. Fists thudded into flesh and bone, they grunted with exertion, hissed with pain, the onlookers roared their encouragement and the fighters became wild beasts, all science forgotten as they reverted to the raw savagery of combat, kicking, biting, gouging, throttling, stumbling and falling locked together to roll over and over on the ground, blood and filth plastered across sweating straining bodies and distorted ferocious faces.

Robert Stafford could hear the shouts as he walked past Clarke's Yard in company with Henry Milward.

'Hark to them,' the older man muttered half-angrily. 'It's my bloody pointers at it already, and barely an hour since they laid their needles down. Ise got a vacancy for another pointer in my mill, and two o' the soft workers be sorting out which on 'um is going to take the saddle.'

Robert Stafford nodded absently. The custom was a long-established one in the district. The pointers had their own jealously guarded methods of recruitment to their ranks. They would not accept any youth until he was well into his nineteenth year. Until that age they considered his lungs to be too weak and underdeveloped to stand the continued assaults of steel and stone dust. Then the potential recruit had literally to fight for the right to take his seat on the grindstone saddle. If several youths wished to apply for a vacancy, then they fought each other, and the overall winner took the job. If there was only one applicant for the vacancy, he had to fight some of the established pointers and prove his toughness and courage before they would accept him.

Robert Stafford had often wondered at the type of mentality such men possessed, who would fight like animals to obtain a job that would kill them in short years. He knew that he himself could never do so, but still he grudgingly admired the courage of those who did, and considered that the high wages they earned were well deserved.

Now however, his mind was too busy with other matters to linger on what the pointers were doing in Clarke's Yard. He had gone to see Henry Milward on business, and had found the man staring disconsolately at the dead gin horse. Anxious for a variety of reasons to ingratiate himself with the needle master, the main reason being his love for Hetty Milward, Robert Stafford had told him of a horse for sale, and was now accompanying the older man to view the animal.

He wished to broach a couple of matters with Milward, and was now considering how best he might begin. The other man saved him from the necessity of making a decision by broaching one of the matters himself.

'Now, young man, what is this gossip I've been hearing about you and my daughter?'

Robert Stafford risked a sideways glance, trying to evaluate the older man's attitude. Encouraged by what he read in Milward's expression, he smiled and said respectfully,

'I should hope that the gossip is not of a deleterious nature, sir?'

The needle master's head wagged from side to side, and he answered with a hint of joviality, 'No it ain't. Because if it was, then I'd be addressing myself to your back wi' a horsewhip, my young buck.'

Robert Stafford assumed an air of gravity. 'The truth of the matter is, sir, that the reason I came to see you today was concerning this very matter. I have to own frankly, sir, that I hold very tender feelings towards Miss Hetty, and to speak plainly, sir, I would ask your permission to pay my addresses to her, and to ask for her hand in marriage.'

'And does my daughter return these tender feelings?'

'Indeed, sir, I have hope that she may not be entirely indifferent towards me. Although, as yet, no words have passed between us concerning the matter.'

'How do you propose to support a wife, young man? Especially one who has been accustomed to a very comfortable style of living, and a high station in life?'

Robert Stafford could barely repress a smile of satisfaction. The conversation was developing along the lines he had expressly wished it to. 'As to that, sir, I have prospects which are even now on the verge of realization. I would trust to be able to provide for a wife with very ample means.'

'What prospects might these be? Pinfield's workshop maybe?' Henry Milward looked slyly sideways at his companion, and chuckled in triumph at the expression of shock on Stafford's face. 'Did you really think to keep it secret, young man?' he demanded rhetorically. 'Why, you'd have had an equal chance of doing such iffen you'd shouted the news out in the middle o' Chapel Green on a mart day, as trust John Pinfield to keep his mouth shut when in his cups.' The needle master could not resist completing the young man's discomfiture by adding, 'Oh yes, and I knows what the carrier brung you from Sheffield as well, my buck, all wrapped up nice and tight in sacking.'

Robert Stafford's smile of satisfaction had become a sickly grimace.

Henry Milward came to a standstill, forcing the other man to halt with him. 'Now listen well, young man.' He prodded Stafford's chest with his forefinger. 'I'm going to speak my mind to you. Ise known you man and boy since you was in your cradle, and I'm quite prepared to accept you as son-in-law, that's always assuming as how Hetty 'ull want you for a husband. I thinks none the worse of you for trying to set yourself up in the trade,

159

even though I knows that youm atrying to poach customers from me, as well as the other masters hereabouts, because that's normal practice, that is. But before you gets to wed our Hetty, then youse got to have made enough to keep her in a manner befitting a daughter o' mine. Is that understood?'

Robert Stafford's shaken confidence was fast returning, and it was again a genuine smile that curved his lips.

'Indeed it is understood, sir, and I thank you for your words.'

'So be it.' The older man nodded bluffly. 'Now let's be pressing on. I wants to see that horse by daylight, not by bloody candlelight.'

The fight in Clarke's Yard finished when one of the youths lay senseless, and while some of the pointers tried to revive him, the others bore the victor into the beer shop to celebrate his acceptance as one of them.

Tom Crawford helped his new-found mistress to serve the clamorous men with drink, pipes and tobacco. The presence of a stranger attracted curiosity, heightened by his injured features and tall strong body.

'Be you a pug?' a gauntly handsome pointer questioned as Tom Crawford placed a pot of beer before him.

Crawford thought a little before answering. He was wise in the ways of the world, and knew that with these men he must tread carefully, particularly at this time when their aggressive instincts had been roused by the fight they had just witnessed. He essayed a deprecating, rueful smile. 'I thought I was, cully, until I copped for this lot.' He pointed to his broken nose and misshapen cheekbone.

The good-looking pointer, Bonny Southall, laughed appreciatively. 'Copped for a tartar, did you?'

'Felt more like a barrowload on 'um,' Crawford joked, and with relief heard several of the other men join in Southall's laughter at this reply. Although Crawford had sufficient gutter-devil in his makeup to fight if he had to, he still much preferred to relieve his temper by hitting women, rather than take on formidable brawlers such as these pointers, for he knew from past experience that strangers to this town could all too quickly and easily find themselves the target for casual violence.

Now he effaced himself quietly and stood near the doorway of the inner room where the barrels of drink were stored, listening to the various conversations going on around him. He knew well that by listening carefully, remembering what was said and collating the disjointed pieces of information, he could be led to unexpected dividends. His time on the fringes of the London and Portsmouth criminal fraternities had sharpened his wits and taught him many things that it would not be possible to find in books.

His close attention was rewarded when he heard his wife's name mentioned in the course of an exchange about the alterations that had been carried out at a place called Pinfield's workshop.

'...her's a sweet piece o' meat that dark-yedded 'un who works theer wi' your missus, arn't her, Bonny,' a man remarked. 'What's her name?'

'It's Tildy summat... Tildy Crawford, I reckon it is.' Bonny Southall's tongue licked salaciously across his strong, brown-stained teeth. 'By the Christ, I'd like to be nestling atween her legs of a night-time, sooner than my bleedin' missus's scrawny shanks.'

'Has her got a man, that Crawford wench?' another pointer questioned, and Bonny Southall nodded.

'Ahr, and that's why my missus took agen her. Bin becalling her summat rotten, Aggie has. Just because the wench has took up wi' one o' them navvies at the Tardebigge Wharf.'

'God fuck me! Why must her take up

wi' a bloody navvy when there's plenty of us pointer lads whom ready and willing to give her what's needful.' A third man laughed, but there was a note of resentment contained within that laughter.

'Oh he arn't just a navvy, the cove her's took up with,' Bonny Southall told them. 'No, her's set her cap a bit higher than that. Her fancy man is the contractor. A cove name of Israel Lee. Lucky bastard that he is, getting his oats from that 'un, and every night as well, I shouldn't wonder.'

'I'll drink to that!' the first man shouted, and the subject was discarded and forgotten in an outburst of laughter.

It was not discarded and forgotten by Tom Crawford, however. His expression became feral as he digested what he had heard.

'Contractor, is he, this Israel Lee. He'll be worth a few bob then. I reckon it's time I was paying that slut another visit.' His eyes suddenly reddened with fury. 'I reckon her's bin laughing up her sleeve at me, ever since I went to see her. Fucking bitch! Got a rich fancy man, and me with me bloody arse out o' me breeches. Well, she'll pay for that all right.'

'What's got into him?' a man lowered his drinking jug to ask, as Tom Crawford suddenly cursed aloud and went blundering out into the fetid alleyway.

Once outside he turned in the direction of Red Lion Street, but as he neared the Silver Street archway his steps slowed.

'It's no use me going threatening and blaggardin' the cow.' He was remembering the stubborn courage his wife possessed in such abundance. 'No, I'll get no surrender that way. But what other way is there of getting the bitch wheer I wants her?'

His thoughts raced until suddenly he came to an abrupt halt and slapped his hand on his thigh. 'That's it! Fuck me blind, for being so thick-yedded. Ise got the very tool I needs alaying in me hands, and I arn't seen it 'til now.

'The kid's mine. I'm his lawful Dad, and it rightfully belongs to me. It's my bloody property.' He grinned with ferocious satisfaction. 'Now what's the best way to go about it, I wonder... What's the best way...'

CHAPTER 15

When the dancing class ended Amelia Boulton's maid brought in trays of cakes and sherbet which the girls ate and drank with gusto. Even the ethereal Augustus

Bartleet displayed a prodigious capacity for the delicacies, and managed to eat and drink three times the amount of anyone else.

Hetty Milward drew Dorothea Stafford to one side.

'Will Robert be coming to escort you home?' she asked, and the other girl giggled.

'It's you he'll be coming to escort, Hetty, and you know that full well. He is foolish enough to believe that we believe his protestations that the town is too rough to permit us to walk home without a protector. He chooses to forget that when he is away Mama is quite content for us to return alone, and walk wheresoever we choose to in the town. We are his excuse to see you... Will you marry him, Hetty?'

Hetty Milward shook her head, then laughed aloud at her friend's expression of mingled shock and disappointment, and said quickly, 'Of course I shall, you goose.'

'Then we shall be sisters, as well as friends,' Dorothea observed happily.

Amelia Boulton, anxious to resume her tête à tête with Augustus Bartleet, who had already intimated his willingness to remain and talk some more, clapped her hands together.

'Come now, girls, it's time you were wending your ways homewards. Your

165

parents will be becoming anxious for you.' She fluttered her eyes in what she hoped was the direction of Augustus Bartleet.

Hetty Milward and the Stafford girls left the house together to find Robert Stafford waiting for them outside. He lifted his tall hat and bowed. 'Miss Hetty, I'm happy to see you.'

She smiled warmly. 'And I you, Mr Stafford.'

He grinned, indicating with a flourish the carriage and pair on the roadway. 'Your Mama has kindly loaned me her carriage so that we all might go for a ride. I have your father's permission also, Miss Hetty, for you to accompany us, if you should so wish, and it is my dearest wish that you should.'

Hetty Milward laughed gaily. 'Try and stop me.'

'Where are we going, Brother Robert?' Helena wanted to know.

'You will know when we arrive,' he told her, and assumed an air of mystery as he whispered, 'I am going to divulge a great secret to you all today.'

Hetty Milward could already make a shrewd guess as to what the secret was. She had overheard her mother and father talking about Robert Stafford's intention to set up in trade for himself. But now

166

she said nothing, not wishing to spoil the young man's pleasure.

He handed the girls into the carriage, and then climbed up to the driving seat and lifted the reins.

'Giddup there! Walk on!' he ordered, and the horses jerked into motion.

Amelia Boulton's house stood on the turnpike road that ran south up the gently rising ridgeway of Mount Pleasant between Redditch and the nearby hamlet of Headless Cross. The carriage rattled smartly over the metalled surface, and they made a merry company as they sang in unison, and waved to passersby.

At Headless Cross, Stafford turned the horses westwards and Hetty smiled to herself now that the direction confirmed her guess that Pinfield's workshop was their destination.

'Do tell us where it is we are going, Brother Robert?' Helena entreated, and Dorothea added her voice to the plea, but the young man refused to answer and only grinned happily, causing his sisters to declare that he looked like the legendary Cheshire Cat. His eyes met Hetty Milward's, and for a moment all the love he felt for her shone unguarded through them. She smiled, blushed, and shyly turned her head away, while Robert Stafford exulted in what he took to be her silent confirmation that she returned his feelings towards her.

Dusk had come by the time the Pinfields' house was reached and the evening air quickly chilled, but youth and vitality kept all of them warm enough.

Robert Stafford halted the carriage, flourishing the long horsewhip in the air before pointing it at the house.

'There, girls, there is the new establishment of Mr Robert Stafford, needle master and factor to the trade,' he announced grandiloquently.

Suitably impressed, the girls ooohhed and aahhed admiringly, and Robert leapt from the seat to hand them down from the carriage.

'Come, ladies, we shall inspect my mill.'

He led the three of them to the side of the house where the refurbished gin creaked ponderously round and round, a powerful shire-horse in the wooden frame and an ancient bent-bodied man driving it on.

'Come and see the new pointing shop,' Robert insisted, his pride and excitement shining in his eyes. 'Of course, there is no one working there as yet, but within the week there will be a pointer sitting on every saddle.'

The girls followed him into the shop; in the dull light of a beam-hung oil lamp

168

they stood beneath the whirling wheels and shafts and the slapping belting and saw the row of grindstones spinning furiously on their axles. They had all seen the inside of a pointing shop before, and Dorothea, always the most vocal and forthright of the sisters, was quick to state this fact, but her brother only laughed as he told her, 'Wait a moment, sister, I intend to show you something that you've not seen before.'

Hetty stared curiously. A pointing-grindstone was always set upon a wooden carriage, the stone's axle being passed through and between two solid wooden blocks rising from the carriage. It was driven by a narrow belt running round a cog-wheel attached at one end of the axle. The pointer himself straddled a wooden saddle on the carriage, his legs and feet stretching alongside each side of the stone, his body bending closely towards it. The needle lengths were fanned between his opposed palms and he ran the points across the face of the stone, revolving them between his palms clockwise and counter-clockwise, the dust of stone and steel jetting upwards in a stream which enveloped his face and head. Hetty felt a touch mystified. She could see nothing different from the norm about these grindstones.

'What do you think to this, girls?' Robert Stafford stood with his nose and mouth covered by a bizarre, long snouted muzzle fashioned from strips of metal and padded with leather around its base where it met the skin of the face. Tapes sewed onto the leather base and tied around the back of the young man's head kept the muzzle in place. 'This is Abraham's magnetic muzzle, of which I am now proprietor. See how it operates.'

He straddled the pointer's saddle, lifting some needle lengths from a box on the floor at his side. He fanned them between his palms to grind the points against the whirling stone. A stream of dust and sparks shot upwards; a myriad of glowing pinpoints spattered against the magnetized metal strips of the muzzle where they clung.

Hetty nodded admiringly, but the Stafford girls did not fully grasp the implications of what was happening.

'Oh la, brother! Is this why you brought us here? Just to show us a funny mask and play at being a pointer lad?' Dorothea questioned disgruntledly. 'I've seen pointers working before. Now let us go home, I'm becoming cold. Come Helena, we'll wait in the carriage.'

Suiting action to words she swept her sister out with her.

'Don't be vexed with them, Robert,' Hetty was quick to tell him. 'They don't understand the import of what you have shown them.'

'Do you understand, Hetty?' he asked plaintively, and she nodded firmly.

'But of course. I can see where the sparks adhere to the magnetized metal. I can understand that the muzzle is gathering the metal dust to itself, and preventing it from penetrating into the lungs of the pointers.' Her enthusiasm took light. 'I think it to be marvellous, Robert. These muzzles will help to prevent the "pointers' rot", will they not?'

'Indeed they will, Hetty.' Robert Stafford laid aside the needle lengths he had been pointing and untied the muzzle. Apart from the thin lines covered by the base pad, his face was layered with a fine dust even from those brief moments he had been bent towards the stone. 'You have perceived the reason for these muzzles exactly. All the steel dust will be caught and held by the magnets. It is the steel dust which damages the lungs most severely. At least, that is what the medical men assert. So these muzzles will render the work that much safer. Men need no longer face certain death from the "rot". I recognized what a boon these muzzles will prove from the first moment I set eyes on them. And from that moment I determined to bring them to this town.'

Hetty smiled with genuine admiration at the young man. 'I truly think it wonderful, Robert. How clever you were to bring this to Redditch. Does my father appreciate what this can mean?'

The young man's exuberance perceptibly lessened. 'This very day I tried to convince him what an impact these muzzles will have on the trade, Hetty. I tried to persuade him to join with me in this venture. But he feels that they don't signify. Those were his very words, Hetty: "These contraptions don't signify. They'll not serve here". And then he bade me to forget about them altogether.' Robert fell silent for a moment, and then could no longer contain his feelings. 'I must tell you, my dear, that this afternoon I also told your father of the tender regard I hold for you, and I asked his permission to pay court to you. To ask for your hand in marriage. No! Hear me out, I pray you.' He gestured her to silence when she would have spoken. 'He was agreeable to my making my intentions known to you, my dear one, but he stipulated that any formal engagement must wait until I have succeeded in my business. Until I can support you in a fitting manner.

'It was after that that he advised me to forget all about the muzzles. He said they

172

would prove no help to me, but on the contrary, would prove a hindrance. But how can I lay them aside when they are central to all my plans? What should I do, Hetty? I feel in my heart that you reciprocate my love, and therefore you have the right to know what conditions your father lays down regarding our future together.'

'No, you must not lay them aside,' she told him forcefully. His disclosure that he had approached her father came as no surprise to her, and she had no intention of behaving like some simpering heroine of a novelette. She knew that their marriage was practically guaranteed if and when she decided to name the day. And being the confident and determined young woman that she was, she was equally determined that her future husband should prove himself capable of standing on his own feet and achieving success.

She knew her father very well, and she knew that in his innermost heart he would like Robert Stafford to fail, so that he could then take the young man into his own business, and thus maintain a domination over his son-in-law and daughter. Hetty Milward wanted to be the mistress of her own future, and now went to the young man and kissed him fully and firmly on his mouth. 'Do not let my father influence you in this matter, sweetheart,' she told him decisively. 'Be your own man. For it is only by being your own man that you can ever become the man I want for husband.'

He drew her to him, and with an equal decisiveness kissed her in his turn. 'Let that serve as my answer, honey,' he whispered. 'And now I have only one more thing to do here, and then we'll return home. Come!' He clasped her hand and led her through to the lean-to at the rear of the house.

Because of the failing daylight the women had finished work, but Amanda Pinfield, acting on previous instructions from Stafford, had kept the workforce back, and now they sat in near darkness waiting stoically for they knew not what. The appearance of Robert Stafford and his elegantly dressed companion was greeted with open surprise and audible comments.

'What does they want here?'

'Why the bleedin' hell have they come?'

'What's this then? Am we a soddin' peep-show now?'

'Hold your bloody rattle, you lot,' Amanda Pinfield shouted. 'Show proper respect for your new master.'

A burst of excited chatter erupted. So this was the reason for the alterations.

Robert Stafford stepped into the centre of the room, leaving Hetty Milward standing just inside the doorway. She wrinkled her nose as the stench of foul breath and unwashed bodies assailed her.

'This is the constant trouble with the poor,' she decided. 'They always stink so badly.'

'Now listen well all of you. I shall not be repeating myself.' Into Robert Stafford's tone had entered a distinct note of arrogance. 'As Missus Pinfield has just told you, I am the new master here. There will be changes, but so long as you work hard and well, you will be able to remain here. Those of you who have menfolk can pass on the word that I am seeking pointers for the new shop here. Tell them who are interested to seek me out at my house during the next few days. In the meantime, you will carry on as normal. Mrs Pinfield will remain in charge of you.'

'That is all, you may go, except for you, Crawford, I wish a word with you.'

As the women and children hastened to leave the lean-to, Aggie Southall whispered spitefully to Tildy, 'I hope he's handing you your sack, navvy-meat.'

Tildy ignored the woman, but at the same time apprehension shivered through her. 'What if he is going to hand me my sack? What will I do for work then? How will I earn money for Davy and me?'

The room emptied until only Stafford, Hetty Milward, Tildy and little Davy were left.

'Come here, Crawford.' Stafford beckoned, and Tildy moved to him, leading her wide-eyed child by the hand.

Hetty Milward also came to stand at her sweetheart's side. She did so with an unconscious motivation that she would not have willingly admitted to if taxed with it. She had seen the beauty of this dark haired woman, and perceived instantly the quality within Tildy Crawford which would draw men to her like moths to a flame. Standing by Robert Stafford's side was her unconscious demonstration of possession, a warning to others that he belonged to her.

Robert Stafford tried to maintain an air of indifference to Tildy's physical attraction. 'Have you done as I bade you, Crawford? Have you learned all you can about the soft work?'

Tildy gravely considered for a few moments, then answered in her soft, low-pitched voice. 'I think I have learned a fair amount concerning it, Master Stafford.'

'Good.' The young man nodded. 'It may well be that Mrs Pinfield will not remain in my employ for very long, Crawford. That miserable face don't suit me. That being the case, I shall be seeking a suitable forewoman to take charge of the women here. It may be that I shall offer you that position? How say you to that?'

To his surprise the young woman did not immediately gush words of gratitude, but instead only stared at him uncertainly.

'Do you understand me, Crawford?' he asked, with a touch of asperity. 'I am telling you that you might well be offered a position which will bring you a greatly increased financial advantage.'

'Oh, I understand, Master Stafford, and indeed, I would be most grateful for it, but...' She hesitated, and fell silent.

'But what?' Stafford was becoming angry. He found that he greatly enjoyed wielding his new-found power, and while he wished to be a benevolent employer to this girl, he also wished her to demonstrate a fittingly submissive gratitude for his benevolence.

'Well, it is Mrs Pinfield. If I should become forewoman here, what will become of her?'

'How should that concern you, Crawford? She is no kin to you, is she? Or even a friend, come to that?' Stafford was genuinely puzzled by this girl before him.

'She is neither of those things, Master Stafford. But I know that she has much difficulty in her life at this present time, and I would not wish to be the cause of

177

adding further burdens to her.'

For a moment, Robert Stafford could only stare in amazement, then he scoffed. 'God strike me! But you're a real goody two shoes, ain't you, Crawford. Do we not all carry burdens through our lives? Why should you concern yourself about a sour-faced hag like Amanda Pinfield?'

In Tildy's mind a fierce resentment exploded, and she vented that resentment without stopping to think of any possible consequences. 'I concern myself about who and about what I please to, Master. Do you think that because you have position in life, and money to buy your way, that those things entitle you to play ducks and drakes with other people's lives? If Mrs Pinfield is a sour-faced hag, then it is because her life has made her so. I'm no goody two shoes, Master. Of course I would like to earn some more money, and of course I would like to become forewoman here if that would be to my advantage. But you know, and I know, that Amanda Pinfield works hard and well, and I know also, even if you do not, that it is her who supports her children and her parents, and that drunken husband of hers as well. Because every penny he gains, and more besides, he drinks or gambles away, and if his wife refuses to give him more money to waste when he demands it, then he beats her unmercifully.

'It is wrong that you should wish to get rid of her for no other reason than she don't suit you because she has a sour face.'

Robert Stafford was by now fuming with anger, but mindful of Hetty Milward's presence he controlled himself, and only snapped curtly, 'You have said too much for your own good, Crawford. Go now, before you cause me to make you rue this day.'

'I'll go, and gladly.' Tildy bobbed a curtsey towards Hetty Milward, and then gathered her child up into her arms and left.

'Damn the insolent bitch!' Robert Stafford exclaimed. 'I've a mind to give her her marching orders when she sets foot in here again.'

He heard Hetty Milward's laughter, and swung upon her incredulously. 'What is it you find so amusing?'

'You!' Hetty told him firmly. 'You were so pompous. Acting like God Almighty, and that girl deflated you like a pricked balloon.'

'I offered her a chance to better herself, and she behaved as if I were some damned tyrant,' he argued.

'You offered her a chance to tread over another woman, and she rejected it because

179

she saw that it was an unjust thing you were doing,' Hetty answered spiritedly. 'Dear God above, Robert! If I did not know you better, I would be tempted to turn away from you myself at this moment. If Amanda Pinfield does not suit you, then be straight about it, and hand her her sack without trying first to ensure that you shall not risk a little of inconvenience yourself in doing so.

'And now, have the goodness to take me direct home. Your poor sisters must be shivering out there in the carriage also. How can you be so selfish? Leaving the poor girls out there in the cold and darkness all this time?'

Disconcerted by this unexpected attack, the young man became flustered. 'I am not selfish, Hetty. You are unjust to so accuse me. When have I ever acted selfishly towards you? Answer me that. When?'

'You are so acting now, by keeping me here in this dirty smelly place against my will.' Without another word she turned her back on him and stormed out of the lean-to.

He hurried after her, beseeching her to wait for him, and in the darkness Hetty smiled to herself. 'How I enjoy to torment you at times, my darling Robert,' she thought gleefully. 'What donkeys you men are.'

Struggling over the rutted muddy track-way towards Redditch, her child in her arms, Tildy felt depressed and angry with herself. 'Why must I always feel driven to challenge those set above me? Why cannot I learn to keep my mouth closed, and to mind my place?' she asked herself over and over again. 'God, I'm such a fool! Such a fool to myself! Why should I care what happens to Amanda Pinfield? She wouldn't have given a hang about me if the positions had been reversed. I could have said yes, and smiled, and showed gratitude to Robert Stafford, and then I'd have been assured of earning more money, and bettering my position in life. I could have afforded to send Davy to a Dame's school, and have him properly cared for when I'm at work. Instead of which, I've opened my mouth too wide again, and lost my job because of it, I shouldn't wonder...'

Behind her there came the jingle of harness and the crunching of iron-shod wheels and hooves. She drew over to the side of the track to let the carriage pass, keeping her head averted from it, knowing it to be Robert Stafford and his party.

The carriage halted just ahead of her, and she sensed the curious stares of the females in the carriage peering at her. Proudly she held her head high, and then Robert Stafford called, 'Crawford,

181

I have chosen to overlook your insolence on this occasion. You may continue with your work tomorrow.' He paused, awaiting her reply, and when at first she made no answer he hissed exasperatedly, 'Do you hear what I say, Crawford?'

Tildy swallowed her pride. 'I hear you, Master Stafford. Thank you. I shall come tomorrow.'

'Don't be later either,' he snapped, and put the horses into motion again.

As the sounds of the carriage faded, and the sight of it was swallowed by the darkness, Tildy could not fight off a surge of self-pity as her clogs squelched and stuck in the clinging mud, and the weight of her child dragged painfully at her shoulders and arms. 'Will I forever have to walk in the dirt, while others ride high above me?' she wondered despondently.

Then, away over the eastern horizons, the clouds rifted and she saw a solitary star shining. It was as if an answer had been sent to her from some mysterious source, and that answer was a message of hope. For reasons unaccountable to her, Tildy felt her depressed spirits lift as she stared at the bright glimmering of light, and she smiled suddenly.

'I'll win through!' She experienced an absolute certainty. 'No matter what lies in wait for me, I'll win through in the end.'

CHAPTER 16

Peg Green was completely besotted with her new lover. He was rough in the bed, at times abusing her body with a sexual ferocity that verged on sadism, but Peg had never known any tenderness in physical love, and took the fierce nightly ravagings of her flesh as a proof of her lover's passionate feeling for her.

Tonight, however, when the last drinker had left and the door was bolted, her lover did not immediately drag her upstairs and throw her down on the bed. Instead he remained seated, nursing a stone bottle of gin in his hands and staring into the turf fire.

'What's amiss, Tom?' she queried, but he made no reply, only kept on staring intently at the dull-glowing clods of turf.

'Tom? Be you feeling all right?' A note of anxiety was in her voice, and Tom Crawford inwardly grinned in satisfaction.

'Tom, what is it? 'As I done summat to upset you? Why wunt you answer me, Tom? What's I done?'

He judged his moment, then slowly shook his head and gusted a weary sigh.

183

'No Peg, it arn't you, it's...it's... Oh, it don't matter, leave it lay.'

She came and knelt at his side, her hands gripping his arm. 'Tell me, Tom. Tell me what's the matter?'

Again he sighed, and then, still staring at the fire, he said, 'I arn't told you afore, Peg, but I've a wife and kid in this town.' He sensed the instant hardening of her eyes, and moved smoothly to avert any outburst. 'I arn't lived wi' me missis for nigh on two years, Peg, I can't stand the sight on her... But I misses my kid summat cruel.' He slowly shook his head. 'I'm fair worried sick about him, Peg, and that's the truth on it. I can't help but keep on thinking how much better it 'ud be for him to be with me, his Dad, rather than wi' that slut of a missus o' mine, seeing her get up to God knows what, wi' the men she sports with.'

Peg Green kept her own counsel and stayed silent, her eyes intent upon the man's face.

Crawford was sufficiently acute to realize that he must go very carefully if he was to win her over to do as he wanted.

'I'm agoing to speak the truth to you, Peg, even though it don't make me sound so good. You see until I met you I never wanted to settle down and lead a quiet steady life with any woman. I couldn't stand being wi' the slut I married, and when I caught her opening her legs for other coves, then I soon upped stakes and ran. But I couldn't forget me son, Peg. He's only a babby yet. It was for him that I came back to this town, and now Ise met you, and wese settled so happy together, well, I can't help thinking how nice it 'ud be if you and me had kids of our own.'

Peg Green, who had borne children to half a dozen men, and let those of her children who still lived roam the town neglected and unloved, shed tears of drunken, maudlin sentiment. 'I knows how you feels, Tom. I understands.'

'Does you, Peg? Does you really?' He cupped her face in his hands and tilted her head so that he could stare into her bloodshot eyes.

'You knows that I does, Tom,' she breathed fervently. 'I'll give you a babby, if that's what you wants. We'll have our own babby.'

Behind his serious expression Tom Crawford was feeling an unholy glee. 'I'd sooner plant a kid in a fucking midden heap, as plant one in you, you old cow,' he thought, but aloud murmured tender words as he cuddled her to him. The woman's tears fell freely as for the first time in her harsh life she really believed that she was being shown loving tenderness by a man.

'Peg, my honey, as well as our own kid, I'd dearly love to get my own son back to live wi' us,' he whispered.

'If that's what you wants, Tom, then it's all right wi' me. I'll be glad to have the little cratur here.'

He smothered her ravaged face with kisses, and rising from his seat he led her upstairs. There he gently undressed her, caressing her slack breasts, pressing his lips to her flabby belly and thighs. Then laying her upon the bed he removed his own clothes and lay down beside her, his hands moving expertly to seek out and stroke her intimate body. He deliberately prolonged his lovemaking until she moaned and cried out aloud as she writhed beneath him. For once he controlled his own needs to tear at her flesh with his strong fingers, to twist, to bite, to inflict pain, and instead brought her to the most shattering, exquisite orgasm she had ever known.

Afterwards, satiated and spent, she lay gazing adoringly at him, and he knew that this was the moment to ask of her whatever he wanted.

'Peg, honey,' he murmured softly, and his hand tenderly cupped and fondled her breasts. 'Peg, to get my nipper back I'll need your help.'

'I'll do anything for you, Tom,' she

promised fervently. 'Anything at all.'

'It wun't take much, Peg, only a few sovereigns at most.'

'I'll give 'um to you, Tom. I'll gi' you whatever you needs. Now love me some more, sweetheart. Please love me some more.'

Grinning in the darkness he moved to straddle her flaccid body once again.

CHAPTER 17

Sunday was a bright crisp day, the sharp easterly wind tempered and warmed by the sun. Israel Lee had come to Redditch to visit Tildy, and taking little Davy they went to walk in the Abbey Meadows, which lay on the valley floor to the north of the town. Once a mighty Cistercian monastery had flourished here, but now only turfy hummocks and mounds denoted the buried ruins of its buildings. Yet carp still swam in the monkish fish ponds, and in the ancient burial yard massive tombstones were inscribed with the Latin scrolls and Papal emblems of the Holy Roman Church.

Tildy loved to walk in these meadows along the banks of the River Arrow and of the watercourses dug by the Cistercians to power their mills and water their Abbey. This day Israel Lee talked almost constantly to her, describing the castles, abbeys and cathedrals he had seen during his roving life on the canals. Tildy listened enthralled, and the hunger to see these wondrous buildings grew strong within her. She said as much to the man, and he was quick to tell her that if she would only agree to become his woman, she would be able to travel and see the country by his side.

'I could take you to London, Tildy, and to Canterbury, or York, or Chester, even Edinburgh and Dublin if you'd a mind to go there.'

She smiled, shaking her head silently, and he sighed and told her. 'I'll keep on asking you, Tildy, because I think that one day in the future you'll say yes, and you'll come wi' me.'

'I don't look to the future these days, Israel,' she remarked quietly. 'I only concern myself with the present. And today I'm enjoying being here with you and my Davy, so the present does me well enough for now.'

'But the life you're leading is no good for you, or for the boy,' he persisted. 'Youm looking real pale and tired, girl. The work at the needles is not good for your health.'

'I'm all right,' Tildy asserted. 'I'm healthy and strong enough. I only look tired because I'm finding sleep a bit difficult these nights.'

'Why is that? Is it because o' that husband o' yourn?'

Tildy nodded, and her expression became troubled. 'I'm worried, Israel, about what Tom Crawford might do.'

'I told you that I'd deal wi' him,' Israel Lee reminded, but the troubled expression remained on Tildy's face.

'If he acts within his rights, then I fear there's not much you could do. In the eyes of the law I'm still his wife, and that makes Davy and me his property. He could do near whatever he wanted with us.'

'That'll be over my dead body,' Israel Lee said grimly, and Tildy betrayed her anxiety by suddenly clutching the man's sleeve.

'No Israel, I'd not wish for you to get into any trouble for my sake. That's the last thing I want.'

'Don't worry, pretty 'un,' he grinned. 'It'll be for me own sake I'd be getting into trouble if that bloody husband o' yourn causes you any more distress.'

As he spoke a cloud masked the sun, and the air abruptly chilled. Tildy shivered slightly, and wondered superstitiously if the blotting out of the sun's warmth was a bad omen for her. 'I think we'd best be getting home, before it gets too cold.'

Tom Crawford had spent the day drinking in company with Bonny Southall and some other pointers at Peg Green's beer shop. Aggie Southall had joined the group, and sunk pot for pot with the men. During the course of their drinking Tom Crawford had told her the story of his marriage, and had found a ready listener as he poured out lies about Tildy's ill-treatment of him, and her affairs with other men. The lies were eagerly accepted by Aggie Southall, whose unreasoning dislike of Tildy had mounted to near-hatred.

'You should break her bloody yed for her, and take the kid from her as well. You said Peg is agreeable to have him here. Ise sin your missus wi' her new bloody fancy man, and it's shameful the way they walks about the town so brazen. Her arn't fit to be a mother. Her arn't fit, bloody navvy whore that she is.'

'Now Aggie,' Bonny Southall remonstrated mildly. 'That babby looks well enough cared for.'

'What 'ud you know about it?' his wife screeched. 'Youm not a mother, and you can't judge these things. No man can, arn't that so, Peg?'

Peg Green was quick to side with her

own sex. 'O' course it's so, Aggie. Us women knows these things, a man can't be expected to understand.'

'Well, I understands, me wench,' Tom Crawford asserted loudly. 'And I understands what's got to be done. I'm agoing to bring the boy here to live wi' me and Peg.'

'And a good thing too!' Aggie Southall applauded. 'And the sooner you does it the better, that's what I says.'

'Yes, youm right theer.' Crawford came to a decision. 'I'm agoing round to Mother Readman's right now, and I'll fetch the boy back here wi' me.'

'Now hold on a minute.' Peg Green was more sober than the rest of the gathering. 'That missus o' yourn is a good mate of Mother Readman's, arn't her. You might well find the whole of the bloody Silver Square lined up against you if Mother Readman decides to take a hand in the matter.'

'Let her try.' Tom Crawford had drunk enough to be reckless. 'I'll take on the whole bloody boiling on 'um if I has to.'

'And we'll help you, wun't we Bonny?' Aggie Southall pledged her support.

Her husband, never averse to a fight, nodded vigorously. 'O' course we'ull. Tom's become a good mate, and we'll all on us stand by him. Arn't that so, lads?'

191

The others in the room voiced rowdy confirmation.

'Right then, let's get to it,' Tom Crawford growled, and with excited laughter and talk the gang of men and women followed him out of the beer shop and towards the Silver Square.

'And I'm telling you that her arn't here.' Mother Readman stood massively blocking her front door, scowling at the crowd clustered around it, her arms akimbo on her huge hips. 'And my advice to you, Tom Crawford, is to fuck off out on it a bit rapid, and not keep on shouting the odds at me.'

'Ise got the rights to take my kid.' Tom Crawford's misshapen face wore an ugly expression of sullen threat.

'I don't give a bollocks about your rights.' Mother Readman was not afraid of his temper, nor of any other man's temper, come to that. 'I'm telling you for the last time that your missus and babby arn't here in the house. So just fuck off, the lot on you.' Her small eyes, slitted in their puffballs of fat, locked onto Bonny Southall. 'Now, Bonny Southall, as you ever known me to spake false?' she demanded.

'No, youse always bin straight as a die, missus, I'll gi' you that.'

'Well then, you knows I'm spaking straight now when I says the wench and her babby arn't here. But I'll tell you this straight as well, that if her was here, and her didn't want to see or goo wi' this bugger, then I'd not let a hair of her yed be touched. Her's a friend o' mine, and I'll stand by her. But I'm telling you true, Bonny Southall, that her arn't here in this house at this time.'

'That's fair enough.' The pointer accepted the fat woman's word. 'Come on, you lot, we'll only catch cold hanging about here. You'll have to try some other time, Crawford.'

With a bad grace Tom Crawford accepted defeat, knowing that without allies he would be very vulnerable in the Silver Square. Already the inhabitants were coming out from their dens to see what was going on at the lodging house, and he knew that despite their internal feuds, they would stick together against outsiders from other streets in the town.

The party retraced their footsteps through the malodorous alley and came out once more at the Red Lion archway.

'Well, we might as well go back to Peg's,' Tom Crawford suggested, and to further bind his new-found allies to him, added, 'I'll be giving you the drinks on the house for the rest of the day.'

Cheered immensely by this prospect the party trooped happily through the town. They had reached the narrow entrance to Clarke's Yard when Aggie Southall's sharp eyes spotted the couple coming across the Chapel Green from the direction of the Fish Hill.

'By the Christ! Theer her comes now, and her bloody fancy man wi' her as well. Now's your chance, Tom.'

Tildy saw the mob approaching, and vented an exclamation of distress. 'Oh Sweet Jesus, it's him! It's my husband!'

The contractor felt his own heart sink as he weighed the possible odds against him if trouble should start. 'I reckon you'd best take the boy and make a run for it, Tildy, while I tries to hold him here. If you can reach Mother Readman's, then you'll be safe.'

Tildy shook her head despairingly, knowing that with little Davy weighing her down she would not be able to outrun any pursuit.

The mob, ominously silent, reached the couple and surrounded them. Tom Crawford stepped forward to confront his wife. Despite the hatred lurking in his eyes, his voice was low-pitched and betrayed hardly any emotion. 'Well now, wife, weem well met. I been looking for you.'

Tildy's voice trembled, but she faced

194

him bravely. 'What do you want with me?'

'I wants my son, you bloody whore,' he spat venomously.

It was now that Israel Lee made the move which precipitated disaster. Unable to bear the sight of Tildy's white drawn features he stepped between her and her husband. 'Leave her alone,' he warned, 'or I'll be giving you more than youse bargained to find.'

He was a formidable figure, and Tom Crawford swallowed hard, hesitant to tackle the man.

But there were others in the crowd who were ready to do so, and Aggie Southall lit the fuse of the explosion.

'Well now,' she sneered loudly. 'Has it come to this? Be the Redditch pointers fritted of bleedin' navvies these days? So fritted that you'll let one of them come between a man and his lawful wedded wife, and steal a man's son from him? Fuck me, your Dads 'ud turn in their graves if they could know about this. They 'uddny have stood by and let a fucking navvy browbeat an honest man arter putting the horns on him as well.'

Bonny Southall was the first to react under the gibe. 'Back off, navvy,' he warned Lee. 'Don't come between a man and his wife.'

'I've no quarrel with you,' the contractor told him evenly. 'Nor with any other of you, except this 'un here.' He pointed at Tom Crawford's face. 'He's the bugger I wants.'

'Well I'm the bugger youm getting,' Bonny Southall growled, and came with a rush, fists balled and swinging.

'Form a ring! Form a ring!' the cry went up, and instantly a space cleared around the fighting men as the quiet of the Sabbath afternoon was shattered by the shouts and cheers of the drunken mob.

Tildy stood as if paralysed, wanting to flee, but not able to bring herself to desert the man who had tried to protect her.

'Now Tom, now's your chance. Grab the kid,' Aggie Southall urged, and Tom Crawford's quick wit grasped that she was right. In one stride he had reached Tildy. Viciously he punched her in the face, and as she cried out and reeled helplessly backwards, he snatched the screaming child from her arms.

Tildy fell to her knees, blood spurting from her nose and mouth, and through eyes blurred by tears of pain she saw her child struggling from his father's grasp. Like a tigress she hurled herself from her knees towards Tom Crawford.

'Grab her! Grab her! Hold her down!' Aggie Southall screeched, and Tildy was caught by strong arms and wrenched back from her terrified son who screamed and strained and fought to reach her in his turn.

Kicking, scratching, biting, Tildy fought like a demented woman to save her baby, but the combined efforts of half a dozen opponents proved too much for her to break through, and she was pinned down on her back in the dirt of the road, helpless to do other than scream and writhe impotently while Tom Crawford bore the hysterical child away. A man's hand clamped across her mouth; she caught the thick fingers between her sharp teeth and bit hard until she tasted the salt of blood and felt the grating of bones.

'Ahhhggghhh! You fucking bitch!' the man bellowed as he wrenched his hand free, then in a paroxysm of fury smashed his fist into her jaw. A jolt of agony exploded through her skull, bright lights flashed before her eyes, and impenetrable darkness fell upon her...

'Davy! Davy! Davy!' Tildy could hear the name shouted over and over. 'Davy! Davy! Davy!' Then suddenly knew it to be her own voice that was shouting. Her head throbbed jarringly, and when she opened her eyes the daylight lanced into them like a sharp knife.

'Lie still, girl.' She recognized the new voice as belonging to the Reverend John Clayton, and she tried to sit up, but a wave of dizzying nausea caused her senses to swim and she fell back.

'Tildy, are you all right, honey?' It was Israel Lee bending over her now, his face cut and bleeding and visibly swelling. Slowly this time she levered herself upright, closing her eyes to fight back the waves of giddiness, biting on the acrid taste of bile in her mouth and throat.

'He's got Davy,' she told the clergyman, who stood looking down at her. 'He's stolen my child.'

Clayton was grim-faced. 'Calm yourself, girl. I have heard what has happened. Gather your senses, and I will hear your version of the story later. But for now, let us first have your injuries looked to. I have sent for the doctor.'

Supported by Israel Lee, Tildy clambered slowly to her feet and stood swaying, holding tightly to the contractor's muscled arm. As her head cleared a little, she was able to look about her. The original mob appeared to have disappeared and now a fresh crowd surrounded her, staring with avid curiosity and whispering excitedly to each other.

'The parson was over in the chapel, lucky for us,' Israel Lee told her. 'When he heard the commotion he came running out and when they saw him coming they scarpered.'

'Are you bad hurt?' Tildy anxiously looked at the bloody cuts and swellings on his face.

He shook his head. 'Theer's nothing broke. That cove could use his fists well enough though, no doubt o' that,' he acknowledged wryly, and then said, 'But you needs looking to, pretty 'un.'

Tildy gingerly fingered her sore jaw, and felt the blood crusting about her mouth and chin. 'I must go after Tom Crawford,' she insisted. 'I must get Davy back from him.' She saw the constable, Joseph Cashmore, in the crowd talking with the onlookers. 'Look, there's the constable. He must come with me, to get my baby back. Will you tell him to do so, Parson Clayton?'

The clergyman could not seem to meet her eyes, and he did not answer her plea.

'Parson Clayton, will you tell him to come with me to get my baby back?' Tildy begged. 'He'll listen to you, and obey you.'

Looking uneasily at her the clergyman said gently. 'I'm feared there is little the constable can do in this matter, Crawford. Your husband has the right to have his child with him.'

From further along the Green, Dr Hugh Taylor, handsome and dandified in his elegant dress, halloed the clergyman, who beckoned him on.

The young doctor cursorily examined Tildy's injuries, and then said to Clayton with more than a touch of asperity, ' 'pon my soul, John, why do you call me from my game for such a trifle? She's merely had her claret tapped.'

'She was lying unconscious when I called for you,' the parson answered testily.

'Well she is on her feet now, and will live by the looks of her. I'll bid you good day.'

With that the young man sauntered away. Clayton pulled out a large gold watch from his fob and glared at it with barely concealed impatience. 'This is too bad. I should have been at Tardebigge Church by this hour, Crawford. I suggest you go to your lodgings and cleanse yourself, then rest awhile.'

Tildy was gazing incredulously at him, as if unable to believe what had been happening in front of her. 'But my baby has been stolen from me, Parson Clayton!' she exclaimed in bewilderment. 'And you are merely telling me to go to my lodgings and wash my face. I want my child! I want him back where he belongs, with me, his mother!'

Again the uneasy look appeared on Clayton's face, and his eyes flicked from side to side as if seeking a way of escape. When he spoke it was slowly and very distinctly as if to a young child receiving its first lessons at school. 'As I understand the law of the land, Crawford, your child is where he belongs. He is with his father. To speak frankly, that is where you should also be. At the side of your lawful husband.'

Tildy pushed herself away from Israel Lee's supporting arm, and went to where the constable was listening to a voluble account of what had happened.

'Master Cashmore, my husband has beaten me with his fist, and he's taken my child from me by force, he's stolen him from me. What are you going to do about it?' Her fear and anxiety made her appear aggressive towards the man.

The heavy-set, taciturn constable stared at her for long moments, then only shook his head. 'There's naught I can do, girl. He's your lawful wedded husband, arn't he?'

Tildy nodded.

'He's on the parish register as the child's feyther, arn't he?'

Tildy nodded.

'The babby was born in wedlock, warn't he?'

Again Tildy was forced to nod.

201

'Well that's about it then, arn't it,' the constable grunted, but his eyes were sympathetic. 'If I went and removed the babby from his father, then I'd be brought before the Justices meself, girl. Your husband has got the right to keep the child with him. Just as he's got the right to make you live wi' him, if he so chooses. Just as he's got the right to give you a belt in the chops if he considers you deserve it. It's the law, girl.'

'But Tom Crawford is a cruel, evil bastard, who treated me worse than he'd treat a brute beast, and who took not a blind bit of notice of my baby, except to shout and curse at the poor little mite.'

'Crawford?' The clergyman spoke from behind her. 'Crawford, I don't doubt the truth in what you say. But sadly, even if your husband was like the Devil incarnate he still has the right to take his son to himself. That is the law of this land. Wife and child are the chattels of the husband in virtual fact.' He softened at the sight of Tildy's distress. 'Listen to me, young woman. I shall be meeting with Reverend the Lord Aston shortly. As you well know he is a magistrate of the county, and one of the justices of the peace for this parish. I shall enquire of him what can be done concerning this matter. Be assured that I have your best interests at heart, Crawford.

202

But for now, do as I bid you. Go to your lodgings.'

'I'll get my baby back myself,' Tildy burst out desperately, tears falling freely down her blood-streaked cheeks. 'I'll go to get him back, and if Tom Crawford tries to prevent me, then I'll kill him. I'll kill the evil bastard!'

'You will do nothing to break the law, Crawford,' the clergyman snapped curtly. 'If you attempt to approach your husband and thus bring about a further disturbance of the peace, then I shall have the constable take you up for committal, and I will guarantee that you will find yourself serving a sentence in the Bridewell. And what will happen to your child then, Crawford? Think well on what I say.'

He turned to the constable. 'I am charging you to have a watch kept on this woman, Cashmore. If she attempts to approach her husband, then she is to be taken into custody immediately.'

He spoke next to Israel Lee. 'You appear to have an interest in this young woman, and to be prepared to stand as friend to her. That being the case, then for her own sake I strongly advise you to take her back to her lodgings and ensure that she stays there until her nerves are calmed. If she refuses to accompany you, then I would further suggest that you use any means you consider appropriate to carry her there.'

To Tildy it was as if a nightmare had invaded her waking hours, a nightmare from which she was powerless to awaken. Sobs tore from her, racking her entire body. Blinded by tears, and utterly distraught, she allowed Israel Lee to lead her gently away.

Back at Mother Readman's, Tildy grew gradually calmer. Drawing on all her considerable strength of character and courage she set her mind to finding a solution to her problems.

Israel Lee wanted to fetch his navvies to go to Clarke's Yard and take Davy back by force.

Initially Tildy was tempted by the idea, but calmer reflection convinced her that that method could only be an act of complete desperation which would inevitably rebound against her in the long run.

'But you and Davy can come away with me, Tildy. Your husband will never be able to find you if weem careful,' the contractor urged repeatedly.

Tildy regretfully rejected his ideas. 'That's just it, Israel. If we were careful. So careful that I'd spend the rest of my life forever looking back over my shoulders. Fearful that someday I'd see

Tom Crawford coming after me. He's a vindictive man, he would spend all his days searching for me to get revenged upon, if I beat him in this way. And he'd have the law behind him, don't ever forget that.'

'The girl is right, Master Lee.' Mother Readman's shrewd mind was also grappling with the problem. She had immediately on Tildy's return despatched one of her spies to Peg Green's beer shop to keep a watch on what was happening there. 'You needn't fret that they'll serve the babby bad at this time, Tildy,' she gave bleak comfort. 'They'll treat him like a little prince for a few days at least, so that folks 'ull not turn agen 'um.'

'But he'll be terrified without me.' Tildy's eyes brimmed with tears as her fears for her baby overwhelmed her once more.

The fat woman chuckled grimly. 'Sweet Jesus Christ, girl! Youm still but a green 'un in some ways, arn't you. The babby has got his mouth full o' sweet suck right now, and he's being fussed and cosseted so that he reckons it's angels has got hold on him. Your babby 'ull not be grieving too much for you while that's happening to him.'

Such cynicism would normally have been unacceptable to Tildy, but now in her desperation she snatched at the statement, drawing from it a curiously perverted type of comfort. Because, if she thought that he was suffering greatly, then her control would become dangerously weakened, and she would be driven almost to breaking point. 'I hope you're right,' she whispered. 'God help me, but I hope you're right, Mother Readman.'

'I'm right, girl, don't doubt it,' the older woman insisted harshly. 'Ise birthed too many o' the little buggers not to know what they'm like. At that age, so long as their belly is full, and theym being fussed, then they don't really give a bollocks who's doing the fussing. Now you can stop this bloody weeping and wailing and get that yed o' yourn working. Youse got to think, and to plan how youm going to get your babby back all lawful and proper.'

'There's no need for the bloody law,' Israel Lee intervened sulkily. 'Ise got two score o' good lads, who 'ull break all the heads that's needful to get the kid back.'

'Hold your rattle, you great numbskull,' Mother Readman scowled. 'Youm talking like a bloody fool still. If Tildy breaks the law by taking the kid back in that way, then her 'ull end up in the Bridewell. Your bloody navvies can't protect her agen the magistrates, and the constables, and the bloody Yeomanry if needs be, can they, and you well knows that. So, the best thing you can do for now is to fuck off back to Tarbick Cut, and be ready to help us when we calls for it.'

The contractor glared at her, muttering angrily beneath his breath, but then Tildy added her pleas.

'Yes, Israel, please do what she says, for my sake. Go now, and wait until I decide what must be done, and then ask for your help. Please...'

Grudgingly he agreed to what she asked, saying as he left, 'But don't you forget for one minute that I'll be waiting.'

Tildy smiled her gratitude, and on impulse gently pressed her bruised lips to his. 'I'll send for you, that I promise. And I truly am grateful for all your kindness to me.'

Greatly cheered by the kiss, Israel Lee set out for the Tardebigge Canal, leaving the women by the lodging house kitchen's fireside.

It seemed to Tildy that hours passed, and rack her brains though she might she could find no idea which gave even a glimmering of hope.

Periodically amid the noise and hubbub of the kitchen's floating population of tramps and homeless transients, the man whom Mother Readman had sent to Peg Green's beer shop would sidle in and make his reports to her.

'The babby's bin put to sleep now, and he looks to be contented enough,' was his final report of the night. Once more Tildy faced the unpalatable duality of reaction upon hearing that her baby was content enough. Relief that he was not suffering, pique that he did not appear to be grieving for her overmuch.

Mother Readman slipped a few coins into the man's filthy paw. 'Theer, that's your entrance money for tomorrow. You'se done well. Make sure you keeps on doing well,' she instructed, and turned to Tildy. 'As for you, my wench, it's time you was up them wooden hills and in Bedfordshire.'

'Sleep! How? How could I think of sleep?' Tildy demanded indignantly.

'Because it's Monday tomorrow,' Mother Readman stated flatly. 'And you needs to be at your work. Wheer else is the money to come from to pay for your bed and board? Don't you dare to argue back wi' me, Tildy, just listen, and listen well.' The fat woman leaned forwards in her thronelike chair, her great meaty hands resting on her massive thighs, and gravely explained. 'I'll tell you what's in my mind now, girl. To stand any chance at all of getting that babby back lawful, youm going to have to have some o' the gentry hereabouts on your side. Now to them theer's only two sorts o' the poor. Theer's the no-goods,

208

and the deserving poor. To be counted as "deserving poor" youse got to slave your guts out all the hours God sends, working for next to nothing all your days. That way, when youm too old and worn out to work any more, they'll say youm a deserving soul, and they'll allow you a few crumbs o' charity out on the money youse helped make for 'um.'

'What has any of this got to do with what happened to me and my Davy today?' Tildy interjected impatiently.

'Shush, 'ull you! I'm coming to that in a minute.' The older woman winked slyly. 'Now I've bin thinking real hard about your troubles, Tildy, and I reckon Ise got an idea which just might...only just might, mind you,' she qualified warningly, 'just might do you a bit o' good in the matter. But for your part, I wants you to goo to work tomorrow.'

The sickening realization that if she did so, she would encounter Aggie Southall, suddenly struck Tildy. Involuntarily she clenched her fists, and almost snarled, 'I'll be seeing Aggie Southall if I go to work, Mother Readman, and the way I feel now, is that when I do see her, then I'll strangle the evil cow.'

'Oh no you wun't!' the fat woman ordered forcefully. 'You'll keep your mouth tight shut, and your hands to yourself, no

209

matter what's said or done to you, and you'll do your work. Then, when the shift's finished you'll come straight home here. You'll keep on like that, and then maybe I might be able to get a bit of help lined up for you eventually.'

'But how can that be?' Tildy pleaded to know. 'What do you intend doing?'

The slitted eyes screwed up tight in their puffballs of fat, and the woman chuckled richly, rocking backwards and forwards, causing her chair to creak and groan and sag dangerously. 'Ask no questions and you'll hear no lies,' she breathed hoarsely. 'Only do as I says. Now off to bed wi' you, girl, and be early to your work in the morning.'

Although Tildy was burning to question the woman more, she knew the futility of trying to draw information from Mother Readman when the older woman did not wish to impart it. Reluctantly she made her way by the guttering smoky light of her tallow candle to her tiny room beneath the eaves, and as she did so she felt a spasm of hope burgeon within her. She knew that Mother Readman had many contacts throughout the district, and in her own way wielded considerable influence among certain groups of people.

'Dear God, let her be able to help me get my Davy back.' Tildy, for the first time in her adult life, knelt by the side of her narrow cot and prayed fervently. 'Dear God, if there is such a being as you, and you can hear me now, I beg you to let Mother Readman be able to help me to get my child back. Please God, please, please, please, give me back my baby...' She knelt for long hours, her head resting on her hands, and eventually, still in that position, she drifted into an unquiet, troubled sleep.

CHAPTER 18

Robert Stafford was facing his own troubles. Only three pointers had come to his house in search of work, and when he had informed them of the proposed rates of pay, they had laughed in his face and told him to do his own pointing. It was in vain that he had emphasized the safety factor to them, they had merely scoffed and walked away.

Now it was Sunday night. He had bought a large consignment of packs of needle-lengths, and until he could get them pointed they were useless to him.

He rose from the evening meal table, leaving his food half-eaten, trying to hide his worries from his mother and sisters, who had been surreptitiously watching him with deep concern.

'Where do you go, Robert?' his mother asked, her face pale and anxious in the candlelight.

'I needs must go out for a while, Mama. I'll not be late home.'

'Are you wandering off to stand beneath Hetty's window, I wonder.' Dorothea attempted to bring a touch of lightness into the gloomy atmosphere. 'La, brother, how smitten you must be to stand beneath her window in the cold of the night.'

He frowned, and snapped curtly, 'Pray don't talk nonsense all the time, Dorothea. I find it increasingly wearisome to have to listen to your inane chatterings.' The moment he had spoken he felt remorse at her hurt expression. 'I'm sorry, sister. Forgive my hasty words. I am out of sorts.'

He went into the hallway and donned hat, gloves and a heavy topcoat before going out into the dank, dreary night. 'I must find some men,' he told himself worriedly. 'If I don't get at least two pointers for tomorrow, then I could find myself in serious difficulties.'

He stared about him, trying to decide in which of the inns or alehouses he would find possible recruits.

'The Royal Oak, that's as likely a spot as any. More than likely James Bray will be there also. I could use him to cry the vacancies around the town as well.'

Bray was the town crier, and it was customary when fresh hands were needed in the mills and factories to use him to spread the news of the vacancies.

The ancient half-timbered Royal Oak was situated at the bottom of the Fish Hill at the corner end of a lane, its ground floor some three feet below road level, and its crooked roof overshadowed by the great new mill of Samuel Thomas. It was a favourite haunt of the pointers who worked in the mills of the north side of the town, and Robert Stafford knew he'd find plenty of them there, drinking and gambling the sabbath night away.

The smoke-filled tap room was well lit by oil lamps and the fire blazing in the grate. Behind his tall narrow counter Tommy Green, short, fat and sweaty, was happily drawing tankards of ale and cider from the huge wooden barrels set on their trestles, and equally happily measuring out horn-tots of rum and gin and brandy. Sunday was always a good night for his trade, and tonight was no exception to the general rule. The big tap room was full, as were the smaller bar-parlour and the snug. These latter rooms were patronized by foremen, overlookers, shopkeepers and respectable artisans. The tap room was by long-established usage the domain of the rougher elements of his customers, among which the pointers predominated.

Robert Stafford entered the bar-parlour and ordered rum mixed with hot water, sugar and a dash of cinnamon, standing where he could see through the intervening service hatch and passage into the tap room. He studied the customers there as they came and went from his view. Ritchie Bint, Luke Fisher, Rammer Perks, Edwin Danks, Sam Styler, John Mogg, Sam Merry, Will Wall, Joe Hill, Hen James, Bonny Southall, Steve Millington. He grimaced as he recognized each individual. Pugilists, brawlers, drunken ne'er-do-wells, every one of them. Not giving a damn for God, man or beast. Reckless of their own lives, and careless of others' lives. Living only for the day and not caring a hang what the morrow might bring them. Robert Stafford wished with all his heart that he did not need these savage men, who at times filled him with fear.

He gulped down the last of his drink, savouring the burning warmth it spread through his body. His courage fortified, he went through into the tap room and halting in its centre he called loudly, 'Gentlemen,

214

can I have a brief word with you, if you please?'

The noise abruptly stilled as men looked up from their cards and dominoes and broke off their talk to stare at the newcomer with a latent aggressive hostility lurking in their hard eyes.

'Now then, young Stafford, make it quick. Youm interrupting good drinking time here.' Ritchie Bint, squat-bodied and broken-nosed, pushed the square paper hat further back on his sandy head and winked at his neighbours. 'Mind you, if youm come about what I thinks you am, then it wun't take but a second to gi' you your answer.'

'You've no doubt heard that I'm looking for pointers then, Master Bint?' Stafford queried.

Bint grinned savagely, showing his broken stained teeth. 'Ahr, I has that, and Ise heard the poxy price youm offering, as well.'

'I'm offering two and a third per five thousand,' Stafford said defensively. 'That's not such a bad price.'

'You must be joking,' Bint jeered scathingly. 'Why, a man 'uddn't gain more than a sovereign and a quarter the week at that price.'

'Maybe not, but a man would keep his health. Because I've introduced a device

215

that will do away with the rot in my pointing shop. Any man who works for me can still earn sufficient to live well on. Twenty-five shillings the week is more than double any of the farm servants hereabouts can earn, even in the summer, and it's three times their winter wages. I'm offering good money by any standards.'

'Not by our standards, you arn't, Master.' Luke Fisher at thirty years of age was old for a pointer, and had managed to last ten years at the trade. But now his sunken eyes and hollow cheeks, his grey face and wasted body, showed that death had him in its grip. Even as he spoke he began to cough chokingly, and was forced to smother his mouth with a huge piece of rag that was already thick with dried blood and sputum.

'Luke's right,' Ritchie Bint agreed. 'You knows what we reckons to earn, young Stafford, and that's up to five pounds the week. Does you really believe that any pointer lad 'ud take your work at your poxy bloody price?'

Stafford could hardly believe the blatant manner in which they deliberately chose to ignore what he was trying to tell them. 'Can you not understand what I'm saying?' he questioned incredulously. 'That by using the new devices I have introduced into my shop, you will not suffer from the rot. Look at Luke Fisher here. His two brothers dead from the rot, and he himself sick almost to death from it. That is what is going to happen to each and every one of you if you carry on with the old ways of working. How can you want that, when I am offering you a safe method of pointing? A method that means you will live long lives, and God willing, live them in full health and strength.'

'Youm offering us long lives to be lived in poverty, Mister,' one man growled. 'Instead of dying sooner from the rot, we'll die later from fucking starvation.'

'At least our way we gets to meet our Maker wi' a full belly and a song on our lips,' Bonny Southall joked, and the room erupted with laughter.

'You go to meet your Maker with the taste of your own blood in your mouth, and your bellies empty because when the rot has you in its grip you are not able to swallow your food. And how can you sing when you can't even draw breath to keep life in you,' Stafford rejoined angrily. 'Are you really so thick-headed that you cannot see I am offering you life?'

The laughter died away and an ominous silence fell upon the room.

Tommy Green, recognizing the signs of impending violence only too well, attempted to intervene. 'Come on now, lads, drink up. Or else I'll be meeting me Maker wi' me coffers empty. I can't have you sat there drinking naught. Me profits be going down summat cruel.' He joked and laughed uneasily, and the walls sent that laughter back to him in solitary echo.

Stafford himself knew instantly that he had overstepped some invisible line in his last statement, and he knew also that at this moment, discretion was the better part of valour. 'I'm leaving directly,' he said quietly. 'If any of you should change your minds, then there will be work for you at my shop.'

Still the hostile silence persisted, and with a nod the young man left.

He had walked only a few yards up the Fish Hill when he heard his name called, and he turned. It was the tall, burly pointer named Will Wall, a quieter, steadier man than his fellows.

'Yes Will, what is it you want of me?' Suddenly hopeful, he added, 'Do you wish to work for me?'

'Not I, Master Robert,' the man answered quietly. 'But because your old mother was good to my missus when her was took badly last year, I wants to gi' you a word of advice. That's if you'll listen to it, o' course. But it's meant for your own good.'

'I'll listen, Will, and gladly.'

'So be it then. My advice is this, Master Robert. Forget all about paying lower rates for your pointing. It wun't serve in this town. No pointer'ull ever work for them rates.'

'But cannot you understand either, Will?' Robert Stafford almost pleaded with the man to comprehend. 'I've introduced a device that will extract the steel dust from the air. It will make the pointing safe. You have no need to throw your lives away any longer.'

'We deliberately chooses to follow the trade, Master Robert.' The man was deadly serious. 'We knows when we takes up the pointing that weem signing our own death warrants in a manner o' speaking. But while weem working, we lives like lords, wi' money in our pockets, good grub in our bellies and as much drink and tobacco and merrymaking as our senses can stand.'

'But how are you benefited in the long run?' Robert Stafford challenged. 'For the most part the wives and children of the pointer lads fare no better than the families of any of the other labouring men in this town. The big money the pointers gain, they throw as quickly on the air. They do not use it to acquire property, to educate their children, to clothe their wives.'

'That's as maybe.' Wall was dismissive.

'But to tell truth, I don't give a fuck for other men's families. It's down to each individual what he does with his own, and 'tis no concern to me.

'Ise only come out arter you to try and do you a favour, and if you wun't listen to what I says, then it's your own funeral, boy. I'll say again, for the last time. You'll have to pay the going rates to get your needles pointed, and forget all about your safe working methods. They don't signify with us, and we don't want 'um neither. Because once the work is made safe, then every Tom, Dick and Harry 'ull be ready to do it, and that 'ud mean the wages dropping, and us pointer lads 'ull never stand quietly by and let that happen. Just remember what Ise told you, Master.'

He turned away and went back towards the inn, leaving Robert Stafford staring disgruntledly after him.

CHAPTER 19

Long before dawn Tildy was washed and dressed, her hair brushed and neatly plaited and coiled on her head. Despite sleeping as she had she felt fresh and strong. The tormented emotions of the previous night had metamorphosed into an implacable resolution to do whatever she must in order to get her child back. Respecting Mother Readman's sagacity Tildy was prepared to follow the old woman's dictates. To go to her work, and try not to react to whatever provocation she might be subjected to there.

'And if Mother Readman's way fails? What then, Tildy? What then?' doubt whispered in her mind, but she met its assault head-on. 'Then I'll find some other method, that won't fail.'

Shawl drawn over her head Tildy picked her way along the filth-littered Silver Street in the morning darkness. From some of the hovels the dimly guttering lights of rush and tallow showed that those within were astir, and even at this hour surly voices raised in dispute sounded from behind the broken shutters and rag-stuffed windows.

She stopped at the wheeled cart outside Holyoakes Manufactury to drink a pannikin of coffee, and was surprised when the stall man refused payment. The explanation for his refusal came from his blowsy wife, who whispered,

'Wese heard what happened up on the Green yesterday when your babby was took from you, my duck. It's a crying bloody shame, so it is, and there's a good many in this town thinks the same.'

It came as no surprise to Tildy to hear that this woman knew what had happened. Most people spent their scant hours of leisure in company with others at inns, beer shops, chapels, in each other's houses. A prime source of entertainment was the exchanging of local news and gossip and consequently any event that took place in the district was eagerly discussed and the news of it quickly disseminated. It was an old joke in the town, which contained more than a grain of truth, that if a complete stranger were to drop dead on the Chapel Green at twelve noon, then by fifteen minutes past noon the entire district would know not only of his death, but also his name, age, profession, marital status, and what he had eaten for breakfast that morning.

Cheered and warmed by the coffee and kindness Tildy thanked the woman and walked on. She pondered on the fact that for perhaps the first time in her life, she did not feel utterly alone in facing her troubles. How strange it seemed to her that hard-bitten characters like Mother Readman and Israel Lee were prepared to stand by her, who could give them nothing in return except heartfelt thanks.

'How strange that I should find such goodness of heart where the prating preachers and praying worshippers would have us believe that only evil and cruelty can be found. In all truth I've found better Christians in Mother Readman's lodging house, and places like it, than I've ever seen going into the chapels with their bibles in their hands.'

Outside the workshop door the crowd of women and children stood waiting in the gloomy darkness. As Tildy approached there was much nudging and whispering. She kept her head high, and with relief saw that Aggie Southall was not among her cronies.

'Thank God for that,' Tildy thought grimly, 'because despite my good intentions I don't really think that I could stand quietly and take provocation from her this morning.'

Tildy came to a halt some little distance from the rest, and stood with her back to them, looking out over the surrounding landscape. From behind her there came an increased volume of whispering, then she heard the sounds of clogs nearing her, and she tensed her body, poised to defend herself if need be. But instead of attack a woman's hand timidly touched her arm. Tildy swung to look into the eyes of one of Aggie Southall's closest supporters.

'Well,' she asked evenly. 'What do you want with me?' All Tildy's resolve to remain passive under provocation abruptly left her, and she cried out silently. 'No! I'll not stand being mocked and bullied by these or any others without making protest. Be damned to being meek and mild. I'm the one that has been wronged here. It's my child that will suffer if I don't get him back. No, if it's trouble they seek now, then they'll find it in plenty.' Outwardly only the heightened colour in her pale cheeks, and a fiery glint dancing in her eyes, betrayed her feelings.

The woman, Janey White, dropped her head and mumbled, 'I knows that youm vexed with us all, Tildy, and God knows wese give you good reason to be so. But we just wants you to know that we all thinks it was a bad, wicked act that Aggie Southall and her mates did yesterday, and if her had come here this morn, then her 'ud bloody soon ha' bin let know how we feels about it. If we can be any help to you in this trouble, then you only needs ask us, and we'll be glad to do any mortal thing we can to help.'

A fervent, low-pitched chorus of affirmation came from the rest of the women, making a huge suffocating lump come to Tildy's throat, and tears brim in her eyes. Hostility from these women, jeers, physical abuse, all these she had been prepared and ready to meet, but this unlooked-for kindness pierced through all her defences.

224

She was only able to utter a single, choked 'Thank you', then was forced to turn away so that the others might not see the tears which she was powerless to hold back.

They possessed sufficient delicacy to perceive that she needed to be ignored and given time to control herself, and reverted to the normal gossip and banter as they waited for the lean-to door to open.

'Come on then, don't keep me standing here in the bloody cold!' The sour face of Amanda Pinfield glowered out of the doorway. 'By the Christ, youm bloody shy of getting in here to do your work, arn't you just. Idle bleeders that you be.' Her eyes noted the fresh dampness of Tildy's cheeks, and she grimaced sympathetically at the sight of the girl's bruised jaw and swollen lips.

When Tildy was seated Amanda Pinfield gently squeezed her shoulder. 'Ne'er mind, my duck,' she whispered. 'Just keep on going. It'll all pass eventually, and God willing, everything 'ull come right for you.'

Tildy forced a smile of thanks for this gesture, and then set herself to deliberately concentrate on her monotonous task in a vain effort to block all thought from her mind...

While Tildy was bending over the work-bench, Mother Readman was moving ponderously down the Silver Street, answering the greetings of its denizens with regal nods of her head. From the Red Lion archway she traversed the mean rows of cottages flanking the stinking Big Pool and went on down towards that easterly part of the town known as Bredon. Her destination was the Fountain, Henry Milward's needle mill, so called because its buildings incorporated an old inn of that name.

Milward's large house, opposite the Fountain, was shuttered and dark, but Mother Readman went confidently to the rear where the kitchen was situated. There was light shining from these windows and the sounds of voices from within. Mother Readman hammered on the door, and pushed past the slattenly scullery maid who opened it.

'Sarah Cull, goo and tell your mistress that I wants a word wi' her,' Mother Readman instructed the skinny-bodied cook, who was sitting by the hearth fire, bleary-eyed and nursing a hangover.

The cook nodded towards the big earthenware teapot on the grate hob. 'Help yourself to a sup o' tay, Missus, and rest yoursen a while. The mistress is down the garden in the privy. Her 'ull be back in a bit.'

Mother Readman accepted the invitation, and sat noisily slurping tea and exchanging desultory smalltalk with the cook. In a few minutes Millicent Milward waddled in from outside, her hair done up in paper curlers, a shabby dressing gown barely covering her massive shapeless form. She smiled in welcome at Mother Readman.

'Well now, what brings you here at this hour, Cousin Charlotte?'

Mother Readman pointed to the chair nearest her. 'Set yourself down, Cousin Milly, I wants a bit of help from you...'

CHAPTER 20

The sound of a child weeping woke Tom Crawford. For a moment or two he lay on his back, his hand across his eyes, painfully aware of the throbbing in his skull and the foul taste in his mouth. Beside him in the bed Peg Green shifted restlessly and broke wind.

'God rot you, you stinking old cow,' Crawford muttered as the foul stench reached his nostrils, and he kicked her flabby naked buttock in a sudden paroxysm of fury. 'Gerrup and shut that bloody kid up, 'ull you,' he snarled, and kicked the woman again.

She moaned and came blearily awake, staring about her with a befuddled air. Crawford glared disgustedly at her, comparing her ravaged sourness with Tildy's fresh, clean beauty. 'That's who should be in my bed,' he thought bitterly. 'Not this poxed old bitch.'

The wails of the child sounded louder, and Peg Green grumbled, 'It's that bleedin' kid o' yourn, the noisy little bastard.'

'Well gerrup and quieten the bugger,' Tom Crawford ordered, and although she glared at him and muttered beneath her breath, she obeyed. Crawford turned over and drew the bedclothes over his head, trying to sleep again and escape the after-effects of last night's drinking, but he heard the woman shout, and the slaps of hands on flesh, and the child's wails became shrieks of fear and pain.

With a vile oath Crawford hurled the blankets from him, and got to his feet. He stood in just his shirt, his hairy muscular legs and hips naked, and groaned as the act of rising caused the painful throbbing in his head to worsen sharply. He opened his mouth to bawl curses at Peg Green, and then abruptly closed it without a sound. For a while at least he still needed this woman's aid. He rubbed his hand across his unshaven chin and grinned to himself. Today he would implement another part of his scheme. But he was going to need a shave, and a clean shirt, and money in his pockets.

'Peg, my sweetheart,' he called. 'Can you come here for a minute?'

He knew exactly what would please her and make her amenable to his demands for money, and when she came in answer to his call he clasped her in his arms and despite her mock struggles and protests dragged her onto the bed and parted her flabby thighs with his own.

Robert Stafford had also risen early from his bed, and now was facing his irate uncle, Tommy Fowkes, in the upper room of the Fox and Goose.

'So then, tell me, what's you going to do about getting your needles pointed?' the innkeeper demanded.

Robert Stafford shook his head. 'I don't know, uncle. I hoped that mayhap you would know of a few pointers.'

'Oh yes, my bucko, I knows of a few pointers all right. In fact I knows of a few score on 'um. But I can't see 'um working for the wages youm offering. Theyse already made that clear enough, arn't they.'

'How about if I bring in young lads to do it?' Stafford ventured. 'Or I recruit in other districts?'

His uncle scoffed at those ideas. 'Bring in men from other districts? By the Christ, boy! They'd not last a day. The bloody pointers 'ud ate 'um for breakfast, and well you knows it. They wun't stand for blacklegs in any shape or form.'

'But if the young lads were local they wouldn't serve them roughly, would they?' Stafford persisted. 'The lads would have kin among the pointers.'

'Of course they 'ud, you bloody fool. And it's bloody unlikely that they 'ud be prepared to goo against their own kin, these young lads that youm hoping to find, 'ud they. The little buggers 'ud be too bloody feared to. Besides, there's summat else youm forgetting, boy. These new-fangled muzzles 'ull only take the steel dust from the air. They wun't take the stone dust, 'ull they. And the stone dust lays on the lungs as well, and causes pain and damage. Young lads arn't got the strength in their lungs to do the work, even wi'out the steel dust, youm still going to need men in their full prime for the work, muzzles or no muzzles.' The pink, hanging jowls quivered violently as the older man negated the idea. 'I reckon it looks as though weem beat afore we starts, boy. You arn't agoing to be able to get pointers unless you pays the full rates, and any profits we might ha' gained depended on cutting them rates. Unless we could have done that, we arn't got a chance of gaining orders, 'as we. No!' Again the pink jowls shook. 'No! I reckon we might as well forget it, and cut our bloody losses.'

Robert Stafford, for all his pampered upbringing, was tough-minded and possessed a strong will to succeed. 'I can do some of the pointing myself,' he said.

'Oh, that's a prime idea, that is,' his uncle answered with heavy sarcasm. 'That's prime. But who's agoing to be out on the road selling our goods while youm spending your days wi' your arse on a pointing saddle? Or be you thinking of paying a traveller to do the business for you?'

The germ of an idea was already wriggling in the back of Robert Stafford's mind, and now it burst its bonds. 'By the Christ, uncle, but I'm stupid not to have thought of it before. Be damned if I'm not! I can get women to do the pointing for me.'

'Women?' His uncle stared as if he feared for his nephew's sanity. 'Women? Women pointers?'

'Why not?' Robert Stafford, snatching at straws, was now convinced he had caught hold of a solid plank. 'They'll be dextrous enough, and some of them are as tough as any man. Besides, if they've been soft workers, then they'll be well accustomed to the trade, and they'll not take any time at all to get their speed up for the work. There's no mortal reason why a woman should not be able to do the pointing as well as a man.'

'But women has never been let on the stones, boy,' his uncle stated emphatically. 'It arn't never been counted a woman's work, and it never will be.'

'Why not?' Robert Stafford challenged. His enthusiasm for his idea growing by the second. 'Why should not women do the work?'

'Because their menfolk 'ud never allow it.'

'Then I'll find women who have no menfolk to forbid them.' Stafford was now eager to be gone. 'I'm going to do it, uncle. No matter what you say. It's the only chance we have of bringing success to our venture.'

Tommy Fowkes recognized the impossibility of stopping his nephew. Grimly he told him, 'If you does this thing, our Robert, then I reckon youm agoing to stir up a whole boiling o' troubles. So be it on your own yed, my bucko. On your own yed be it...'

CHAPTER 21

At midday the women and children at Pinfield's workshop were allowed half an hour for their dinner. Today, when Amanda Pinfield told them to lay down tools, Tildy followed her usual practice. She would always go outside to eat her bread and cheese; the scant time spent in the clean air looking out over fields and woodlands refreshed and strengthened her, and enabled her to complete the remaining long hours imprisoned in the foul-smelling, dirty workshop.

The weather was blustery, but mild for November, and Tildy welcomed the cool damp cleanness of the wind upon her face. She couldn't eat however—the thought of her child took away all appetite for food. Instead, she walked away from the house to stand gazing at the nearby woods, which still bore masses of yellowing leaves.

Lost in anxious reverie she was unaware of the approaching man until he was only yards behind her. Then she heard his footfalls and swung to face him. A spasm of hatred, so intense that it tightened her throat and constricted her breathing, struck through her.

'How bist, wife? Ise just come to let you know that the kid is thriving.' Tom Crawford, fresh-shaven, clean-shirted, his tailcoat brushed and his billycock hat set at a rakish angle on his black curly hair, ran his gaze appreciatively over his wife's slender, full-breasted body. 'Fuck me, but she's a tasty piece, right enough,' he thought lustfully. 'I keeps on forgetting just how ripe her is.'

'When are you bringing him back to me?' Tildy spat the words into his face, and so venomous was her expression that Tom Crawford actually stepped back a pace.

'Now calm yourself, wife,' he said. 'I arn't walked all this way to fight wi' you. Ise come to see you as a friend.'

'A friend? You? A friend?' Her hand went unconsciously to the bruises his fists had left on her face, and she asked bitterly, 'When were you ever friend to me, Tom Crawford?'

Inwardly the man itched to smash this defiant girl into submission, and then abuse her body until she begged for mercy. But outwardly he remained calm and reasonable in his manner. 'I admit I was a rough husband to you, girl, and I'm sorry for it now. That's why I came back to this town to find you. I came to tell you that very thing.'

'And to steal my baby from me,' Tildy accused angrily. 'I want him back, Tom Crawford, and I want him back this very day.'

'Theer's no reason why you shouldn't have him back, wife,' he told her, a taunting gleam in his eyes. 'Ise found us a place to live together. This very morn, in fact. And that's what Ise come up here to tell you. You can come and live wi' me and the kid, and be a proper wife to me agen.'

She gaped at him in astonishment. 'Be a proper wife to you again?' she repeated, then vented a shout of bitter mirthless laughter. 'Be wife to you again? You who raped me, and made me pregnant? Who beat and misused me all the time I was with you? I think I hated you from that very first night, and I hate you now. I'd sooner be wife to the Devil than share your bed, or dwell under the same roof as you.'

Fury reddened his eyes, but although his hands bunched into fists, he made no move towards her. Instead, he grinned maliciously. 'Well Tildy, as I sees it, you arn't got any choice in the matter, not if you wants the kid back.'

'So that's your game,' she told him with

loathing in her voice. 'You'd try and force me back to your bed by using my Davy.'

The malice in Tom Crawford's eyes metamorphosed into an emotion akin to pure evil, and when he answered his voice was hoarse and strained. 'You hear me well, bitch! I'm still your lawful wedded husband. If I chooses I can knock you arse over tip right now, and fuck the living daylights out of you, and it's my rights to do so. There's nobody can say me nay. Youm still my missus, and that makes you my property, to do wi' as I pleases.'

In the capacious pocket of Tildy's white apron was a hunk of bread, and a small square of hard cheese. There was also the sharp-bladed knife which she used to cut up her food. As she sensed the looming threat her husband presented, her hand went into the pocket and her fingers locked on the wooden haft of the thin blade.

'I'm not your property,' she stated defiantly, and her courage rose and expanded until she felt that she could defy not only this man before her, but a hundred others like him. Fuelled by her bitter memories, she went on, 'I want my baby back, Tom Crawford, and I want him back this very day. I'm giving you fair warning that if you don't give him back to me, then I'll do whatever I must to get him back, and not you, nor anyone else, will frighten me off.'

Tom Crawford's wits had been honed in the thieves' kitchens and brothels of London and Portsmouth. He had noted her hand going to the apron pocket, and guessed that she had a weapon of sorts there. He also recognized that in her present mood she could well be provoked into some act of desperation. Her bold stance, and the absence of any noticeable fear of him, also disconcerted Crawford. He had not expected this response from a girl he had once kept in a state of fear and subjection, although he was by now remembering other times when she had stood defiantly against him.

But this was a new, stronger person who now confronted him. Abruptly he changed his tactics. 'Now, Tildy, there's no call for you to get all fired up,' he told her, forcing a smile and holding both hands out in a placatory gesture. 'All I'm suggesting is that you might like to come and live wi' me and the kid. I'm not saying that youse got to bed wi' me, am I. Ise already admitted that I warn't very good to you afore, and Ise said I'm sorry for it. All I'm asking for now, is for you to gi' me the chance of making it up to you. Of showing you that I've changed, and that I'm hoping I'm a better man to live with.'

He took a step towards her, and instantly the knife flashed out.

'You lay one finger on me and I'll use this. I swear I'll use it,' Tildy warned, and such was her agitation that her voice rose to a high-pitched keening cry. 'And if you harms a hair on my baby's head, then I'll use it.'

Suddenly in a complete change of outward mood, the man roared with laughter.

Tildy stared in puzzlement, unable to understand what was causing him such amusement. Equally suddenly his laughter stopped, but still grinning, he told her, 'If youm concerned about the kid, my wench, then you'd best think agen about what youm saying. Because if you turns that knife agen me, then you 'ull certain sure be hung or transported, and what 'ud happen to the kid then?' He slowly wagged his head from side to side. 'No, Tildy, as I sees it, you got no choice in the matter at all. If you wants to be wi' the kid, then you'll have to come back and be a wife to me. If you don't do that, then the little bleeder 'ull just have to take its chances, wun't it.'

He nodded pleasantly. 'Think about it, Tildy. I'll be back for your answer in a day or so. Tara now.'

He sauntered off whistling a gay tune,

238

and as Tildy stared after him she was suddenly assailed by despairing helplessness which struck her to the heart.

That despair was still dominating her when the seemingly endless day drew to a close and she set out on the return journey to her lodging house. One thought continually recurred, gradually insinuating its horrifying attraction into her mind.

If Tom Crawford were dead all her present troubles would be over. It was as simple as that. His death meant her and her child's release from fear and pain.

Tildy, on her solitary walk back to Redditch, forced herself to face the question squarely. 'Could I kill him myself in cold blood?' she pondered. 'Could I face Davy as he grew older and keep from him the knowledge that I had killed his father? Could I face myself in the mirror each day, knowing that I was a murderess?'

She tried to reject any notion of committing such an act. 'No! I could never bring myself to commit murder. It's wicked even to think of such things.' But a tiny voice in her mind kept on reminding her, 'You would be free of an evil man at last, Tildy.'

'And what good would that do Davy or me, if I were taken up and hanged for it?'

she argued with the voice.

'There's ways to do it and not be caught, Tildy.' The voice was increasingly seductive in tone. 'There's potions to be had, which slipped into his food or drink he wouldn't taste. Those potions would kill him quick and easy, and no one would ever know what it was that killed him. No one would ever know...'

By the time Tildy had reached the Chapel Green it was full night and the wind had risen, bringing with it gusting rain and sleet. The streets were empty, which meant that nobody would see in which direction she walked, and a name kept reverberating in her mind. 'Esther Smith. Esther Smith. Esther Smith. Esther Smith.' The syllables seemed to keep time with her hurried footsteps, and as Tildy quickened her pace in an effort to leave the name behind her, it too quickened its progress and stayed dinning through her brain. 'Esther Smith. Esther Smith. Esther Smith. Esther Smith.'

Between Tildy's full breasts there nestled a small leather pouch containing her total worldly wealth. Three shillings and four pennies.

'I need only pay her a shilling to enquire of her about such things,' Tildy thought defensively. 'Not to buy anything from her, but just to find out what sort of potion

240

would make a man ill.'

It seemed then that the voice in her head laughed in satisfaction, and then scoffed at her, 'Don't beat around the bushes, girl. Have the courage to face facts. You really want to know what sort of potion would kill him, not merely make him ill. Don't be a hypocrite to yourself, girl, have the courage to face the facts.'

'All right then, I will,' Tildy muttered aloud in defiance. 'I'll go to Mapple-borough now, and I'll find Esther Smith and ask her what sort of potion would kill a man.'

The inner voice appeared to change, to become anxious and concerned. 'And what of your immortal soul, Tildy? If you were to someday kill Tom Crawford in cold blood, what about the foul stain on your immortal soul?'

Her familiar demon of stubbornness now had Tildy firm, and she would not be deflected from her purpose. 'If I should someday be driven to kill Tom Crawford by whatever means, then my immortal soul must take its chance, as my mortal body must do.'

Mappleborough Green was the name given to a straggling area running along the edges of a range of low-lying, heavily wooded hills some three miles to the east of Redditch. To reach this area Tildy's route took her past the church and rectory of Ipsley, where she had worked with, and married her husband. The sight of these buildings and the memories they invoked further hardened her resolve.

The woman she was on her way to see, Esther Smith, bore a sinister reputation. Popular belief considered her to be a black witch, and many were the tales of her casting the evil eye on those who offended her, and of her causing livestock to sicken and die, and crops and fruit to rot in field and on branch. Many men and women visited Esther Smith despite her evil repute. Some came to seek revenge on their enemies, others to seek knowledge of their future. Some wanted love charms so that they might win the hearts of their chosen ones. Many women came hoping to rid themselves of the fruits of their love. There were several such witchwomen and cunning men in the needle district, but old Esther Smith was considered the most powerful and well-versed in the occult arts.

The single-storied, mud-walled cottage with its unkempt thatched roof was a hummock on the edge of a stretch of wild heathland, practically indistinguishable in the darkness from the wooden hillside behind it. Guided by the dim light flickering from its small window Tildy approached, carefully picking her way across the heath, brambles catching and tearing at her long skirts, squelching mud clinging to her clogs.

She shivered slightly in a surge of apprehension, remembering with some degree of irony how she herself had once warned a young girl against going to see this very witch-woman she now sought. As she neared the cottage a dog began howling, a sound eerie in the night, and for a brief instant Tildy was tempted to turn and flee from this ominous place. But screwing up her courage she went on, and the howling changed to a frenzied snarling and barking.

Tildy halted, peering about her, eyes straining to pierce the darkness and find the animal, fearful that if it could, it would attack her.

A door opened in the cottage and a small figure appeared, silhouetted against firelight.

'Who is it out theer? Spake up, or I'll loose the bloody dog at ye.' The voice was gruff and hoarse, hard to define in gender.

'Are you Missus Smith?' Tildy called. 'Mrs Esther Smith?'

'Who is it wants to know?' The woman returned question for question. 'Be you alone?'

'My name is Tildy Crawford, and yes, I'm alone.'

'Then come forrards, wheer I can see you clearer,' the woman instructed, and Tildy dutifully obeyed.

'Hold hard, stand theer,' the woman shouted, moving so that the light cast from the door could dimly illuminate Tildy's features. Then she came forward herself.

Tildy's heart missed a beat as she saw for the first time the saw-toothed, wickedly curved billhook the old woman had in her hand. 'I mean no harm by coming here,' she hastened to reassure. 'I'm seeking only your advice, Mrs Smith, that's all. And I'm able and willing to pay for it.'

'Then you'd best come in.' Esther Smith led Tildy into the cottage.

Once inside she looked about her curiously, surprised to find it clean and fragrant with the varied scents of the bunches of dried herbs that festooned the lime-washed walls and hung from the roof rafters. The light came from the big fire in a great stone inglenook which filled one entire end wall. By the side of this fire sat an elderly man engrossed in a large open book tilted towards the firelight. His lips moved soundlessly as his forefinger traced the lines of words. His hair was long and white, hanging down each side of his face,

244

and he wore a countryman's smock and gaiters, with heavy thick-soled boots.

'That's my husband, you need pay him no mind.' Esther Smith herself was a tiny, wiry-bodied woman, clad in a black gown with a heavy black shawl about her thin shoulders. Her stringy grey hair was uncovered, and dressed in coiled plaits around her ears. Her thin, weather-browned face, deeply lined, looked commonplace except for her dark, bright eyes which had such a piercing quality that Tildy experienced the fanciful notion that the old woman was able to see into her very mind and read the thoughts contained there.

The furnishings were sparse, a small square table flanked by two wooden stools, a couple of chests against one wall, a storage barrel, a bucket, some utensils and food pots upon the shelves. A doored wooden partition bisected the interior of the cottage, and Tildy guessed that the bed-chamber lay behind it. The floor of hard-packed earth, smooth as any flagstones, had several small rush mats strewn upon it.

The old woman showed isolated blackened fangs of teeth which she grinned knowingly at Tildy, and said, 'It arn't what you was expecting to find, is it, young 'ooman?'

Tildy blushed, and began to stammer an apology for staring so rudely, but the other woman waved it aside.

'Don't thee fret yoursen, young 'ooman. I knows well enough what people thinks to find in my house. Bats and toads and human bones, and a big old iron pot abubbling and stinking, that's what they thinks to see, and me sitting by the pot chanting spells and charms.' She cackled with gruff laughter. 'Bloody fools, they ben. Bloody fools... Set you down theer, young 'ooman.' She indicated one of the stools, and Tildy seated herself.

The old woman lit a tallow candle at the fire, and placed it in a candlestick on the table before seating herself on the other stool opposite Tildy.

'Now let me see you.' She stared closely at Tildy for some moments, then continued, 'It'll be man-trouble, wun't it, young 'ooman. And you'll be wanting rid of him, wun't you?'

Such accuracy caused Tildy to widen her eyes, and the old woman again cackled with laughter, then shook her head.

'It arn't witchcraft that tells me that, so you needn't look so took aback, my duck. It's nary but a bit o' common-sense. A girl as bonny as you 'ull be able to get any man her wants wi' just a wink of her eyes. So you arn't come to me to seek a man for

246

yourself. It's a man you wants rid of.'

Tildy could not help glancing at the man in the inglenook, and Esther Smith told her, 'You need pay him no heed, my duck, because he arn't apaying you or me any. You could say that he's on this world, but not of it. You can spake plain and open here, because it's only me who'll be hearing your words.

'Now tell me what your trouble is, my duck, and tell me true. For if you lies, then I'll know, and I'll not help anybody who tries to tell me lies. The powers don't like being lied to, it makes 'um angry.'

A strange impulse suddenly burgeoned in Tildy's mind. An impulse to tell this old woman everything. Powerless to stop herself, she began to speak, and continued without pause until the entire truth had been told. Afterwards she felt relieved, and strangely light-headed as if some tangible substance had been extracted from inside her skull.

Esther Smith remained silent for some considerable time, her dark eyes intent on Tildy, until the young woman began to feel uneasy under the unblinking scrutiny. Then, with a visible jerk, the old woman straightened and said, 'Youse told me the truth, Tildy Crawford, and because you has, then I'm agoing to help you. What money do you have?'

This last sentence created an instant inner conflict for Tildy. Suspicion that this old woman was a trickster who wanted only to fleece her dupes battled with the need to believe that Esther Smith could invoke powers which would aid her, Tildy, in her troubles. The need to believe finally won, and surrendering absolutely, Tildy said,

'I've three shillings and four pence with me now, but on Saturday I shall get my wages, so I'll have another seven shillings almost.'

'For tonight two silver shillings 'ull be enough,' Esther Smith informed her, then rose and went to the nearest shelf. From it she brought back a small white-glazed bowl and a stone bottle. From the bottle she poured a dark oily liquid into the bowl, and moved the candle so that its light shone across the liquid, creating a lustrous sheen upon the oily surface.

Seating herself on the stool Esther Smith placed her hands palms uppermost on the table at each side of the bowl, and told Tildy, 'You must place a silver shilling on each of my hands, girl, and then place your own hands on top of mine. When youse done that, you must keep your gaze fixed on the black pool here, and think as hard as you can about what's troubling you, and don't stop from it.'

Tildy nodded and took out two shillings from the leather neck pouch. She placed a coin into each of the clawlike hands, placed her own hands over them, then stared hard at the black liquid in the bowl and concentrated as intensely as she could upon the visual image of Tom Crawford. In her turn, Esther Smith also gazed into the bowl.

The seconds lengthened into minutes, and the minutes followed one on another until Tildy lost all track of time. The only sounds in the room were the breathing of the women, the crackling of the fire, and the rustle of paper as periodically the man in the inglenook turned the pages of his book. Tildy found that her concentration wavered at intervals, when other thoughts forced their ways into her mind. Her worries for Davy constantly intruded.

After some considerable time she became aware of an alteration in the pattern of Esther Smith's breathing, and glanced up, unable to restrain herself. The old woman's jaw had fallen open and a trickling of saliva wormed its way down her chin from one corner of her slack mouth. Her breathing was harsh and stertorous and her eyes bulged hugely in her head, the pupils shrunk to pinpoints, the whites preternaturally dominant. A sheen of sweat covered her brown face, now a sickly liverish hue.

Tildy wondered nervously if the old woman was suffering a fit of some sort, and she took her hands away as she tried to decide what to do. Then Esther Smith's tense erect body suddenly sagged, and her head fell forwards, her eyes closing as it did so. Her breathing eased to become a series of long-drawn gulpings of air. Then her head lifted, and her eyes opened and fixed on Tildy's.

'The powers has bin good tonight, girl,' she whispered hoarsely. 'Theyse shown me much. But they 'ull never show me all.' She paused, swallowed, and lifted her hands to wipe the saliva from her lips and chin. Her next words sent a tremor of superstitious fear through Tildy, finally convincing her that this old woman was truly a witch who could converse with unseen beings. Unseen beings who had the power to read people's innermost thoughts.

'The powers has told me that you wants a potion from me. A potion to use against the enemy who torments you. I might give you such a potion, girl. But firstly, you mun gi' me five gold sovereigns. Then, if I gives you that potion, you must never spake of it to a living soul. For if you should do so, then the powers 'ud strike you down dead in that instant.' She lifted one hand and brought it down hard with a chopping motion, to emphasize the threat. 'And there's one more thing the powers has shown me girl, and that's a grey horse. A grey horse is going to help to bring your troubles to an end.'

Tildy stared in puzzlement. 'A grey horse?' she questioned. 'What grey horse?'

The old woman shook her head. 'I can say no more, girl. For the powers has shown me no more at this time. Go now, for I'm tired to death.' She closed her eyes, letting her head sink forward upon her chest once more.

Tildy, still under the spell of superstitious dread, rose to her feet and silently tiptoed from the cottage. As she hurried away across the heathland the unseen dog began to howl, its mournful wailings borne towards Tildy on the wind long after the cottage had merged into the looming darkness of the hills.

Walking back to Redditch. Tildy was torn by inner conflict. She had no doubt now but that Esther Smith could provide her with the means to rid herself forever of Tom Crawford. But, the question was, could she ever bring herself to use those means?

'I would be a murderess!' She recoiled with horror from that word yet, rack her brains though she might, she could think of nothing else which would set her free and save her child.

Once back in Redditch, Tildy was irresistibly drawn towards Clarke's Yard. 'I must see Davy. I must be sure that he is well and being looked after properly.'

The Yard's fetid rottenness enveloped her as she entered its black shadows. To one side was the high blank wall of a warehouse, to the other side the row of mean hovels in which Peg Green's beer shop held the centre stage. Because of the weather, doors were shut and broken shuttering veiled the majority of the small windows.

Tildy reached the door of the beer shop and stood for some moments straining to hear what was happening inside. All she could distinguish was a meaningless rumble of voices. She pushed the door open and went in. The small lamplit room held only three men, dressed like pointers. They were huddled around the rusty firegrate, nursing flagons of beer, smoking clay pipes and spitting frequently into the smouldering fire. One of the men, gaunt-featured, but still handsome, smiled at Tildy and held out his pot.

'Does you want to take a sup of my ale, sweetheart?'

She ignored him, only drew her shawl

tighter about her head, while her eyes swept the room. The entrance to the rear room was doorless and she could see the dim outlines of the barrels in there, but no sign of her child.

Bonny Southall blinked his eyes and looked more closely at the girl, then recognized her. 'Fuck me! It's Tom Crawford's missus, arn't it?' he ejaculated, then shouted loudly, 'Tom, your missus is here. Get your breeches on and get down here.'

Tildy heard the thump of feet on the low ceiling boards above her head, moving towards the staircase in the rear room.

'Well, well, well, if it arn't my sweet wife come acalling.' Tom Crawford, dressed only in shirt and breeches, his calves and dirty feet naked, stood facing her.

'If you wants a bit, then you'd best get her upstairs a bit rapid, Tom,' Bonny Southall advised jokingly. 'Because Peg wun't be long away.'

His companions laughed and passed lewd comments, and Tom Crawford scowled and jerked his chin upwards. 'We'd best go upstairs. We can talk theer in private.'

'I've not come to talk,' Tildy told him. 'I've come for my child.'

The man's tongue ran across his lips as he stared speculatively at Tildy, his eyes lingering hungrily on the bodice of her dress. 'The kid's asleep upstairs,' he told her. 'Come on up if you wants to see him.'

Suspicious though she was of her husband, and fearful of what might happen should he trap her in a confined space, still Tildy's need to see and hold her child impelled her to follow the man up the short staircase to the single upper room which stretched across the width of the hovel. There was no protecting bannister around the stairhead and the stairwell was an open hole in the rough bare boarding. A lamp was hanging from the rafters by whose dim light Tildy could see clearly enough. On one side of the stairhead stood a double bed strewn with dirty, bad-smelling blankets, on the other side in one corner lay a heap of musty rags. This was Davy's bed, on which he slept, legs drawn up in a foetal position, his thumb in his mouth. He lay so still and his breathing sounded so heavy that Tildy realized instantly he had been dosed with Syrup of Poppies. The laudanum-based cordial which was given to small children to drug them into sleep, and which could kill if too much were given.

'Oh Dear God!' Tildy moaned in distress and went to go to her child, but Tom Crawford blocked her way.

'Now then, missus, what's it to be?' he asked, his face so close to hers that Tildy felt the moist warmth of his breath on her skin, and the reeking foulness of it filled her nostrils. 'Do you come back and be wife to me, and so get to look arter him, or does he take his chances wi' me alone?'

Tildy's brain was a confused jumble of thoughts and impulses. In her apron pocket she still carried the knife, which for a moment or two she considered the chances of using to frighten Crawford into letting her take Davy. Almost as if he had divined her thoughts, Tom Crawford's gaze dropped to the apron pocket; without any warning he brutally back-handed her across the face, and as she cried out and raised her hands to protect herself he rammed her bodily against the wall, his forearm crushing against her throat while his other hand snatched the knife from the pocket.

He brandished it before her eyes, and taunted savagely, 'Planning to use this agen me, like you did afore? But too slow this time, warn't you, bitch!' He brought the sharp point towards her face until it hovered barely a hairs-breadth from her eyeball. 'One flick o' my fingers now, and your fucking eye 'ud be running down your face, 'uddn't it,' he hissed.

Hardly able to breathe, her throat feeling

as if it were being crushed, her face aching from the blow, Tildy could feel terror building up in her. She closed her eyes and bit her lips to stop herself surrendering to that terror, to hold back the shrieks, sensing that if she did break and cry out she would tilt this man over some mental abyss to unleash beyond recall the ravening beast that was in him.

Waves of nauseous faintness broke over her, making her shudder involuntarily. The pressure of his forearm increased, threatening to block her windpipe completely, and she gagged and choked and scarlet-streaked blackness swam before her eyes. 'He'll kill me if I don't get away,' she thought desperately. 'I must get away.' She tried to summon strength, but all strength had left her as if her body were paralysed. 'Oh Davy I'm sorry!' she cried out in her mind. 'I'm so sorry to have failed you.'

Drowning in her agonies she was unaware of the knife clattering down the stairwell, and the greedy fingers tearing her bodice open and squeezing and mauling her breasts. Suddenly the terrible pressure on her throat slackened, and she was able to drag breath into her tortured lungs, then Tom Crawford's wet mouth clamped on hers, and she was dragged to the bed. Grunting like a wild boar Crawford struggled to hold her down and to unlace the front flap of his breeches. Tildy bucked and writhed and fought yet still she could not scream out. She tried to, opening her mouth wide and striving to force the screams from her throat, but nightmarishly all that emerged were strangled gasps and moans. Inevitably the man's vastly greater strength began to tell, and Tildy's struggles grew weaker as her muscles and sinews slowly exhausted their strength. He managed to wrench her gown up around her waist, though she writhed and twisted frantically as his knees bludgeoned her thighs apart and his hands sought and found their goal and guided his maleness to it. She felt him enter her, at which the screams at last tore free.

'Shurrup you bitch! Shurrup, damn you!' he snarled, trying to smother her mouth with his hands, but she heaved and twisted and screamed and screamed and screamed until it seemed the very dead in their graves must awaken to the tumult. Then shouts came from the street below, followed by iron-shod clogs clumping up the staircase. The man's plunging battering weight was dragged off her, as she heard the pointers laughing and telling him,

'Theer's a bloody mob down below, you fool. They'll ha' sent for the fucking constables by now. Everybody reckons there's murder being done.'

Under their lustful stares and mocking jeers of laughter, Tildy pulled her dress down over her naked belly and thighs, and tied her bodice across her breasts. She felt no embarrassment, only a terrible burning anger. Then, before anyone could move to stop her, she darted across the room to the corner and snatched her drugged child up in her arms.

Even in this unnatural depth of sleep he cried out in pain, and Tildy now saw the thick rope tied about his waist which secured him to a hook set in the wall. She put him down on his rag bed and started to untie the rope, but before she could do so Crawford was on her, grabbing her hair and heaving her bodily backwards. She wrenched free but stumbled and fell down the open stairwell, cannoning against the walls and thudding onto the earth floor so hard it knocked the breath from her body.

She tried to move, but hissed in agony as a sharp pain lanced through her lower ribs. Laboriously she got to her hands and knees and lifted her head. Tom Crawford was struggling to break free of the men restraining him and follow her down, but, laughing as if it were some huge joke, they held him back.

Forcing herself to disregard the pain in her ribs Tildy clambered to her feet.

She would have gone back upstairs, but Bonny Southall came to hold her back from doing so.

With a broad grin on his handsome face he told her, 'You'd best get away from here, girl, afore that bugger up there kills you. And if he don't do it, then it's certain sure Peg Green 'ull, when she hears about this commotion.'

'I want my child,' Tildy told him doggedly, and tried again to push past him.

Suddenly serious, he forced her back as he repeated, 'Get you gone from here, and leave the kid wheer he rightfully belongs, wi' his Dad. This is wheer he should be, not living wi' a navvies' whore. Now just fuck off, afore I tells the lads to let Tom loose so he can get at you.'

Sick with pain and weariness, Tildy recognized that she could not hope to take her child this night in the face of such hostility and numbers. Reluctantly she forced herself to accept temporary defeat, and retreated from the house, pushing past the curious onlookers clustered around the doorway, and holding her shawl close around her head to shadow her face and hide her tears.

Out of the Chapel Green she crossed to the chapel entrance porch and in its shadows gently explored her damaged ribs

259

with her fingers. She concluded thankfully that nothing was broken.

Her bodily contact with Tom Crawford had left her feeling soiled and unclean in more than a physical sense. 'I must wash him away,' she told herself. 'I must swill every trace of him from my body.'

She knew that in the fields to the east of the town there were springs and freshets. Disregarding her bodily weariness and pain she hurried to find one, stripped off her clothing and despite the coldness of the night immersed herself in the icy water. For long minutes, teeth chattering with cold, breath caught in gasps, she scrubbed and laved her body until she felt cleansed and purified once more. The cleansing had also served to calm her tortured nerves, soothing away the horror of the night's happening.

Afterwards, as she slowly made her way back towards the town, Tildy told herself, 'Very well, I may have lost a battle tonight, but I'm still here. I can still think and plan and prepare to fight again. This is a war now, and after what Tom Crawford did tonight I'm prepared to use any means that I have to, to win it. I really am prepared to use anything now...' 'Even the potion? Even murder?' The tiny voice whispered in her mind. Tildy nodded grimly. 'Even that, if everything else should fail. Even that.'

CHAPTER 22

Early next morning in the lean-to workshop Robert Stafford faced the women and children, and coughed to clear his throat. His cough triggered off a burst of coughs and throat-clearing from his audience, so that it was some time before silence was restored with the aid of Amanda Pinfield's virulent scoldings.

As Stafford's eyes moved across the faces ranged before him, his thoughts wandered fancifully. 'There are all shades of intellect registered in these faces. From the bright to the dull, the gentle to the brutal, the happy to the sad, mayhap even the near-genius to the absolute cretin...' With an effort he dismissed his roaming fancies and came to the business at hand. Now the time had come to broach the subject, the young man was assailed with doubts.

It was true what his uncle had said, the pointing had always been considered men's work, ever since the first dry-grinding process had been introduced into the industry. No woman or child had ever been allowed to do it. What he was about to propose was a revolutionary step, and now it had come to it, he was afraid of a complete rejection of his idea by these women before him. He coughed nervously again, then took a deep breath and plunged into the matter.

As he explained his needs, he saw their faces first mirror surprise, then rejection. He pressed on with the fast-increasing conviction that he was wasting his time. He came to a finish and waited, hoping for comment, or enquiry, or acceptance. Only silence came. He spoke directly to Aggie Southall.

'Well Aggie? With all the children you have, do you not wish to earn treble your present wages?'

She shook her head sullenly. 'The rot is already taking my kids' Dad, it arn't going to take their Mam from 'um as well, that's certain sure.'

'But have I not told you repeatedly that with the muzzles the steel dust will be extracted from the air?' he said wearily. 'I know that there will still be stone dust, but that is not half so harmful as the steel. You will stand an excellent chance of escaping any harm at all.'

'But the pointing is men's work, Master Stafford,' Janey White spoke up. 'It's never been known for a woman to do it.'

Stafford had been expecting this argument, and was ready to counter it. 'It was only considered men's work because of the steel dust. A woman's lungs, being weaker than a man's, cannot stand the shredding caused by the steel. But using the muzzles there will be no steel breathed in, only stone, and that is of a softer, rounder texture and cannot do the same damage to the tissues.'

He looked about him, experiencing a sense of defeat as he saw the sullen closed expressions that confronted him. Then, from the rear of the crowd, a voice queried, 'How much can be earned, Master Stafford?'

All heads swung to stare at Tildy Crawford.

A springing of hope caused Stafford to smile at her. 'Two and one third per five thousand is the rate I'm offering. When you achieve speed at the work you will be easily able to earn in excess of a sovereign the week.'

'How much in excess?' Tildy wanted to know.

He shrugged expansively. 'Perhaps five shillings or more.'

Tildy was as frightened of risking the rot as any woman present. But if she could earn so much money as that, she would be able to clothe and feed Davy properly. To pay for his schooling. To find a decent, peaceful place to live. Another, darker incentive which she tried not to acknowledge was the fact that earning this amount of money she could very quickly afford to obtain a potion from Esther Smith.

For some moments indecision racked her. The rot was a very real and terrible presence among the needle workers, and no matter how emphatically Robert Stafford claimed that his new muzzles removed most of the danger, still doubt remained. Then Tildy shrugged her shoulders and thought fatalistically, 'What real choice do I have? I must earn more money, and this offers me the chance to do so. If it is to be my destiny to become afflicted by the rot, then that is fate, and inescapable.' Aloud, she said quietly, 'I'll point your needles for you, Master Stafford.'

'You'll not regret doing so, Crawford,' he told her. 'Now here is one woman who is not afraid to earn herself a small fortune,' he said to the rest of the group. 'Can it be true that no one else among you will not join her?'

Although he detected a definite wavering in two or three of the faces, still no one voiced acceptance. He was a reasonable judge of character, so he decided to let matters rest for the time being. He was now fairly confident that once they had actually witnessed him pay Tildy Crawford her first big wage, greed would win over some of the others to the pointing.

'Very well then, it is your loss, not mine. Go back to your work, all of you, except for you, Crawford. You can come with me.'

He led Tildy into the pointing shop. The old man whose task it was to drive the horse gin was lying on some sacking, snoring loudly, until Robert Stafford's highly polished Hessian boot kicked him into wakefulness.

'Get the horse in the cradle, Sim, and start the gin turning.'

Yawning and knuckling his rheumed eyes the old man shuffled out. Before long the ponderous gin wheel began to turn as with a slapping of belting and clattering of shafts, cogs, and screechings of axles the pointing shop's machinery jolted into motion.

Robert Stafford had to shout to make himself clearly heard above the noise. 'I'll show you how it is done, Crawford, then you can carry on by yourself. Do not try to achieve speed today, just concentrate on grinding smoothly and accurately. I'll not be unduly concerned about the waste for a couple of days, at any rate.'

He demonstrated the work, then Tildy took his place on the saddle. As he tied the muzzle laces around the back of her head, she grimaced at the cumbersome discomfort the heavy metal and leather contraption caused her. She fanned the first batch of needles between her palms and bent to the work. A fountain of glowing sparks erupted making the pungent smell of burnt metal fill her senses.

The first day was a purgatory of cramped muscles, aching spine, buttocks, hips and arms. Her grit-filled eyes watered, skin was ripped from her hands as she inadvertently touched them against the whirling stone. Friction-heated white-hot sparks burnt her; but worst of all, perhaps, was the terrible dryness of dust and smoke, the sickening sulphurous taste, and the pains in her chest as the dust caused her to heave and gag and cough raspingly.

The second day was if anything worse, because there was no longer even the novelty of the work; it had become a dragging monotony.

By the third day she was achieving a smoothness of finish, and by the fourth an accuracy of point length. Her speed imperceptibly increased, and by the sixth day she was achieving a reasonable rate of pointing. But for every advance in skill she was paying an awful price.

When dusk fell on the sixth day and the whirling grindstone squealed slowly

266

to a halt, Tildy laid the final batch of pointed lengths into the box at her side. Weary beyond belief she sat slumped on the saddle. She pulled the muzzle from her nose and mouth, and buried her dust-caked face in her filthy, oily hands. Even with closed eyes she still saw the showering sparks. Her head span dizzily because the constant whirling of the wheel disoriented her sight, so that it took long minutes before she could focus with stability.

'Dear God, I'm not sure if I can continue to bear this vile work,' she whispered aloud, remembering the countless moments during the past days when she had wanted to hurl the needle lengths away from her, and run from the deafening clattering jerking machinery out into the clean fresh air. As she lifted her head she hoped fearfully that it was only the unnatural constriction of the chest muscles during the long hours bending over the grindstone that was causing pains in her chest.

'I couldn't be getting the rot this quickly,' she tried to reassure herself. 'It couldn't be possible. It takes years to cause that much damage to the lungs.'

Despite this rational conclusion the fear stayed constantly with her, reinforced by her vivid imagination which kept on picturing flesh torn asunder by steel and stone.

CHAPTER 23

'Onnne tup three! Onnne tup three! Onnne tup three! Onnnee tup three! Grace full ly! Grace full llyy! Grace full lyyy! Wonne tup three! Wonne tup three!' Augustus Bartleet whispered the cadence into the delicate pink ear of the deliciously rounded, blonde-haired Emily Cutler as they waltzed around the room before the admiring gaze of their audience. At the piano Amelia Boulton's short fat fingers hammered out the tune as she jealously strained her myopic eyes to watch the expressions on the couple's faces. But unfortunately for her own peace of mind, she could only distinguish shapeless blurs of flesh and hair.

Around her salon ranged on chairs were the dowagers of the town with their spouses and dependants, all sweating profusely in the stifling heat of the room with its flaming masses of wax candles adding to the warmth from the twinned fire-places. The fans in the white-enamelled, be-ringed hands of the women clicked open and shut, waving furiously in impotent attempts to stir the sluggish air into a breeze to cool their flushed, rouged faces, and powdered shoulders and necks.

Hetty Milward was seated demurely at her mother's side. Behind the women's chairs Henry Milward and Robert Stafford, uncomfortably hot in their thick broadcloth coats and high-stocked cravats, wore fixed expressions of boredom as they watched the proceedings.

It was Amelia Boulton's idea that periodically Augustus Bartleet's pupils should demonstrate their accomplishments at the 'dance' to their doting Mamas and Papas, and thus advertise their teacher's expertise in imparting graceful poise to them. It was a testament to Amelia Boulton's shrewd business brain, because no parent would ever dare publicly admit that their marriageable daughters were not constantly benefiting from these very expensive dancing classes.

As the demonstration waltz came to an end, Augustus Bartleet bowed with a flourish and his partner curtsied while the spectators applauded politely.

'And now, ladies and gentlemen, we shall have a pause for refreshment,' Amelia Boulton announced. Trying not to display any unladylike lack of decorum, she managed to insinuate her plump, befeathered presence in between Augustus Bartleet and the distractingly pretty Emily Cutler.

Bartleet, scented, rouged, enamelled, and extravagantly elegant in lavender and pink court dress complete with silk stockings and gold embroidered dancing-pumps, frowned in pique at being so rudely separated from the nubile young blonde, before he remembered his dependence on the Widow Boulton for the use of her salon, finances and musical talents. He smiled charmingly at the widow and with another sweeping bow offered her his arm.

'Let us also partake of a glass of wine, dearest Amelia.'

Blushing like a virgin girl the widow allowed herself to be promenaded into the adjoining room where tables laden with a sumptuous display of food and drinks had been prepared.

Robert Stafford bowed to Mrs Milward. 'May I fetch you a platter and a glass of something to refresh you, ma'am?'

She regarded him disbelievingly, then told him bluntly, 'Theer's no call for you to smarm around me, young Stafford. Wese already as good as gi' you our permission to wed our Hetty, so you've naught to gain by trying out your fancy airs and graces on me. If I wants a bite o' grub, and a glass o' drink, I'm perfectly well able to go and fetch it meself. Mr Milward wants to have a word wi' you anyway. So this is as good a time as any to have it, while me and our Hetty goes about our own private business.'

Robert Stafford was not disconcerted by his prospective mother-in-law's blunt manner. He genuinely liked the woman.

'As you wish, ma'am,' he acknowledged and turned to her husband. 'I am at your service, sir.'

'Ahr, right then. Let's go outside and get a breath of air, Robert, this place stinks like a dolly-mops' privy.' Henry Milward could on occasion be as crudely outspoken as his wife.

They made their way through the French windows at the end of the salon and out into the garden, where others were also taking advantage of a breath of fresh air. From a night sky clear and sharp with frost, the moon lit the surrounding countryside with a pale clarity. With a jerk of his head Henry Milward led the younger man out of earshot of the other people in the garden, and when satisfied they could not be overheard said, 'Youse got yourself a pointer-'ooman then, Robert. How is her shaping up?'

'She is doing uncommon well,' the young man told him with some enthusiasm. 'Considering she has only been a week at the work.'

'And you reckon her 'ull stick at it, does you?'

271

'I'm sure she will, and what is more, there will be other women who will join her at the work after tomorrow.'

'Why so?'

'Because, sir, I intend to pay her a full sovereign in front of all of them. When they compare that to the wages they will receive, I do not doubt but they will all be clamouring to become pointer-women themselves.'

The older man appeared to carefully consider that affirmation, and then said with a reflective air, 'It's causing a lot of talk in the district, Robert. Why, only yesterday Abel Morral himself come up from the Green Lane to visit me at the Fountain, and ask me what I thought about this bloody pointer-'ooman. It being common gossip that you might well become my son-in-law in due course, he thought I'd summat to do wi' what you was about.'

This information came as no surprise to Robert Stafford. Since his uncle's inn, the Fox and Goose, was the favoured meeting place of the needle masters, he already knew through his uncle of the stir that had been created in the district by this employment of a woman to do his pointing.

'Well, sir, what is the consensus of opinion among the needle masters concerning what I'm about?' Robert Stafford enquired, and the older man frowned thoughtfully.

'It's a bit mixed, Robert. A bit mixed. Some on 'um thinks youm a bloody young fool whose got too big for his breeches. But mostly they'm waiting to see what happens afore they comes to make any hard and fast ruling on it.'

'What do you yourself think, sir? Am I a fool? I shall not take offence whatever your answer, because I highly value and respect your opinion.'

Like his wife before him, Henry Milward regarded the young man with some degree of ambiguity. Men did not become needle masters by being easily gulled, or by being susceptible to gushing flattery, and if a fool followed in his needle master father's footsteps, he very soon found out that it took more than the accident of birth and position to fill those footsteps successfully. Henry Milward chuckled grimly. 'My oath! But youse got a smooth tongue, arn't you, boy. But I'm too old a bird to be caught by honey on a limed branch. I'll tell you straight and plain that it's my belief that you reckons youse backed a winner.'

Robert Stafford was not happy with this answer, and he pressed the other man. 'With all respect, sir, you still have not given me your personal opinion of my venture.'

The needle master grinned with a hint of brutal satisfaction. 'My own reckonings be that youm agoing to come a cropper, my bucko. A real bloody cropper.'

'But how can that be?' The young man protested vehemently. 'Women can do the work. Tildy Crawford is proving that fact. And once I have more women at the grindstones, then my production will match any of the smaller mills hereabouts, and my selling prices will undercut them by a third or more. How can I fail, when my prices will be so much lower than any of the other manufacturies? Tell me that? To speak plainly, sir, your attitude smacks of sour grapes more than anything else. Mayhap because I'm young and modern-thinking enough to have bettered the old men who dominate this trade at their own game.'

Henry Milward's plump features became hard-set, and his manner altered dramatically from pleasant to hectoring. 'I'll tell you how you'll fail, my bucko. You'll fail because when they so chooses the "old men" 'ull combine agen you, and drive you into failure. Does you really believe that youm the first young puppy who's ever tried to teach us old dogs some new tricks?

'How does you think that we built this district into being the centre of the needle trade? It warn't by being bloody soft-hearted, or soft-yedded, I'll tell you. The Welsh, the Sussex, the Cheshire needlemakers, all on 'um through the years has been forced to move here and join with us, or else shut shop. The Buckinghamshire needle men, down in Long Crendon theer, theym even now in the process of transferring their businesses to this district. Because they knows that if they don't come in wi' us, and meet our terms, then they'll be driven to the wall.'

He paused, his eyes raking the young man up and down contemptuously. 'And now there's you, coming to take our trade from us single-handed, because you reckons that youse got hold of a new invention that's agoing to revolutionize the whole industry.

'Does you think that youm the first that has thought o' making the pointing safe, boy? Because let me tell you very definite, that you arn't. Muzzles, magnets, hoods, they all bin tried afore, and a dozen other notions as well. But that's neither here nor theer, boy. Youse asked me to tell you how you could fail? Well, you could fail whenever us old men decides it's time for you to fail. But it wun't be from us that the reasons for your failure 'ull come, boy. It'll come from the very direction youm least expecting.

275

Just wait and see, my bucko. Just wait and see.'

The young man's jaw had dropped in astonishment. 'But why should you yourself wish me to fail, sir? Am I not your son-in-law to be? What could you possibly gain by my failure, which could only bring distress to Hetty? I own myself astonished and distressed that you, whom I respect, and count my friend, should wish failure upon me.'

'Did you not think that I would be astonished and distressed when I found out that you was trying to poach some of my best customers from me, boy?' the older man questioned mockingly, then laughed raucously and answered his own question. 'Of course I warn't. Because that's the way o' business. We'll any one on us, acting as men o' business, lie, cheat, steal and stab in the back to gain the orders we needs to ensure our own survival. But it's no use aweeping and awailing if you finds the same actions being took agen you. Youse got to learn your business, boy. Youm not swimming wi' tadpoles in a little puddle now. Youm in the big river, and there's pike and otters theer, boy, wi' sharp senses, and sharp teeth and even sharper hungers.' He paused, and his manner softened. 'Listen, Robert, it's not that I wishes you to fail, and I know that facts be sometimes hard to face, but the way I sees it, you'll have to learn to face even the unpleasantest of facts sooner or later in your life. It's better you should face 'um sooner, when youm still young and strong enough to start agen.'

'But you are talking as if my failure were already assured, sir?' A note of petulance had crept into the young man's voice, and the older man heard it with a wry amusement.

'It is, Robert, sadly, it is,' he stated quietly. 'But remember, you must learn all you can from the lessons you'll be getting. That way you might even gain from it in the long run.'

From inside the salon the tinkling notes of the piano started up again, and Henry Milward nodded towards the sound. 'Come, boy, the womenfolk 'ull be nagging at us if we arn't there to stand like bloody stuffed mawkins behind their chairs.' He took hold of the young man's arm affectionately. 'You must not take what I been saying as anything against you personal, Robert. I still wants to see you and our Hetty wed and settled. But I can't help thinking that you and her 'ud have better prospects if you was to come and work for me. I can always find a position for you in my mill.'

'I thank you for that offer, sir, but I

feel that I really must try and succeed by my own endeavours,' Robert Stafford told him, and inwardly added, 'Because I've no intention of coming to work for you, you damned old tyrant. I've seen how you treat those who are dependent on you for their bread.'

CHAPTER 24

It was the custom in the needle district to pay out the wages to the workpeople in inns and alehouses. Each master normally favoured a particular establishment to do this in, and inevitably an interested enquirer would find that the master had either a business agreement with the landlord, or was in fact the actual owner of the premises himself.

Another wide-spread practice was the 'truck' system. This was the paying of wages partly in coin of the realm and partly in metal tokens and scrip struck or printed by the employers themselves. These tokens and scrips were only redeemable at certain shops and beerhouses designated by the employers. The wares were of poor quality and the prices very high in these 'Tommy shops', and again an interested enquirer would inevitably find that the employer was also the owner of the 'Tommy shop', or had a financial agreement with its proprietor.

The workpeople bitterly resented the 'truck' system which had arisen during the long wars with the French because of the shortage of specie. But those wars had been over for more than seven years, and the shortage of specie rectified. Yet still 'truck' flourished more strongly than ever, and unscrupulous employers fleeced their own workpeople mercilessly. Grumble and protest though they might, the workpeople were powerless to alter the system. The Combination Acts ensured that they could not act in concert and demand their wages be paid in good coin of the realm, because if they did band together in this way against their employers, then they could face transportation, or even the penalty of death.

One advantage the workers at Pinfield's had possessed was that they had always been paid their wages in coin of the realm. Robert Stafford would have continued that practice, but his Uncle Tommy Fowkes was not the man to allow any chance of profit, however small, to slip through his fingers.

On the morning of the Saturday payday, Robert Stafford went to the Fox and

Goose to arrange about the money for the wages. His uncle immediately broached the subject of 'truck'.

'We shouldn't be paying out in good money. We should pay out in "truck" tokens, or scrip.'

'No employer in the district pays out solely in "truck", Uncle, not since the war ended anyway,' Robert Stafford pointed out amusedly, knowing from long experience his uncle's appetite for gold. 'Even the greediest of the masters are forced to pay half the wages in good coin. The justices ruled on that point.'

'Then that's what we'll do,' Tommy Fowkes asserted.

'But the expense of having tokens struck or scrip printed for the amounts we are having to pay out at present, is hardly worth it,' his nephew argued. He was no supporter of the 'truck' system, which he considered an unfair imposition. 'Besides, we've no Tommy shop to exchange them in, have we.'

'That's as maybe.' His uncle was dogged when in pursuit of profit. 'But wese got an alehouse we can use as a "Tommy" shop, arn't we. It's this 'un, Tommy Fowkes' alehouse.'

'But I employ only women and children.' Robert Stafford was half-amused, half-irritated by his uncle's incessant greed.

'They don't go to the beer shops to drink their money away.'

'Maybe they don't, but it's certain sure that their bloody menfolk 'ull be drinking the money for 'um. Youse bin brought up in this town, arn't you? You knows very well what happens to the money the kids earns. Their Dads takes it from 'um afore it's got warm in their pockets. It's always bin like that, as long as I can remember. The buggers puts their women and kids to the trade to earn a bit o' beer and bacca money for 'um, and you knows that as well as I does. So let's try and make certain that some o' the money we pays the sods comes back into our own pockets.'

'By the Christ, Uncle Tom, but you are a pike, sure enough.' The young man was experiencing a fast increasing distaste for his relative. Whatever faults Robert Stafford possessed, excessive greed was not among them. Nor did he wish to exploit his workpeople beyond those limits necessary to make his venture successful.

The hanging jowls before his eyes quivered as the fat man blew out his purple cheeks in explosive indignation. 'Don't you go calling me a bloody fish, my fine gentleman, or you and me 'ull be having a falling out. And anyways, it's no use you arguing the toss, because Ise already made arrangements... Here, cop hold of this.' He handed his nephew a small cloth bag which weighed heavily and clinked as Robert Stafford put it on the table. 'Them's tokens from Will Bartleet and Will Hemming. There's values for shillings, tanners and pennies in theer. Pay half and half.'

Robert Stafford grudgingly agreed, and his uncle remonstrated, 'Christ on the Cross, boy! Don't look as though you'd lost a pound and found a penny. Ise already made us a few bob with this arrangement, and that's what business is all about. You must always remember, if a man's got a shilling in his pocket, then that shilling needs to transfer itself to your pocket afore it can do you any good.

'Now, another thing. You'll pay out in the tap room here, and remember, keep the buggers waiting as long as you can. That way they'll be bound to get thirsty and sink a few pots while theym waiting. Has you got that?'

'Yes uncle, I have it,' Robert Stafford answered impatiently, and promised himself. 'Once I've succeeded, then I'll buy this damn Shylock out, and I'll run the business in my own way; and that won't be by stripping my workpeople of their wages at every turn.'

The news that the wages were to be paid

out in the Fox and Goose created a minor uproar of protest at Pinfield's, because previously they had always been paid out at the workshop itself. For some of the women and children it meant having to walk the two miles into Redditch, and then three or even four or more miles back to their homes in the hamlets beyond the Pinfield's house. The forewoman, Amanda Pinfield, shared the general disgruntlement, and now she sat by Tildy in the pointing shop watching the young girl finishing the final batch of needle-lengths for the day, and grumbled about the new arrangement.

'Bloody Stafford! He's just the same as all the other bloody masters, for all his soft way o' talking to us. It's bloody unfair, so it is. Some of the poor buggers here 'ull have to travel six or seven miles afore they gets home tonight. There 'ull be trouble for some o' the women as well, when their men gets home and finds no fire in the hearth or grub cooked and on the table.'

Tildy finished the batch, laid them aside, then pulled the swathing rags aside and removed the muzzle from her nose and mouth.

'Well, at least I'll not have that trouble, Mrs Pinfield. That's one advantage of being alone, I suppose.'

The forewoman stared quizzically at the young girl, thinking how beautiful she was, even with the black-grey dust caked upon her face and the dark rings of exhaustion shadowing her eyes. During the time Tildy had been working here, Amanda Pinfield had grown to like and respect the girl for her quiet, dignified comportment, and her lack of whining complaints about the harshness of her life.

'It's a real puzzle to me, Tildy, why a pretty wench like you chooses to do this sort of work?'

Tildy smiled wearily. 'What other work is there for the likes of us, Mrs Pinfield?'

'Well, you must have many chances o' settling wi' some decent man who'd care for you and your babby.'

Tildy's smile instantly disappeared at this reminder of her child, and Amanda Pinfield saw that she had unwittingly distressed the girl.

'I'm sorry, Tildy,' she said hastily. 'I was forgetting about where your nipper is at present.'

'It's no matter,' Tildy told her quietly. 'I'll get my child back someday. I'm determined on that.'

The other woman held her hands up with her fingers steepled as if in prayer. 'I'll wish Amen to that, my duck.' Then suddenly burst out, 'By Christ! But I wish I had your courage, Tildy, and that's the truth.'

'My courage?' Tildy repeated wonder-ingly.

'Yes, my duck, your courage. The way youm brave enough to stay apart from your husband, and do work like this to support yourself and your kid. Not asking favours from anybody, and what's more, keeping yourself straight and decent living. There arn't many women I knows of who'd have the courage to go it alone like you does.'

Tildy pondered this for some moments, and then slowly shook her head. 'It's not courage, Mrs Pinfield,' she murmured sadly. 'But sheer necessity.'

'But you could easy find a man to look arter you, girl. Look at that contractor, Israel Lee, he'd try and get you the moon if you asked him for it. He'd take care o' you like a shot, given half a bloody wink.'

A sudden fierce resentment sprang into flame in Tildy's mind. 'Why should we women have to so depend on men to look after us, Mrs Pinfield?' she demanded angrily. 'Why should that be the only solution we can ever seem to think of for whatever problems assail us? Find a man to look after us, to protect us? We put up with bad usage, abuse, beatings, poverty, from these very men who we look to for protection in this life.

'It's wrong, Mrs Pinfield! It's totally

wrong that we should ever have to endure such treatment from them. We work harder and longer than they do. We slave for a pittance of wages. We care for the kids, we nurse the sick, we clean and cook and wash and iron, and then we are supposed to lay down and let them use our bodies any way they've a mind to in the night. No! It's wrong! It's totally wrong! And I'll never put up with such treatment ever again.' She looked directly at her companion, her dark eyes glowing with conviction. 'I think it takes more courage to live as you do, Mrs Pinfield, with a man who treats you like a dog.'

The forewoman stared blankly, unable to comprehend these outlandish ideas, expressed by the young girl before her, and Tildy, realizing this, smiled wryly and said gently, 'If we are to collect our wages before the night is spent, then we'd best be making our way to Redditch, Mrs Pinfield.'

Although a mutual antagonism still existed between Tildy and Aggie Southall no further clash had taken place between them, and as if by unspoken agreement they ignored each other. Aggie Southall was also being virtually ignored by the other women because of her part in the snatching of Tildy's child. To do her justice, Aggie Southall herself was by now regretting her involvement in that affair. Her husband drank regularly at Peg Green's; she sometimes joined him there, so she had seen the way little Davy was being treated, and felt guilty whenever she heard him weeping, or saw him bawled at and hit by Tom Crawford and his paramour. Paradoxically the guilt made her even more resentful of Tildy, and so far it was only the knowledge that the rest of the women supported Tildy that kept Aggie Southall from provoking a fresh confrontation with her.

In the Fox and Goose tap room Aggie Southall sat alone and listened to the easy banter and laughter of the rest of the group. Inwardly she seethed with anger because they were deliberately excluding her from the conversation. Tommy Fowkes bustled in and out of the room, pressing the women to drink while they were waiting for Robert Stafford to come and pay them, and nothing loth, some of the women had taken up his offer of credit and by now were merrily half-tipsy. The drink wasn't making Aggie Southall merry however. Instead it only served to heighten her resentment at her exclusion, and it fuelled her anger against Tildy Crawford, who with a twisted logic she blamed for her own present unpopularity.

Tildy was sitting with Amanda Pinfield,

sharing a pot of beer. Tildy rarely drank and now was only taking the occasional sip so as not to appear deliberately unsociable. She was aware of Aggie Southall's rabid glares at her, but tried to ignore them. 'After all,' she told herself, 'I've more troubles than enough to be going on with. I must concentrate only on getting my Davy back, and not waste energy in fighting with Aggie Southall.'

Robert Stafford made his appearance to be greeted with ironic cheers and applause. He smiled good-naturedly and called for Amanda Pinfield to bring the tally book to him. This was the big ledger in which each worker's hours and production was entered. He wanted more of the women to join Tildy at the pointing, and had already decided to pay her first so that all of them would witness how much more she had earned than themselves. To drive the lesson home, he had so decided that she, and only she, would be paid fully in coin of the realm.

He laid two money bags on the table, one of them containing the tokens. Then from his valise he took an inkpot, a pen-holder with a brace of feathered quill pens, and a shaker of blotting-powder. He spent some time in arranging the items before taking his seat behind the table and opening the ledger. The women and children quietened, eager to learn how much their fellows were being paid. Every one of them jealously computed and totalled everyone else's earnings, with frequent, bitter altercations and complaints if they decided someone had unjustly gained a penny or two more than they deserved.

Stafford ran his fingers down the neat entries made by Amanda Pinfield until he came to Tildy's name. He rapidly computed sums in his head, then entered the amount to be paid her in the designated column. It had become so silent in the room that the scratchings of his quill pen across the thick paper could be heard distinctly.

'Matilda Crawford?' He beckoned her to the table. When she was standing before him, he smiled and announced, 'Twenty-two shillings wages.' With a flourish he opened one of the bags and counted out silver coins onto the table top. As the coins spread across the stained wood a sighing of envy rustled through the watchers.

'More than a guinea for a week's work! More than a guinea! And earned by a woman!'

Tildy's own hands trembled as she picked the money up and felt its weight growing in her palm. 'Twenty-two shillings, for just a week's work!' She felt momentarily richer than Croesus.

'You'll doubtless be earning more than that next week, Crawford. Now that you've gained familiarity and speed at the work.' Robert Stafford was secretly delighted with the effect created among the other women at seeing one of their number pick up such wages. 'Now Crawford, are you not pleased that you took up the pointing?' he asked, and overawed and excited as she was by receiving such a sum, Tildy forgot all the sufferings of the past days as she blurted happily,

'Oh yes indeed, Master Stafford. Indeed I am.'

'Good!' He smiled benevolently. 'Off you go now, Crawford, and spend some of that money. Take care for highwaymen on your way home,' he joked. 'Such a sum as that would tempt Dick Turpin from his grave.'

She left the tap room, the envious stares of the women following her out.

Robert Stafford was about to follow his original intention of asking if there were now any volunteers to become pointer women. Then he abruptly changed his mind. 'Let them receive their own wages, and then they'll come clamouring for me to let them at the pointing. I can pick and choose, then,' he said to himself.

'Janey White?' He signalled the woman to the table and reckoned up her total.

'Five shillings and seven pence.' As he had anticipated, the comparison struck home immediately, and struck even harder when Janey White saw the tokens among the coins.

'What's this then, master?' she questioned angrily.

'That's your wages, White,' he told her.

'But we don't get paid in bloody truck money,' she remonstrated.

'You do now, and from this date on you'll be getting half your wages in truck,' he calmly informed the room, hiding his own distaste for that fact behind a façade of indifference. He was deliberately modelling his manner towards the workers on the examples of behaviour he had witnessed among the old needle masters.

A storm of loud protest broke out, but he quelled it with a single shouted sentence. 'If you don't like it, then don't come back to work on Monday.'

A hard-bought knowledge of how difficult it could be to find other jobs closed mouths and leashed back tempers.

Sullenly Janey White picked up her wages and began to turn away, then swung back to face him. 'I'll do pointing next week, master.'

Stafford toyed with the quill pen in his fingers, inwardly savouring his triumph, then looked up at her. 'I don't know about that, White. I've had a lot of people come begging me for pointing work these last few days. I'm going to have to think carefully about who I'll accept for the work. Ask me again on Monday morning. Naturally I'd like to give the people who already work for me the first chance at it if possible. Be off with you now, there are others eager to be paid here.'

By the time the wages had been given out, Robert Stafford had more volunteers than he needed for his pointing shop.

Tildy did not go to the lodging house. Instead she went on past the Big Pool, through Bredon towards Mappleborough Green. In the clean frosty night sky the stars glimmered blue-white beyond the crescent moon. Once again the howling of the unseen dog greeted her as she approached the mud-walled cottage, and once again Esther Smith stepped out of the door while Tildy was still a full two-score yards distant. This time, however, the old woman made no challenge; she merely waved Tildy on silently and the girl shivered nervously as she crossed the threshold of the cottage. The old man was not at the fireside tonight, Esther Smith was alone. She wasted no time in preamble, but asked straight away, 'Has you brought the money?'

Tildy, fighting to hide her nervousness, was equally direct. 'I can't get hold of such a sum all at once. But what I can do is to pay you fifteen shillings each week until you've got the full amount.'

The old crone sucked her blackened fangs of teeth ruminatively, and then told Tildy, 'Listen to me, girl. I'm willing to hold to such an agreement, for to my mind youm an honest cratur. But there are things I must obtain, which will mean I'll needs to have all the money afore I can procure you what you seek. And for your purpose I reckons the time you'll take to pay me, 'ull prove too long.'

A chill of dread struck Tildy. 'How so? How will it prove too long?'

The old crone lifted her hands, and in the wavering firelight they seemed to be talons seeking to hook a helpless prey. 'Ise dreamed dreams these last nights, girl,' she whispered hoarsely. 'And the powers come to me in them dreams, and showed me many things. Hark to me now, girl, for what I'm agoing to tell you is them things which they showed, that I reckons concerns you.' She paused for some time, her mouth working soundlessly, her bright dark eyes intent on Tildy's face. 'They showed me a coffin, girl. A coffin that was small and fit for a child.'

'Oh my God!' Tildy moaned aloud as a sickening, fear-induced faintness assailed her, causing her head to spin and her knees to buckle for an instant.

The bright dark eyes never wavered in their scrutiny of her expression. 'Yes, girl. They showed me a coffin. But the coffin was still empty.'

Snatching desperately for reassurance, Tildy questioned eagerly, 'Does that mean that it's not certain then? That the child's death is not assured?'

Esther Smith grinned and nodded as if congratulating an apt pupil. 'Indeed that's just so, young 'ooman. That's just what it means. The child's death is a possibility, but the powers arn't yet decided on what's to be done.'

'But how will they decide? Cannot you tell me that? Is there nothing I can do to influence them?' Questions volleyed from Tildy, and the old crone's taloned claws waved in admonishment.

'Don't you dare to voice such things, girl. That's what makes the powers angry, when we tries to influence 'um. We mortals must never never pester the powers. It's only that Ise got the gift o' the second sight, that I gets to know what I does. And then they only tells me what theyse a mind to.'

Outside the dog started to howl again, and the doleful unearthly lament caused shivers to run down Tildy's spine despite the warmth of the room.

'Hark to that,' Esther Smith whispered. 'There's summat evil acoming this way, that's what my cratur out theer is telling me.'

Tildy's eyes widened with superstitious fear. Despite her courage and intelligence, she was still a child of her time, and like the vast majority of her peers she believed implicitly in the forces of witchcraft, and the existence of witches' familiars, those earthbound spirits which could assume animal forms.

Now her overstrained nerves distorted her powers of logical reasoning still more, so that she fully accepted that the unseen howling dog was indeed Esther Smith's familiar. In spite of Tildy's desperate desire for Esther Smith's aid, her fears now burgeoned unbearably, and all she wanted was to run from this place and find a haven among the rough noisy company of Mother Readman's lodging house.

As if sensing what was in Tildy's mind, the old woman urged her. 'You'd best go quick from here, girl. You can leave your money on the table. I'll do what I can to conjure the powers to help you. But mind what I say, you must bring the full amount just as quick as you can. Because time is running short. It's running short, girl. It's running terrible short.'

Tildy hastened to obey her, her agitation so great that her hands were shaking violently, causing her to fumble and drop the money as she tried to count it out on the table. The howls of the animal redoubled in intensity, and Esther Smith shouted hoarsely, 'Be quick, girl, be quick, for there's summat coming this way that'll do you no good to meet with. I needs to be alone to stop it causing harm. Go quick now, girl, and bring the rest of the money as soon as you can. Remember, the coffin wun't stay empty for much longer.'

CHAPTER 25

The first day of December brought snow to Redditch, massively drifting swirls of it to blanket the earth. The day also brought Abel Morral, of Green Lane, Studley village, to the Fountain Mill on his old spavined horse. Abel Morral, in his mid-forties, still wore his hair queued and pigtailed in the fashion of the previous century, and with his red bovine face, and bulky smock-clad body, topped with a broad-brimmed hat and tailed with leather gaiters and hob-nailed boots he looked like a yeoman farmer, rather than what he was. A one-time pointer who had used his wages to set up in business for himself before the rot could grip him, and had become one of the foremost needle masters in the district.

He faced Henry Milward in the latter's office with its glass-fronted cases of needle samples, mounted on the wall and said bluntly, 'I bin trying to get hold o' that bloody son-in-law o' yourn this morning, Henry, but I arn't seen hide nor hair of the bugger. Wheer's he got to?'

'If you means Robert Stafford, Abel, he arn't yet my son-in-law, and at this moment in time he arn't welcome to be, neither. And as for his whereabouts, then your guess is as good as mine.'

Abel Morral studied the other man's face, then stated, 'Youse had you post from the North Country, I reckon, Henry.'

'So I have, Abel. It come yesterday afternoon, and from your being here now, I'm led to the conclusion that youse had your post from theer as well, and that it contains much the same tidings as mine did.'

'Cancellations?' Abel Morral raised his busy eyebrows interrogatively.

'Just so.' Milward nodded. 'Three orders lost to me.'

'And two 'o mine, one on them a real

297

good 'un too,' Abel Morral added, then demanded, 'Well? What's to be done, Henry? The young bugger is poaching our customers left, right and centre. I don't mind a bit o' fair competition, but he's cutting his prices so close that if I was to sell at the same price I'd be making my bleeding needles at a loss. You can't tell me that the young bleeder is making any profits at the prices he's quoting.'

Milward stroked his smooth double chins reflectively. 'I should think that he's barely covering his wage and material bill, and his running costs at present Abel, if that even, but to my mind...'

He broke off speaking as his wife came bustling into the small room. She was wearing her working dress of old black gown, white apron and floppy mobcap, with heavy clogs on her large feet. Millicent Milward still used her skills as a soft worker in her husband's mill several days of the week, and her dirty, oily hands now bore testament to where she had just come from.

'I saw your old nag from the shop window, Abel,' she greeted the Studley man, 'and I don't doubt but that youse come to moan at us because young Stafford is poaching your customers. Am I right?'

'Youm part right, Milly.' The two were old acquaintances. 'Ise come about Stafford

298

poaching my customers right enough, but I arn't come to moan at you and your man about it. No, my wench, what Ise come for is to see if we can get together and do summat about it. Because if it keeps on the way it's going at present, there might well dawn a day when the young bastard 'ull end by driving us both to the wall.'

Millicent Milward smiled grimly. 'He's proved he arn't so green as cabbage-looking, Abel. Why, I can remember how last month you was laughing at his magnetic muzzles, and you near on pissed your breeches when I told you he'd got women pointing his needles.'

'All right, Milly, all right, theer's no need to rub bloody salt in it, is theer. Arter all, you and me has always bin good friends, arn't us.' He winked slyly, and the fat woman, remembering certain moonlit nights when she was more slender and tender than today, chuckled richly for a moment, then abruptly became stern and businesslike again.

'Right then, has you got any ideas about how to deal wi' young Stafford, Abel?'

'Oh ahr, that I has,' he offered with a ferocious facetiousness. 'We could string the bugger up on the Chapel Green, and I'll pull on one leg and you pull on the other to send him on his way to Paradise.' He sobered, and went on,

'I suppose we could always try and get the rest o' the masters wi' us, and band together to undercut his prices. Use our combined resources to stand the losses we'd have to take until we'd drove him out o' business.'

'That's no good,' the woman rejoined curtly. 'It 'ud play havoc wi' the trade, and can you see the rest o' the Masters helping us? They'll only be concerned about Rob Stafford when he takes their customers from 'um, and if just we does such a thing alone then it's a recipe for our ruination. Neither on us could afford to take such losses and still stay in business.'

She had automatically assumed the dominant position over her husband, as she always did in times of crisis, and for his part, Henry Milward was content to defer to his formidable mate.

'Well, how about if we makes him an offer for the magnetic muzzle?' Morral tried again. 'Once we had it ourselves, then we could afford to cut our own prices.'

'Youm talking sarft, Abel,' Millicent Milward scathingly dismissed the suggestion. 'If we made an offer like that, then he'd know he'd got us over a barrel and he'd demand a king's ransom from us for the muzzle. You'll needs think on.'

Abel Morral's bovine features seemed

to undergo a mysterious transformation, and for a brief instant the tough, reckless, ferocious-brawling pointer usurped the place of the respectable needle master. 'The young bugger could well meet with an accident. The roads be terrible treacherous underfoot what wi' the snow and ice. He 'uddn't be the fust 'un to fall wi' his horse and break his skull, 'ud he?' He paused and stared speculatively at the couple. 'But then, I expect that 'ud prove a terrible grief to you two 'uddn't it, him being your intended son-in-law?'

'It arn't us who's wanting to share the young sod's bed, Abel. It's our Hetty,' Millicent Milward told him bluntly. 'I'd not be grieved overmuch if such an accident came about. But then, I 'uddn't rightly want to see our Hetty caused such grief, so I hope the Good Lord, 'ull look over and protect the young bugger from that sort of harm... For the present, at least.'

'There's one way we could put a spoke in his wheel,' Henry Milward ventured diffidently.

'Oh yes, Milward, and what's that way? It'll be summat good, I'm sure, coming from you who's always so bold and sure in the face o' trouble.' The fat woman was aggressively sarcastic, but Henry Milward for once did not retreat before her attack.

'Just keep quiet and hear me out, both

on you,' he rejoined heatedly. 'And don't interrupt me until I've finished.'

At first his listeners wore expressions of open derision on their faces. But as he continued to speak the derision changed slowly until it became an eager concurrence with what he proposed.

'That's bloody good, that is, Henry,' Abel Morral affirmed. 'I reckon that might well do the business.'

'By the Christ, Milward, I never knew you could be so devious!' his wife exclaimed jocularly. 'Like Abel says, it's bloody good, and I reckon it'll serve for us. It'll serve very well.'

CHAPTER 26

Israel Lee was sitting at Mother Readman's fireside, deep in conversation with the old woman. The subject of that conversation was Tildy Crawford; the contractor's mood became increasingly sombre as the talk went on. At length he took his leave and went back to the stable yard of the Red Lion where he had left his borrowed pony and trap.

Snow was falling as he drove out of the town along the Salters Way. It was nearly dark when he reached Pinfield's house and muffled though he was in a thick greatcoat he shivered with the cold as he waited for Tildy to appear, the snow mantling the canvas-shrouded b k of the horse, and the barrelled tarpau roof of the trap.

The lean-to door opened to let the crowd of women and children stream out, some of the smaller children beginning to wail as they felt the cold wetness of the snow enveloping their bare feet and legs. The older children by contrast whooped with glee and immediately set to throwing snowballs at each other. The women didn't whoop with glee, they merely exchanged glum comments and curses, dreading the freezing damp such weather created in their ramshackle homes.

Israel Lee searched for Tildy among the be-shawled heads, and when he saw her walking apart from the others, her head bent, her slender figure drooping with a tired listlessness, his heart filled with a loving pity. He stepped down from the trap and went to meet her. When she saw him she smiled, then the smile disappeared to be replaced with an expression of wariness.

'What brings you here, Master Lee?'

'My name is Israel, or have you forgotten?' He grinned at her. 'And I've come to give you a ride home in my trap.'

303

As he avidly studied her features his grin faltered. Beneath the caked dust of the grinding, her face looked drawn and thinner than before, and her eyes held a feverish, strained quality which disturbed him. 'Come on, Tildy, let's get under cover,' he urged gently, and Tildy, weary to her very bones, was thankful to climb beneath the barrelled roof and slump down onto the padded leather seat.

For a while they were silent as the pony plodded on, its legs sinking fetlock-deep into the snow, which by now was falling so heavily that it had already filled and overlayed the tracks left by the trap's wheels on its approach to Pinfield's.

Israel Lee grunted in exasperation as the vehicle veered to one side and the wheel hit the raised verge of the track causing a jolt and judder to shake them. 'Jesus Christ! We could easy lose the track and end up in the bloody ditch if it gets any worse nor this.'

'Mayhap it's best if I walk back to Redditch,' Tildy suggested. 'Because if this snow keeps falling you might find it hard to get back to Tardebigge.'

'No matter,' he smiled. 'If it gets too bad I can always put up at one of the inns. If worse comes to worst, I'll have to share your room. I'll sleep on the floor, naturally.'

Tildy showed no appreciation of his attempt to lighten her mood. 'I don't want you to have to go to the expense of an inn on my behalf, and there's no place in my room for you to sleep.'

In sudden exasperation he turned to stare at her. 'By Christ, Tildy! I was only joking about staying in your room, so don't look so bloody sour about it. Why are you talking to me as if I was a bloody stranger to you. I arn't seen you for weeks, and youm acting as if you wished you hadn't seen me now.'

In all truth Tildy's sole desire at this time was to regain her child. All her waking thoughts were filled with that sole object in view, and she resented any necessity to make conversation or give attention to anyone. But at the same time she had no desire to hurt those who tried to show her friendship, so now, contrite, she tried to explain herself to the man beside her. 'It isn't that I'm not pleased to see you, Israel, but all that now concerns me is my child. I mean no offence to you, but I've no wish to talk of anything else except getting my Davy back, and I've no real interest in anyone else. I won't have, until I've got him back with me again.'

'But haven't I told you time and time again, that I'm ready to get him back for you,' the contractor broke in impatiently.

305

'I've told you afore that I'll take my lads to that beer shop and we'll have the kid out on it, come hell or high water.'

Tildy's own exasperation mounted. 'And haven't I told you that I don't want you to do that?' She shook her head helplessly, searching for words to explain emotions and motivations within her that she could barely comprehend. 'It isn't that I'm ungrateful for your offers of help, Israel. Indeed, I am grateful to you for them, truly I am. But I just feel that I must get Davy back through my own efforts. If others get him back for me, then somehow he will no longer be fully mine. I feel that this is my battle, and mine only, and that I must fight it by myself. And if I should be beaten to the ground time and time again while fighting it, then time and time again I must rise up and go on fighting until I achieve the victory. But I must achieve that victory by myself, else it will mean nothing in the greater scheme of things. If others win it for me, then it will be their victory, and not mine, and I shall not really have regained my son.'

'Youm talking like a bloody fool, girl,' he told her roughly. 'What youm saying makes no sense. Besides, how can you fight the odds ranged agen you? There's your husband, his woman, and his mates, and he's got the law on his side as well.

You've got no chance against all that. No chance at all.'

'Oh yes I have! I've got a chance all right, and don't you try telling me different.' Her eyes were hot and wild, and she nodded her head jerkily. 'I've got things afoot that'll win the day for me, and that's certain sure. It might take a bit more time, but it will come and I'll get my Davy back, and get him back through my own efforts, you'll see. You'll all see.'

'Look, Tildy, stop babbling like a bloody lunatic,' he shouted, 'and let me help you.'

'You just let me be, master. Keep away from me and let me go my own way.' She trembled with the force of her feelings. Before he realized what was happening she had leapt from the trap and struck out towards the woodland that lay in the direction of the town.

'Tildy? Tildy, come back here,' he shouted after her, and jumped from the trap himself to go in pursuit, but she halted and turned.

'Keep away from me, Mr Lee.' Her voice was very firm, and her thin face as unyielding as granite. 'I don't want your help. Mayhap some day we can meet again and be friends, but all I want from you now is your good wishes, and your distance.' With that she went running to

307

be swallowed up by the swirling flurries of falling snow. Israel Lee stood still and let her go, miserably aware that in her present mood to give chase would only compress her obduracy into greater hardness.

By the time Tildy reached the Silver Square her clothing was saturated. Although reluctant to do so, she was forced to go into the lodging house kitchen to dry herself at the fire there. It was the only source of heating that Mother Readman permitted on her premises. Too many of her doors and floorboards had ended as ashes in the fireplaces of the other rooms when she had allowed her guests to have fires in them.

The old woman was enthroned in her massive armchair, her ragged courtiers ranged about her by the fireside, when Tildy entered.

'Shove over, you lot, make some room for the girl,' Mother Readman ordered, and told Tildy, 'Bugger me, my duck, but you looks bloody nigh on perished. Come here next to me and warm yourself right now.'

Gratefully Tildy took her seat on the stool which had been vacated for her next to the old woman, and stretched out her hands, blue and pinched with the cold, towards the leaping flames.

'Here, my duck, get this down, it'll

stick to your ribs and warm you.' Mother Readman ladled stew from the great iron cauldron hanging on chains above the fire, and handed the steaming bowl to the girl.

Tildy was voraciously hungry. She murmured her thanks, then quickly filled her mouth with the greasy gristly mess, uncaring that it tasted slightly rancid. She was conscious only of the overwhelming need to still the painful achings of her empty stomach. When the bowl was empty Tildy sat with it upon her lap and gazed blankly into the fire, her body held in motionless thrall by sheer muscular exhaustion.

From time to time Mother Readman glanced at the young woman at her side and on a couple of occasions was about to speak to her, but each time had second thoughts. In the event it was Tildy who broke their mutual silence to tell the older woman, 'Israel Lee was waiting for me when I left my work tonight.'

'I guessed he would be. He was here earlier, talking to me.'

A spasm of annoyance twisted Tildy's full lips, and the old woman smiled knowingly.

'I take it you give him his pass for the route, my duck.'

Tildy nodded, and a hint of sadness

came into her eyes. 'There was naught else I could do.' She glanced about her to see if any of the others at the fireside were trying to listen to their low-toned conversation, but all were lost in their own reveries, or engrossed in their own gossiping, and satisfied she was being ignored by them, Tildy explained, 'I'm not going to lead him on, Mother Readman. He's too good a man to do that to. If things had been different for me, then perhaps he and I might have become close. Who can tell? But with troubles on me like they are now, I've no wish to have tender dealings with any man.'

'That's more or less what I tried to tell him, my duck.' Mother Readman's small slit eyes were gentle as she looked at this girl for whom she had a deep and genuine fondness. 'But being pig-yedded, like all men be when they thinks themselves to be in love wi' a maid, he 'uddn't accept what I told him, but must needs hear it direct from you.

'Still, let's talk about other matters right now. Like how much money has you give old Esther Smith, for example?'

Tildy jerked her head round to stare in shock at her companion. She had truly believed that no one knew of her visits to the witch woman.

'Ise told you afore, Tildy, there's naught

310

stays secret in this town for long, and I'm usually one of the first to hear about any goings-on. In this case I reckon there's only me who knows. Me, and whoever it was that told me, that is. Now, out wi' it, how much?'

Realizing the futility of denial, Tildy told her. 'Nigh on two sovereigns so far.'

Mother Readman nodded sagaciously, then dropped her voice to a whisper. 'And what is it youm buying from her Tildy? And give me a true answer.'

For some moments Tildy fought an inner battle with herself, but the sheer necessity of having some one, some friend, in whom she could confide fully, finally drove her to admit, 'It's a potion. To rid myself and my Davy of that evil devil who so persecutes us.'

Again the old woman's head nodded sagaciously, and for a while her lips moved soundlessly as she ruminated over the information. Then she grimaced, and told Tildy, 'Youm taking a terrible risk, girl, by considering such a method of ridding yourself of a husband. God only knows, the bugger well deserves it, and he 'uddn't be the fust in this town to be got rid of so by the poor wenches theyse served bad. I for one 'ud think none the worse of you for using such a way. But has you really thought it out proper, Tildy? Has you thought about how youm going to slip it to the bastard, for example?'

Tildy, to her own surprise, suddenly realized that she had not ever really planned how she could make use of the potion. To her it had only been, until now, the all-powerful talisman which would enable her to turn the tables on Tom Crawford, and regain her child. Now, she was forced to shake her head.

'No, I've not thought it out, Mother Readman. Truth to tell, all I've been thinking of up to now was how to get hold of the potion, and how I could pay for it.'

'How much is she wanting?'

'Five sovereigns.'

'Hmmm!' The older woman again fell silent and ruminated over what she had heard.

'Mother Readman?' Tildy touched the fat grimy hands. 'Mother Readman, do you think me evil and mad to think of doing such a thing against Tom Crawford?'

The old woman recognized the inner turmoil that was tearing at the girl, and sighed heavily. 'Youm only acting as you've bin drove to act, Tildy. Youm not evil, nor never could be, but I has to say that I thinks youm mad to be planning to use one of Esther's Smith's potions. Listen girl, Ise known old Esther since I was only a kid. Her was a grown 'ooman then, so God only knows how many years she's acarrying now. Her's always had the gift of the second sight, and her's always bore the name of a black witch, in league wi' the bloody Devil.

'Different people has had her fetched before the magistrates a dozen times and more in the past, accusing her of all manner o' things. From abortion, to making 'um barren, to putting plague on 'um, rotting their crops and their cattle, setting fire to ricks and barns, even sodding murder by witchcraft. But always, she's walked away free, and always, harm has come later to them who tried to harm her. So I arn't going to try and tell you she's gulling you now, girl. I reckon old Esther is in league wi' summat or other than arn't o' this world. If the evil old bitch says her can give you a potion to destroy Tom Crawford, then I for one believes she can do just that. But for your own soul's sake, Tildy, I reckon you ought not to take anything from her.'

'But if I don't have her help, then my Davy will soon die,' Tildy moaned in distress.

'How so? How is he going to die?' the older woman demanded to know.

'I don't know exactly, but Esther Smith has told me that she sees a coffin, a child's coffin, waiting to be filled, and if I don't manage to pay her the full five sovereigns and get hold of the potion very soon, then it'll be too late for me to get Davy back, because by then he'll be dead and filling that coffin.'

The other woman's tallowy, moonlike features darkened ominously. 'You hark to me, my duck. If your babby is fated to die, then it'll be because God wants to take him, and it'll be naught to do with whether youse got Old Esther's bloody potion, or not. Of course her can tell you that she can see a babby's coffin waiting to be filled. I could do that right now, and take you to half a dozen houses hereabouts wheer the poor little craturs be sickening nigh to death. That's common knowledge, arn't it, what wi' four out of five that am birthed in these bloody slums being took off afore they reaches four years of age. She's just aplaying on your fears, my duck, and now youse told me that, I'm of a mind to goo and sort the evil old bitch out good and proper.'

Superstitious fears thrilled through Tildy. 'Don't do that, Mother Readman. God only knows what she might do against you, or what harm might befall you.'

The woman's hands slapped down on her massive thighs and she laughed grimly, her ponderous body shaking until the old chair creaked and groaned beneath her shifting weight. Then her laughter stilled, and she became serious and intent. 'Don't you fret on my account, my duck. I've yet to see the witch-woman or cunning-man who could harm me, or scare me even. I knows a trick or two meself, you needn't moither.'

'But if Esther Smith doesn't help me, then who will?' Tildy asked desperately. 'You yourself said that you might have good news for me, but you've said nothing more about it since.'

'Because there arn't bin anything I could say yet, my duck.' Mother Readman patted the girl's slender shoulder. 'I went to see my cousin about you, and she's having words wi' people she knows, including a man who's an attorney at law. His name is Richard Hyde Guardner, but at present he's away in London. That'll cost you money though, Tildy. I was pleased when you got that chance to earn more at Pinfield's, even though the work's a bloody killer. But I thought you could do it just for a few weeks, and you'd be putting the extra money aside, and you could use that to pay Guardner, when he gets back here.

'But now you tells me, that youm giving all the extra to Esther Smith, so wheer's the money to pay Dickie Guardner agoing to come from, girl? I got a few shillings saved, which you can have and welcome, but that wun't be sufficient, and he'll be back any day now.'

It took Tildy a little while to digest the implications of this fresh information. 'But who is your cousin, that she should have access to an attorney?' she questioned. At her level of society to have dealings with an attorney or any legal practitioner other than as a defendant in a Criminal Court was practically unheard of. It was a profession reserved for the use of the gentry and the rich.

'My cousin is Mrs Milward, wife to Henry Milward, the needle master.' Mother Readman could not hide her pride. 'Her's a good sort, and unlike many I could name who come from nothing, our Milly has never forgot her was born in the Silver Street, and her's real John Bull about it, as well. She arn't shamed of her birth, and them that don't like it, can lump it, is her motto.'

'Does she really think that I can go to the law to get Davy back then?' Tildy asked wonderingly, because in all her experience the law had only ever proven an enemy to her, never a friend, or protector.

'She don't really know what to think, Tildy.' Mother Readman was brutally honest. 'But she says that if anybody can help you wi' the law, then it'll be "Slippy Dicky". I remember us calling Guardner that when he was younger, and the bugger's proved himself slippy all right since them days, I'll tell you. And what's more, arter hearing my account of you, our Milly has said that her's prepared to stand as character reference for you if necessary. That was good of her, warn't it.'

'Truly good,' Tildy murmured, experiencing a sense of gratitude that a woman she had never personally met was ready to help her in such a way.

'It's like I said afore, Tildy. In this world you needs the gentry on your side. If I was to stand reference for you, the bloody magistrates 'ud piss their breeks, but if a needle master's wife stands reference, then that's a different story. The magistrates looks at the clothes and the horse and carriage you see, girl, never at the heart. Still, that's the way o' the world, arn't it.'

'It is.' Tildy nodded in heartfelt agreement. 'But I would dearly like to thank Mrs Milward for her kindness. It's rare to find a gentry-woman prepared to help our sort in this way.'

The lodging house keeper chuckled hoarsely. 'Don't you ever let our Milly hear you calling her a gentry-'ooman, girl. Her's got no kind words for that lot when in private, I'll tell you.'

'But what can I do about Esther Smith, if I go to the attorney and have to pay him whatever money I earn?' Tildy asked with concern. 'After all, I've made the bargain with her to pay her in full as quickly as I can. It's fearful to think what she might do against me if I should break my word to her. You admit yourself that she has strange powers.'

'Don't you moither about that, my duck,' Mother Readman affirmed solemnly. 'I don't agree with the way the old bitch has gone about getting your money from you. She ought not to have scared you by threatening your babby's death like that.'

'But perhaps she genuinely did see it.' Tildy was reluctant to condemn the witch-woman without full proof that she had indeed been acting in bad faith. 'And there's another thing.' Doubts were flooding through her mind now. 'Suppose this attorney hears me out, and then tells me he can do nothing to help me? Then, where else can I turn? At least Esther Smith will provide me with a weapon, even if I don't know yet how I will be able to use it.'

'That's summat to consider, right enough,' Mother Readman conceded. 'To be straight wi' you, Tildy, I hadn't thought about that meself.' She suddenly became aware of how drawn and deathly pale Tildy's face was, and how large and black the rings beneath her eyes. 'Jesus Christ, girl! But you looks all knackered out. There's naught to be gained tonight by worritin' your yed about the matter. Arter a good night's sleep things always seems clearer, don't they. We'll both on us sleep on it, and tomorrow we'll put our yeds together and decide what's best to be done. You get off now, and no argument!'

Reminded of her utter weariness Tildy became aware of just how worn-out she felt, and she recognized the good sense of the other woman's advice.

'I'll bid you a Good Night, then Mother Readman. And thank you for your kindness,' she could not help but add, before climbing slowly up the stairs to her tiny room.

But when in bed, desperately tired though she was, true rest evaded her. The confusion as to the direction she should take engendered by the conversation with Mother Readman reduced her thoughts to a troubled, jangling maelstrom, which invaded her sleep as nightmares and brought her continually back to wakefulness throughout the long dark hours of the night.

CHAPTER 27

No one appeared to know from where the rumour originated. But, like all rumours, it spread rapidly, and was as rapidly given full credence by many of those who heard it. As was usual in these cases the person likely to be most affected by the rumour was among the last to hear it.

Robert Stafford was well content with life. It seemed that all his hopes for his business were fast coming to fruition. Six grindstones were now worked by women in his pointing shop, and his last brief trip to the North Country had produced very favourable results concerning orders.

Hitherto he had been forced to sub-contract out certain of the finishing processes of the work, such as the hardening, straightening, scouring and polishing of the needles. But now Robert Stafford was seriously considering expanding his operations and setting up his own workshops for these processes. Of course his meteoric success had caused adverse comment and a certain amount of open hostility directed towards him by some of the needle masters, but the young man was unconcerned about that. It was, he reasoned, a tribute to his business acumen that they should be so jealous of his success.

Another happening that had given him great satisfaction had occurred only days before as well. Abel Morral, of Green Lane, one of the most acute and respected needle masters in the district, had enquired in strict confidence whether he, Robert Stafford, would be prepared to contract for Abel Morral's own pointing operation, and the older man had strongly hinted that there were several other needle masters who were thinking along the same lines.

The idea held a strong appeal for the young man, as a source of potentially immense profits. He could well envisage a situation where he would do the pointing for the entire district. Of course, he realized that such a monopoly could not endure for long. The other masters would strain every nerve to find a way of making their own pointing shops safe, so that they in turn could once again employ their own pointers at lower rates. But at this moment Robert Stafford held the whip hand. It would cost him little to expand his pointing operation. A few more grindstones and saddles, extra shafts, belting and cogs, and of course a few more pointer women...

A smile of pure satisfaction curved his

lips as he stood now in the doorway of his pointing shop and watched the women bending low over the whirling, screeching stones, showers of white-hot sparks jetting up before their muzzled, rag-swathed faces as deftly they fanned the needle points backwards and forwards, backwards and forwards.

'By God, Robert, you are truly a genius,' the young man congratulated himself facetiously. 'And such a simple idea, as well... But then, are not all ideas of genius simple? The trick being, merely to think of them in the first place.'

His eyes came to rest on Tildy Crawford. Even here amid the noise and dirt of the shop, her nose and mouth covered by muzzle and rags, her hair hidden by the turbanned kerchief she wore over it, the girl emanated a graceful sensuality which pleased the aesthetic sense of the man watching her.

'What a beauty she would be, dressed in fine clothes and set in surroundings more suited to feminine charms than this stinking workshop,' he mused idly as he stared at her.

As if she sensed and was disturbed by his stare she turned her head and looked directly at him. As her luminous dark eyes met his Robert Stafford experienced an almost physical shock in full recognition of her beauty.

'God Dammee! But she truly is lovely,' he acknowledged, and instinctively raised his hand in greeting and smiled at her. She nodded her head gravely, before turning once more to her work. The young man's emotions became a confused jumble; to his own dismay he found himself wondering if he had developed an infatuation for Tildy Crawford.

'I must be suffering a fit of temporary insanity.' He attempted to treat the disturbing notion of infatuation as a joke, and moved away from the door and back into the lean-to workshop. 'I love and honour Hetty,' he told himself. 'How could a factory wench mean anything more to me than as a potential trollop to sport with on occasion?'

Yet somehow his inner protestations lacked conviction, and again he wondered why it was that Tildy Crawford should so suddenly have had this disturbing effect on him. 'A momentary fancy, that is all it can be. It will pass as quickly as it has come.'

He tried to dismiss all thought of Tildy from his mind, but at the same time he felt an ever-strengthening need to return to the pointing shop and to talk with the girl.

'Be damned to this nonsense!' Taking a firm grip on his errant fancies, he left the premises. Outside, the raw cold air helped him to regain control of his urges. Not wishing to risk another such disturbing interlude he mounted his horse and turned towards Redditch.

'I'll take a dram at Uncle Tommy's,' he decided, 'and mayhap read the newspaper there.'

To cater for his clientele, Tommy Fowkes went to the expense of having *Berrows Worcester Journal, Aris Birmingham Gazette,* and the *Worcester Herald* brought by the carrier's waggons from those cities, and with their midday broiled beefsteaks and chops the needle masters would peruse the newspapers and discuss their contents with their fellows.

Robert Stafford's anticipations of an hour or two's pleasant converse about world affairs were however rudely shattered on his arrival at the Fox and Goose. His uncle immediately beckoned him upstairs to the private parlour, and once there launched into the attack.

'What's all this bloody talk I'm hearing then, our Robert? What the hell has you bin getting up to?'

The young man blinked in puzzlement. 'What talk, Uncle?'

'Why, the talk that youm agoing to

contract for all the pointing work in this town.'

Robert Stafford made no immediate reply; instead he grinned with a wry amusement at how rumour could spread so easily in the district.

'Well?' his uncle demanded impatiently. 'What about it? Don't tell me youse forgot how to spake, our Robert.'

'No, I've not forgotten how to do that,' Stafford chuckled. 'But this is all news to me, uncle, and I'm wondering how such a tale got about in the first instance.' He went on to describe the brief talk with Abel Morral, and the hints given to him that other needle masters might be contemplating sub-contracting their pointing to him. 'But that is all that has passed between myself and any of the other masters, Uncle Tommy,' he finished. 'I did not think it even worth mentioning to you, unless it developed into a definite offer.'

'Well, my buck, it's all over the bloody town that within a few weeks youm agoing to be the contractor for all the pointing work hereabouts.'

'Is it indeed.' The young man smiled. 'I could only wish it were true.'

'Wipe that fucking smile off your face, nephew, or by the Christ, I'll bloody well wipe it off for you,' the fat man

325

shouted, his face purpling with sudden rage, and Robert Stafford stared at him in amazement.

'What is amiss with you, uncle?' he asked. 'Why are you so angry about a mere rumour, which if it should prove eventually true, could only be of immense benefit to us?'

'Benefit to us?' his uncle almost screeched. 'Benefit to us? How can it be a fucking benefit to anybody to have their premises burned down around their fucking yeds? Answer me that, 'ull you? Answer me that?'

Taken aback by the vehement fury of the older man, Robert Stafford could only lift his hands placatingly. 'Look uncle, would it not be better that you should explain fully to me what is amiss here? I swear I've heard nothing, and know nothing about this rumour.'

With a visible effort the fat man forced himself to speak in a quieter tone. 'There's bin trouble this morning at some o' the mills wi' the pointer lads. They've bin told by somebody or other, that shortly all the pointing shops be agoing to shut down, and all the work given to you and your bloody pointer women to do.'

'But surely their employers told them that there was no truth to the story?' In Robert Stafford's mind a disquieting notion was beginning to germinate and bud. A notion which exploded into full bloom as his uncle told him,

'No! None o' the bloody masters denied the story. Not one on 'um did...'

The younger man's agile brain grasped the full implications of the situation. 'This is the masters' way of stopping my gallop. They start this rumour, then refuse to tell the truth, and instead implant in the pointers the notion that they'll be losing their work because of me.'

'That's it exactly.' Tommy Fowkes scowled. 'And the bleeders 'ull be bound to cause trouble for you now.'

Despite his anxiety Robert Stafford was forced to smile at how quickly his uncle had begun to shift the burden entirely onto his, Robert Stafford's shoulders. 'Trouble for me alone, uncle?' he questioned mischievously. 'Not for me alone, surely? But trouble for us both. After all, we are partners in this venture, are we not?'

'Partners?' The fat man spluttered and waved his hands in the air. 'I was just trying to help you get started in business, that's all. Trying to do my best for a kinsman. 'Tis no fault of mine that the pointers should lose their work. It was you who brought that bloody muzzle to the town, and you who put women to the pointing, not me. I had naught to do wi' that, my buck. Naught to do wi' it.'

'All right, uncle, all right, calm yourself do.' The young man was half-amused, half-disgusted. 'I'll accept the charge. More importantly now, what is to be done about the situation? What do you think the pointers might do?'

'Might do?' Tommy Fowkes' jowls quivered violently. 'What might they not do, more like? Theym a pack o' wild beasts, my buck. Theym capable of any bloody mischief. Talk is theyse called for a mass meeting of all the pointers in the district.'

'When will that take place?' Stafford asked.

'Two days from now, at the White Hart up at Headless Cross.'

The young man nodded grimly. The White Hart inn was kept by another ex-pointer and local prize-fighter, Nail Styler. For the sake of his profits he would be pressing them to drink, and with that to further inflame their tempers, Robert Stafford dreaded to think what might happen. He sat silently for some moments, and his uncle fidgeted impatiently, then burst out, 'Well? What's you agoing to do about it? Youse brought this trouble down on our yeds, and it's up to you to get us out from under it.'

'I'll go to that meeting myself,' the

young man finally decided. 'And I'll tell the men that there is no truth in the rumours.'

'If you shows your face theer when theyse got a skinful o' drink, they'll bloody well murder you afore you gets a chance to open your mouth,' his uncle said gloomily.

Stafford frowned grimly. 'I don't think I've the choice to do aught else, Uncle Tommy, but to go and face them. And what's more, I'll see if I can persuade some of the other masters to come with me, and confirm what I say.'

'They wun't be likely to do that, nephew, because theym all on 'um set on seeing you bite the dust. You was too quick to poach, my buck. It caused a hell of a lot of bad feeling agen you. The buggers don't take kindly to Johnny-come-latelies taking their customers from 'um. I reckon you'd do better to go to the constable and let him goo up theer and warn the pointers off.'

His nephew shook his head. 'No, Uncle, they'd pay no heed to Joe Cashmore, in fact it would probably act on them like red rags to bulls. But to think on, for a moment. Mayhap we are allowing ourselves to become unduly perturbed. After all, the lads are only meeting together to discuss what is merely a rumour. If I go and explain to them how that rumour developed, and why it was put about in the first place, then surely to God they'll see reason, and we'll have no trouble from them.'

'I hopes so,' his uncle breathed fervently. 'I truly hopes so. But remember, nephew, whatever else you might say, don't you even whisper that I'm your partner in this matter. It might mean this place getting smashed up, and at the very least it 'ud be the ruination of my trade here.'

Stafford could appreciate how his uncle was feeling, even though he felt a sense of contempt for what he saw as the man's cowardice. So he reassured him, 'Do not worry, uncle. I'll deal with this matter by myself. Your name will not even be mentioned...'

CHAPTER 28

The first trouble came even sooner than Robert Stafford expected. He rode to the workshop early next morning to find that only a handful of his workforce were present.

'What is happening here, Mrs Pinfield?' The forewoman followed him through the almost deserted workshop and into the pointing shop. Only two of the grindstones' saddles were occupied, one by Janey White, the other by Tildy Crawford.

'The rest of 'um be feared to come to work, Master Stafford.' Amanda Pinfield's face was grey and haggard and one of her eyes was bruised and closed by swollen flesh.

Knowing what the answer would be, Robert Stafford was still constrained to ask, 'Is it the pointer lads' doings?'

'Yes, Master. I had a row meself wi' Pinfield about it, last night.'

The young man glanced sympathetically at her damaged eye. 'Yes, so I guessed, Mrs Pinfield. Do you know any details about what has happened?'

The woman seemed near to tears. 'I should think the same as happened to me, master. Them whose menfolk be pointers arn't bin let to come, and the others has most probably bin warned off.'

'But you are here in the workshop, Mrs Pinfield. Do you intend to work?'

Her toil-scarred hands lifted her apron and wrung and twisted it as though squeezing out water. 'I'm only here in the shop to tell you what's happened. I'll not be doing any more tasks. In fact, I'll not be working for you any more from now on, Master Stafford. Pinfield's forbid me.'

'Is he at home now?' Robert Stafford asked, and the woman nodded.

'Then I'll have a word with him myself.'
Without waiting for her reaction he went
through to the hallway and from the foot of
the staircase called, 'Master Pinfield, can I
have a word with you?'

The man came to the head of the stairs
and stood sullen and silent.

'I've no wish to shout my business for
the world to hear, Master Pinfield. Can I
come up?'

The man nodded assent, then turned
and went into one of the rooms leaving
Stafford to join him.

Inside the room the young man came
straight to the point. 'Now what is amiss,
Master Pinfield? Why do you forbid your
wife to work for me? I pay her a fair wage,
do I not?'

'That's as maybe.' The pointer glowered.
'But at the same time youm taking the
fucking bread out o' my mouth, arn't you.'
The stench of stale drink and tobacco from
his debauch of the previous night hung
about him like a miasma.

'Listen to me a moment,' Stafford tried
to reason with the man. 'These rumours
that I'm to take all the pointing work in
the town are only rumours. They have no
foundation. They have been put about only
to damage me, I swear to you that there is
no truth in them.'

Pinfield's yellow teeth showed as his lips

drew back in a snarling grimace. 'True or false, it don't matter a fuck now, master. The point is, that the lads chooses to believe 'um, and whatever I might think about what youm atelling me now, don't signify. If I lets my missus go on working as your forewoman, then I stands a bloody good chance of having this place burned down over me yed. Some of the lads are roiled up enough to do just that, master. It's only because I'm a pointer meself, that's kept it from happening already.'

'But the rumours are false!' Stafford re-stated emphatically.

'False or not, the lads chooses to believe 'um,' the pointer re-stated doggedly.

'What must I do to prove to them the truth of what I am saying?' Stafford questioned with exasperation in his voice.

'What you must do, master, to my mind at any rate, is to get rid o' them fucking muzzles and the women whom wearing 'um. And if you wants pointing doing, then pay the proper rates to the proper pointer lads.'

In Robert Stafford's mind's eye he saw again the face of Will Wall, and heard the man telling him, 'Once the work is made safe, then every Tom, Dick and Harry 'ull be ready to do it, and that 'ud mean the wages dropping, and us pointer lads 'ull never stand by and let that happen.'

With the memory came the conviction that nothing he could say would make any difference. The pointers had thrown down the gauntlet, challenging him to either pick it up, or abandon his plans. He drew a deep breath, and said quietly, 'I cannot do that. My business depends on the use of the magnetic muzzles.'

'Then be it on your own yed, master,' Pinfield warned him, and nodded towards the door. 'And now I'll thank you to let me be.'

'Very well.' Stafford turned to go; the pointer followed him out to the stairhead and bawled down, 'Manda? Gerrup here. And look fucking sharp about it if you knows what's good for you.'

With downcast eyes the forewoman brushed past Stafford and went up to join her husband.

Back in the pointing shop the young man tapped Tildy and Janey White on their shoulders and signed for them to follow him outside the house.

The girls unlaced their cumbersome muzzles as they walked, glad to rid themselves of the discomfort for even a short space of time. Outside the snow crunched beneath their clogs and the wind was chill on their faces.

Janey White shivered and whispered to Tildy, 'I hope he wun't keep us long here.

I'm bleedin' froze already.'

Stafford heard her and smiled glumly. 'Don't worry, White, I'll not keep you here overlong. But I don't wish anyone to overhear our talk. Firstly, I want to ask you if any threats have been made against you if you should continue with the pointing?'

Both girls shook their heads, and as he looked at them, Robert Stafford again felt the impact upon his emotions of Tildy Crawford's beauty. 'By God! But the wench works a powerful effect on me,' he thought, and could not help but compare her with Hetty Milward, to the latter's detraction. 'Damn your eyes, Stafford?' he remonstrated with himself. 'Keep your mind on business, will you. Haven't you troubles enough to contend with, without adding females to them?' Aloud he said, 'I'll speak plainly to you both. I think it highly possible that you might well be in danger of insult, perhaps even physical assault from the pointers if you should continue at this work. God knows, I am grateful that you have continued, but my conscience will not allow me to attempt to persuade you with false assurances to carry on with the pointing, without making it fully plain to you both what the situation is at this moment.'

He paused, watching for their reaction

335

to his blunt honesty. It was Tildy who spoke out.

'What exactly is the situation, Master Stafford? Naturally we've heard some wild talk, but neither of us are clear in our minds as to what is really happening.'

As truthfully as he could the young man explained about the pointers' attitudes concerning them and the muzzles. 'You must understand that I really do not know myself what they intend doing now. But, knowing them as I do, I can only fear that violence will ensue. I cannot guarantee to be able to protect either of you from the results of that violence, should it occur, so whether you continue here or not must be your own decision. I shall think no less of you if that decision is to stop pointing.'

Again he paused, and saw the doubts clouding their faces.

'Ah well,' he tried to console himself. 'At least I have been a gentleman, and have told them the complete truth.'

He had practically resigned himself to the fact of losing these last two pointer women also, and was trying to come to terms with defeat, when Tildy again spoke out.

'Master Stafford, I'll not lie and tell you that I'm not afeared of what the pointers might do to me. I am frightened. But there are personal reasons which force me to earn as much money as I can at this time. So my answer is this, if you are prepared to pay me, then I am prepared to carry on with the pointing.'

Janey White was at this time the sole wage-earner in her home. Her husband was ill and her children too young to work. She also needed every penny she could earn. 'I'm with Tildy in this, master,' she said determinedly. 'While you pays, I'll work.'

Admiration for the courage of these two women flooded through Robert Stafford. 'So be it,' he told them simply.

Greatly troubled as he was, Robert Stafford decided to go down to the Fountain Mill and have a word with Henry Milward. At the mill however it was not the needle master who came to the office to speak with him, but Millicent Milward.

'Mister Milward's away today,' she informed. 'But if youse come about the troubles youm having, then I can give you the same answer you'd get from my husband.'

The young man smiled wryly. 'I think I can hazard a guess as to what that answer will be, ma'am. It will be that I must make my own way through these difficulties, will it not?'

'Youse got it right fust go, Robert.' The woman's attitude was not hostile, but he

337

could discern no hint of sympathy in her for his predicament. 'And that's the answer that you'll get from every other needle master in this town, my lad.'

'I see,' he answered quietly, and then remarked, 'Do you know the aspect of this affair which gives me greatest cause for astonishment, ma'am? It is the fact that I am offering a way of pointing which is designed to prevent sufferings and to save lives, and the very people whom it would benefit the most are the ones who are most strongly opposed to it. I proffer to them a blessing, and they return me only curses.'

'Don't prate like a bloody parson, my bucko,' Millicent Milward jeered. 'You brought in them muzzles to try and steal a march on us established needlemakers. You did it for your own benefit, not to bring blessings on the working folk in this town. Look at me, boy.' She indicated her shabby working dress, and her oily filthy hands. 'Youm not talking to some addle-pated, soft-living gentry-'ooman now. My Dad was one of the fust dry-grinding pointers in this town, and me brothers all died o' the rot, 'cepting for the youngest, and he was killed when his grindstone blew up. They all knew the price they'd have to pay, and the lads whom doing it now knows the same bloody thing. They knows the wages they wants from the masters, and us masters knows we'll have to give 'um them wages if we wants the pointing doing.

'Everybody is well satisfied with the way things am. Mayhap there 'ull come a day when the pointers 'ull put a long life afore a full pocket, but that day arn't dawned as yet, and to my mind it'll be a bloody long while afore it does, and anybody who thinks any different is naught but a bloody fool.'

The young man listened without comment, forcing himself to face the unpalatable fact that at the moment nothing would change the present system. He also forced himself to accept the truth inherent in the woman's jeers about his own motivation for introducing the muzzles. Primarily he had done so for his own ends, and although he might possess some philanthropic instincts, those instincts had in all truth been very secondary to his main purpose.

'At least now, I can truly say that I have learned something about myself,' he thought ruefully. 'Perhaps that knowledge can be put to good account at some time in the future. Mayhap even help me to become a better man.'

'What are your intentions now, Robert?' Millicent Milward's voice had lost its jeering edge, and she appeared to be genuinely concerned. 'Because I reckon that you'll have to abandon this business, wun't you.'

After a while he shrugged. 'I really cannot say what my intentions are at this moment, ma'am.'

'You'll not lose much anyway, Robert. So that's some comfort for you. Mayhap your pride's bin dented a bit, but that's all to the good at your age. Young 'uns tends to get a bit too much above themselves when all goes their way too easily. What you must do now is to put this behind you and give some careful thought to your future prospects. I knows that Mr Milward 'ud like to see you work for us at the Fountain here, if and when you and our Hetty should get wed.'

Stafford sighed heavily. 'I must settle my affairs first, ma'am, before I can give thought to my future. I own that what concerns me most is what is to happen to those who at present are dependent upon me for their employment.'

The woman sighed also. 'It's always a bad business when a workplace closes, Robert, but I shouldn't worry your yed too much about the people. The trade is picking up lately, so I should reckon that most on 'um 'ull find other work afore too long.'

'Let us hope so,' Stafford said, and took his leave.

CHAPTER 29

Before dawn next day Robert Stafford was at Pinfield's house. He entered the lean-to and went through to the pointing shop. After some time he came back into the lean-to carrying a weighty sack bag which he tossed into a corner.

When Tildy arrived, Janey White, one other woman and two small boys were seated in the lean-to. They comprised the sole workforce. Robert Stafford was staring grimly out of the end window at the wintry landscape. No fire had been lit and the shop was cold and damp, the breaths of the small gathering pluming visibly from their mouths. Even before Robert Stafford spoke Tildy sensed what he was going to say, and her spirits sank.

As if he had read her mind, Robert Stafford nodded glumly at her. 'Yes Tildy, it is all over for you with the pointing. I'm sorry for it, but I have thought much about it overnight and there really is no other choice open to me, than to close this venture down. I am going to pay each one of you here a full week's wages, and I will speak on your behalf with Mr Milward of the Fountain Mill should you wish to seek work there.'

Pulling a small bag from his coat pocket Stafford counted out coins into the hands of the small boys and the woman. When they had left he gave Janey White and Tildy a gold sovereign each.

'It is small reward for your bravery in being prepared to carry on with the pointing,' he told them with genuine regret. 'And I meant what I said about speaking on your behalf with Mr Milward. I am sure he will be able to find work for you at the Fountain.' He essayed a touch of humour. 'Though not as pointers, I'm afraid.'

Tildy was too sick at heart to return his smile. Once again life had dealt her a heavy blow. Without the pointing work how could she hope to earn enough money to pay for the attorney or for Esther Smith's potion?

She would have left with Janey White, but the young man stopped her from doing so.

'Hold hard, for a moment, Tildy, I wish to speak with you.' Once alone with her he said with apparent concern, 'Tildy, I know that you face many difficulties at this time. Is there any way in which I can help you with them?'

Normally Tildy's pride and caution would have prevented her from accepting an offer of this type. She knew from past experience that in return for their help men exacted a heavy price from women under obligation to them. Now, however, her desperation impelled her to answer. 'Indeed, Master Stafford, I am in sore need of help. I need money urgently, perhaps as much as ten guineas, to enable me to recover my child. Could you loan me such a sum?'

'It's a deal of money,' he observed. At her instant recoil at a possible rebuff, he added hastily, 'But I think it possible that I could help you with it. Why exactly do you require such a large amount?'

Tildy explained about the necessity to pay the attorney, but made no mention of Esther Smith.

When she had again fallen silent, Robert Stafford regarded her speculatively, and found himself becoming sexually aroused at the sight of her full breasts pushing against the thin material of her bodice. Driven by an urge he could not control, he asked her. 'And what would you give me in return for my help, Tildy? What could I expect from you in token of your gratitude? A few kisses perhaps? Or maybe something more?'

Contempt filled the luminous eyes, and the young man felt instantly ashamed. 'Please forget I said that,' he stammered

343

with embarrassment. 'It was unworthy of a gentleman, and a mean action on my own part.'

Tildy shrugged, and said coldly, 'I'll bid you good day, Master Stafford.'

'No! Wait! Don't go. I am truly sorry for what I said, Tildy. Please believe me.'

Tildy accepted that he was sincere in his protestations, and told him, 'No matter, Master Stafford. I took offence because I had thought you to be different from most other men, and when you said that, I felt angered as much at my own gullibility as at the insult you offered me.'

Stafford now felt driven to prove that he was not the same as the other men she referred to, and that he was not seeking to take advantage of her in any fashion. 'Hear me out, Tildy,' he asked quietly. 'Only stay and hear me out, I pray you.'

'Very well, master,' she agreed evenly. 'I'll hear you out, but let me tell you plainly, that I'm not prepared to act the whore for any favours. I would only ever consider that should all other hopes forsake me.'

'I will be plain and open with you in return, Tildy,' he answered her gravely. 'I will fully admit that I find you very beautiful, and that I feel a strong desire for you, as a man naturally feels for a woman. But what I am going to propose to you now is quite divorced from any desire that I might feel for you. Please believe me when I say that.

'Now, to help you, I propose to make you a loan of ten guineas, for which you will sign a receipt, and for which you will sign an undertaking to repay as soon as you are able. The sole condition attaching to the loan is this...' He paused, and Tildy waited with heightened tension for what he might say next. 'The sole condition is this...that you look upon me as your friend, and that you believe me when I tell you that I am making this loan to you as a true friend. No more, no less, than that.' He grinned, and asked, 'Is that condition acceptable to you, my friend?'

Suddenly all Tildy's doubts as to his motives left her, and she relaxed her tense muscles as she smiled back at him.

'Indeed it is most acceptable to me, Master Stafford, and I thank you from my heart for your kindness. I will pay you back every penny of the money just as quick as I can.'

'That's settled then,' he told her. 'Be off with you now. I'll have the money delivered into your hands at your lodgings before nightfall. But first I have other matters to attend to.'

When he was alone the young man grinned ironically to himself. 'God dammee,

345

Stafford. What a philanthropist you are. And how righteous the doing of a good deed has made you feel. Who knows what rewards you may be vouchsafed in Heaven for such an act.' His mood sobered as his eyes encountered the sack lying where he had thrown it in the corner of the room, and he moved to pick it up.

The pointers had begun to gather at the White Hart for their meeting when Robert Stafford rode up to the inn and dismounted. He walked into the already crowded tap room and surveyed those present with hard eyes. With an equal hardness the pointers glared back. With a sudden movement Stafford up-ended the contents of the sack he carried onto the floor.

The magnetic muzzles tumbled into an haphazard pile, and the young man took a heavy headed hammer from the pile, and brought it smashing down in a rapid series of blows, crushing the muzzles. Then, as if satisfied, he straightened his back and pitched the hammer down onto the mangled remnants. He nodded to the watching men.

'There you are, my lads, I've saved you the trouble of doing that yourselves. And there's no need for you to go up to my workshop either. I've closed it, and shut shop. I'm no longer in any way of business. Good day to you.' He walked out of the room, leaving the pointers staring bemusedly at each other, and at the shapeless heap of metal and leather.

CHAPTER 30

Two days after Tildy had lost her pointing work a messenger sent by Millicent Milward came to the lodging house and spoke with Mother Readman. After hearing the message the old woman shouted for Tildy.

'Get your shawl, Tildy. Me and you are going to call on Slippy Dicky. He come back to town yesterday, and our Milly has had a word wi' him about you.'

The chambers of Richard Hyde Guard-ner, attorney at law, were almost directly opposite the town lock-up, and despite the grandiloquent title consisted merely of a small single room above Professor Parr's barber shop. The access to the room was an outside wooden flight of steps at the rear of the building. Mother Readman looked at the steep pitch of the rail-less steps and shook her head.

'I arn't able to manage them, Tildy.

You'll ha' to goo up them by yourself.'

Nervous at the prospect of consulting a professional gentleman by herself, Tildy hesitated, but the older woman scowled and pointed, and obediently Tildy mounted and knocked on the warped, paint-peeling door.

'Come!' a voice shouted from inside, and she pushed the door open to be met with a cloud of acrid smoke which caused her to cough and her eyes to smart and water.

'Come in, damn you, and shut the door. Are you trying to kill me with the cold?' The testy voice came from the tall man busily feeding ribbon-tied rolls of parchment documents onto the smoking fire in the grate. The man straightened and turned towards Tildy. He was much younger-looking than she had expected, and colourful in his wide-skirted sky-blue riding coat and baggy Cossack trousers, bright yellow waistcoat and multi-spotted billowing cravat. His hair was a wild unruly greying cloud around his smooth pink face and bulging blue eyes.

'Don't tell me! Don't tell me! Don't you dare tell me!' He pointed an ink-stained forefinger into Tildy's astonished face and stepped towards her, bending so that his eyes were on a level with her own. 'Don't breathe a word, young woman, as you

348

value your life, don't breathe a solitary word,' he commanded warningly, then circled her, moving sideways like a crab so that he faced her at all times. Back in front of her once more, he yet again repeated, 'Don't tell me. Don't utter a single word!'

He took a pace backwards, straightened to his full height, then recited rapidly: 'Matilda Crawford, needle worker, presently residing at Mrs Readman's lodging house in Silver Square. Husband, Thomas Crawford, at present residing in Peg Green's beer shop in the Clarke's Yard. No known employment. Subject of dispute between them, the custody of David Crawford, their infant son.'

Tildy could only stare in bemused wonderment as the tall man recited these facts. 'My fee is six guineas, young woman, payable in advance.'

Tildy wordlessly handed him the coins. He wrapped them in a small screw of paper and carelessly tossed the small packet onto a table strewn with books and rolls of parchment, and then told her, 'You will go directly from here and find the constable, Joseph Cashmore. You will lay a complaint against your husband, stating that in the month of March 1821, he ran away leaving you and your child chargeable to the parish authorities. The said charges although initially falling upon the overseers to the poor of the parish of Bromsgrove, were eventually transposed upon the overseers to the poor of the parish of Tardebigge, this being your place of settlement by birth, and the place of settlement by birth of your child, the said David Crawford.

'By his actions your husband has committed a criminal offence under Statute Seventeen, George Second, Section Four of the Vagrancy Acts.

'The overseers to the poor of the parish of Tardebigge will act as the plaintiffs in this matter, and I shall represent them in the action, which will be heard by the magistrates here, and not at Sessions, since it is your husband's first offence of this nature.

'You may be called upon to testify as witness for the plaintiffs.'

For the first time since she had entered the room, Tildy had a chance to speak. 'And what will happen after the case has been heard, sir?'

'Why then the magistrates will give their ruling on the case, young woman. Now please go. I have many pressing matters to attend on, and can spare you no more of my time at present.' When she would have spoken again, he pointed his forefinger into her face. 'That is all, young woman. Now

350

will you kindly leave my chambers.'

Realizing the futility of remaining, Tildy left.

At the foot of the stairs Tildy related what the attorney had instructed her to do, and Mother Readman watched the girl intently while she spoke.

'Youm still a mite troubled by this, arn't you Tildy?' she asked when Tildy had finished.

The girl nodded. 'Yes, I am. Even after all he has done against me, yet Tom Crawford is still my child's father, and somehow now the time to act has come, I am still reluctant to put the law on him. I know I am stupid to feel such reluctance, and I cannot understand myself why I feel so, but yet I can't help it.'

Mother Readman nodded sympathetically, and thought hard for a few minutes, then said, 'I'll tell you what we'll do, Tildy. Me and you 'ull go to Peg Green's right now, and we'll give the bugger one last chance to hand your babby back to you. We'll give him a warning that if he refuses it'll be the worse for him. But we wun't tell him that we'em laying the law agen him. The bastard might give leg-bail if we does that, and to spite you he'll be bound to carry the babby wi' him if he does a runner.'

Tildy nodded agreement, and experienced a definite sense of relief. 'Yes, let's do that. It makes me feel easier in my mind to give Tom Crawford this last chance.'

Crawford was half-drunk when the two women came to the door of the beer shop. He swore vilely when he saw them and came to confront them at the entrance. Mother Readman signalled Tildy to remain silent and to stay in her rear, then faced Crawford across the doorway. 'Just shut your bloody rattle for a minute, Cully, and hark to me.'

Aware of how formidable an opponent she could prove, Crawford snarled, 'If youse got summat to say, then say it quick and fuck off from here, and take that bleedin' slut of a wife o' mine wi' you.'

'I'll fuck off all right, don't you worry. I've no liking for this bloody hole, or the rats who dwell in it. But before I go I wants to ask you one last time to give Tildy her babby back.'

'Piss off!' Crawford swore.

'You'll bring trouble on your yed if you don't give us that babby back now,' warned Mother Readman.

The man laughed raucously, then glanced spitefully at Tildy and shouted back over his shoulder, 'Peg, bring that fuckin' kid down here, 'ull you.'

Tildy pushed forward, unable to bear

to remain where she could not see into the room. But with a massive strength Mother Readman encircled the girl's arms and body with her own meaty arms, and held her powerless to move.

In the gloomy interior Peg Green came into view holding little Davy in her arms.

Tildy vented a moan of distress when she saw the pathetic spectacle her child now presented. Thin, filthy, ragged, he lolled in the woman's grip so drugged with Syrup of Poppies that he was too dazed to know what was happening to him.

'Theer now, wife,' Crawford grinned wolfishly at Tildy. 'You can see the good care I'm taking of the little fucker, can't you. Now piss off!'

As he slammed the door in their faces, Tildy with a sudden heave broke free and launched herself at the rough planking.

'Give me my baby! I want my baby, give him back to me! Let me go, for pity's sake let me go!' she shouted at Mother Readman, but the older woman only dragged her bodily down the alley and back into the main roadway once more.

Abruptly Tildy ceased struggling, and Mother Readman whispered hoarsely into her ear, 'If I lets you go now, what 'ull you do, Tildy?'

The young woman's face was deathly pale and drawn with anguish, but a hard determination had entered her eyes. 'If you let me go, then I'll go straight to Joe Cashmore and lay complaint against Tom Crawford,' she said harshly. 'I swear I'll bring the law down on him now, and do it gladly.'

Mother Readman cackled with satisfaction, and released her grip.

To Tildy's surprise Joseph Cashmore also appeared to know the purpose of her errand before she even began to tell him what she had come to him for.

'All right, my wench. Mrs Milward's had words wi' me. Her husband's the senior overseer to the poor this year in the parish, so he'll be the one acting for the parish against Tom Crawford. All I wants from you is your signed deposition that your husband run off and left you and your babby wi'out means of support, and so you became chargeable to the parish!'

'Do you not need me to testify to the magistrates?' Tildy asked puzzledly.

The man's taciturn features softened into a rare smile. 'No, my wench. It wun't be necessary in this case. Theer's a lot o' sympathy for you in this town among certain people. And Mrs Milward is taking a great interest in your case. Her's a powerful friend to have, girl, and her's got the ear of Lady Aston.' The man winked broadly. 'No needs for me to say more, is there, girl. Be off wi' you now. Wait in your lodgings until you hears from me agen.' He suddenly remembered something and chuckled wryly. 'I was forgetting, you'll needs gi' me your deposition fust. Can you write?'

Tildy nodded. 'Yes, I can write.'

'Good, because that 'ull save me struggling to scribe it for you. Here's pen, ink and paper...'

Outside once more, Tildy excitedly related to Mother Readman what the constable had told her, and the older woman laughed with satisfaction.

'Theer now, didn't I tell you that our Milly was one o' the best. It'll be Reverend the Lord Aston who'll be hearing the case, you'll see. Our Milly is very thick wi' his missus, and his missus rules him wi' a rod of iron. You'll get your kid back now for sure, Tildy.'

Tildy's heart was pounding so that she could hardly breathe. 'I must go and thank Mrs Milward,' she burst out, but Mother Readman frowned at this.

'You'll do no such thing, my wench, at least not yet awhile. What's bin done for you by our Milly has to stay hidden. Otherwise folks 'ull start saying that the gentry uses the law to suit themselves.'

'But everyone knows that to be a fact already,' Tildy pointed out, and the old woman chuckled and winked slyly.

'Ahr, that may be so, but nobody is supposed to admit to knowing that, am they, girl. It's what you might call an open secret. So, my duck, you'll keep right away from our Milly until that husband o' yourn 'as bin put wheer he belongs. And then you can go and thank her. All right?'

Reluctantly, Tildy agreed.

At three o'clock in the afternoon of the following day, Joseph Cashmore came into the kitchen of the lodging house. In his arms he carried little Davy. The child was sleeping, drugged with Syrup of Poppies. As Tildy tenderly enfolded her baby in her arms, Cashmore told her, 'Doctor Pratt had a look at the babby. He says he's all right, and to let him sleep quiet until the cordial passes through him.'

Tildy could not hold back tears of relief and joy, and brokenly thanked the constable over and over again until he waved her to silence.

'Wheer's Tom Crawford? What did he get?' Mother Readman wanted to know.

'He's in the lock-up. Lord Aston heard the case this morning. He's give Crawford a month at hard labour in the Worcester House o' Correction, and a public whipping.'

'A whipping?' Tildy looked anxious.

356

'Don't worry, girl, I wun't kill the bugger,' Cashmore assured her. 'He's to be whipped at the cart tail through the town tomorrow, and then I'll take him on to Worcester. You just worry about that kid, and pay no mind to Tom Crawford.'

After the constable had gone, Tildy tenderly stripped and bathed her comatose child, and wept further tears as she saw the bruises on his small body, and the red swellings of vermin bites. 'Tom Crawford deserves everything he gets,' she told herself angrily. 'Everything!'

CHAPTER 31

The crowd outside the lock-up was continually augmented by newcomers until it seemed that half the population of the district was gathered there. The mood was good-humoured and as the drink circulated the horseplay and badinage intensified so that it resembled a fair day. But underlying the merriment was the ancient atavistic lust to see pain inflicted and blood shed.

Together with Mother Readman, Tildy stood in the crowd, shivering with cold and the dread of what she was to witness. Now that her time of vengeance had come, she found that it was not the desire to see her husband suffer for what he had done against her and her child that was paramount in her mind. Her need to be present here was to demonstrate to herself and to the world, that she believed in the justice of the punishment to be inflicted on a man she truly regarded as evil.

With a swift movement she slipped the shawl back from her head onto her shoulders, so that her features were in clear view. 'Let those who would condemn me for informing against my husband see now that I am not ashamed or feared of seeing justice done to him,' she thought defiantly.

The crowd was a cross-section of the town, workmen, shopkeepers, farmers, pointers, housewives, young girls, children, and around the outskirts young bloods on horseback and fur-cloaked gentry women standing on their carriage seats for a better view, their well-clad menfolk standing beside them with an equal avid eagerness.

'The cart's acoming. The cart's acoming.' The news spread quickly through the crowd, and as the blue-smocked butcher Vincent drove towards the lock-up the close-packed heads swirled and eddied to make a path for his horse and cart, and applauded wildly as if he were a showman come to entertain them.

Tildy's breath caught in her throat as she saw the animal. Its colour was grey: a vivid memory of Esther Smith's words came to her. The grey horse! The grey horse that would bring her troubles to an end.

The cart lurched to a standstill outside the tall arched doorway of the lock-up, the doors creaked open and Joseph Cashmore, wearing a caped greatcoat, tricorn hat, and carrying his crowned long-staff of office, came out from the dark-shadowed interior, with Tom Crawford, flanked by two assistant constables, following close behind. Crawford was wearing only a dirty shirt and breeches, his calves and feet bare. Grey-faced, he was shivering visibly, his throat and jaws heavily stubbled, his black hair tousled and greasy. His eyes flickered wildly across the crowd, which emitted a curious baying howl like hounds scenting their prey.

With the pieces of rope they carried the assistant constables tied Crawford's wrists and arms to the high tail-board of the cart, stretching the limbs wide so that he resembled a human cross; all the time his terrified eyes flickered wildly across the faces crowding about him. Dr Pratt came from the lock-up together with the parson, John Clayton, both men funereal in black coats and trousers, and tall black hats perched upon their white tie-wigs.

From the floor of the cart Butcher Vincent lifted a wooden bucket, its contents giving off wisps of steam, and an excited murmur of recognition came from the crowd.

'Fresh brine! Fresh brine to treat the bugger's back arter it's done. That'll make him burn! That'll make the bastard cry out!'

The overseers to the poor were the next to file from the lock-up and arrange themselves in a loose rank at the side of the cart. The senior overseer, Henry Milward, proffered a long-handled, thick-thonged whip to Joseph Cashmore. The constable took the whip and cracked it loudly several times. Tom Crawford blanched and flinched and trembled violently as each sharp crack split the air, and the crowd laughed gleefully as a wag shouted, 'Don't you dare faint yet, Tom Crawford, the ball ain't even started.'

The burly constable removed his greatcoat and hat, handing the articles to one of his assistants, and stood in his shirtsleeves and waistcoat. Slowly and carefully he rolled up his right sleeve to display his thick-muscled forearm, and again cracked the whip. He looked expectantly towards John Clayton who, pale and grim looking, signalled to Butcher Vincent to take the horse's head, then nodded to the constable.

Cashmore stepped up to Tom Crawford, and with a single brutal heave ripped the shirt from the prisoner's back. Crawford cried out, and again the crowd roared with laughter as the wag shouted, 'Don't scrawk yet, you windy bleeder, save some breath for the first Quadrille.'

Cashmore stepped sideways, his brawny right arm went high in the air and then slashed downwards. The leather thong bit deep across Crawford's naked shoulders and his body jerked grotesquely, his head went back, and he screamed. A long, long scream that seemed to go echoing through all the streets of Redditch. The old grey horse started, shivered and sweat steamed on its hide. As it tried to rear, it took the combined strengths of three men to hold its head down and prevent it bolting. Again the whip slashed down, now making blood spray from the pallid, grimy flesh. The cart lurched forwards and Crawford's legs gave way so that his feet dragged behind through the muddy slush, and Cashmore followed, his arm rising and falling. Each time it fell screams bubbled from Crawford's slack, wet mouth, and the front of his breeches stained and steamed as he staled himself. Some among the crowd turned away from the spectacle, fingers pressing their ears to shut out the hideous shrieks, but more moved onwards with the cart, shouting

361

hysterically, laughing, jeering, cat-calling. Tildy tasted bitter bile in her mouth, and her senses swam sickeningly, but she forced herself to stumble after the cart also.

'It's because of me he is suffering like this,' she reiterated over and over again in her mind. 'I must have the courage to witness what I have brought down upon him...'

Slowly the cart moved on, bumping and lurching over the rutted road. By the time the crossroads of the Chapel Green had been reached, Crawford's back was a scarlet mess of criss-crossed bleeding weals and the rear of his breeches was saturated by the blood which had run down and soaked in. The cart turned to travel along the main street towards the Front Hill. Joseph Cashmore was panting now from his exertions and his flushed face was covered with the sheen of sweat, but still his arm rose and fell with a terrible iron strength.

Tom Crawford's screams were cut short as he fainted. Dr Pratt shouted the cart to halt, and went forward to examine the limp hanging body, feeling for the heartbeat, checking the eyes and breathing.

'Fetch a pail of water and sluice him down,' the medical man ordered. 'When he comes round, you may continue.'

Willing hands brought buckets slopping

362

over with filthy stinking liquid which was hurled over the slumped figure until, coughing and spluttering, Tom Crawford was roused to consciousness.

Tildy's white teeth bit on her lips until the blood came. Her hands shook so badly that she was forced to press them hard into her heaving breasts to still their motion.

'No more!' she jerked out. 'Please God, let them stop now.'

Clayton signalled to the butcher, the cart jerked into motion once again, and once again Cashmore's arm raised and came slashing down, tearing a high-pitched shriek from Tom Crawford's ravaged throat.

'No! No more! No more!' Tildy ran forward and clutched desperately at the constable's raised arm. He stared down at her, shocked by her intervention, then looked across at John Clayton for guidance, as Tildy also turned her head towards the clergyman, and beseeched, 'Parson Clayton, for the love of God, stop them. I beg you to stop them. Stop it now!'

'But this is his lawful punishment, Crawford.' The clergyman's ugly features were mystified.

'He's been punished enough already,' Tildy stated vehemently. 'To continue now is only to torture him.'

'But it was you who laid the complaint against him?' John Clayton was struggling to comprehend her present action. 'It is because of you that he is being whipped.'

'I know I laid the complaint,' Tildy answered, and her voice sounded unnaturally loud and shrill in the sudden hush which had fallen upon the crowd. 'And I would do the same again. But I only wanted a just punishment to be given out to him. I did not want him beaten nigh to death like this.'

At this moment Tom Crawford groaned loudly, and fell limp again. Dr Pratt came forwards, pushing Tildy and the constable aside. After a brief examination he brutally cuffed the limply hanging man on the side of his head.

'You damned coward! You're trying to gull me.' The doctor turned to the clergyman and overseers. 'This damn white-livered hound is shamming,' he grated out. 'Lay on again, man, and lay on hard,' he told the constable.

'No!' Tildy thrust herself between the constable and Tom Crawford. 'Leave him be now, he's been punished enough.'

'Let her take his place then, it's obvious her wants to join the bloody dance as well,' the wag in the crowd shouted, and the mass erupted with cheers and clappings.

'Get hold of her,' Cashmore growled at his assistants, but before they could move,

Mother Readman came battering through the crowd.

'You leave her be,' she shouted warningly, as she came. 'I'll take her out on it.' Gently she touched Tildy's cheek. 'Come on out of it, my duck,' she said softly. 'There's naught you can do to stop what's happening here. And this bastard is only getting what he well deserves. It arn't worth you getting your own yed broke to try and save him from a bit more pain.'

Realizing the futility of further struggle, Tildy allowed the older woman to lead her away, and began to weep softly as behind them, with the crowd roaring approbation, the cart moved and Cashmore's whip cracked sharp and loud...

While the two women walked side by side towards the Silver Square, Mother Readman urged, 'It's finished now, Tildy. It's past you and over and done with. You must think only of caring for your babby and making your way in the world now. Try and forget what's gone.'

'But what will happen when Tom Crawford comes out of prison?' Tildy wondered aloud.

'Well, he's got a full month in the Worcester house o' Correction to do furst, arn't he. And then there's talk that the Bow Street Runners be arter him for some devilment he got up to in London. No...'

Mother Readman shook her massive head. 'I don't think he'll show his face here agen. I reckon wese sin the last of the bugger in this town.'

'I pray it may be so,' Tildy wished fervently.

The older woman grinned at her. 'You just think on one thing, Tildy, and that's that your babby is waiting for you at home.'

Tildy's mood suddenly altered dramatically, and her spirits soared. She laughed in joyous happiness. 'So he is, Mother Readman. So he is. My child is waiting for me to come home...'

This Large Print Book for the Partially sighted, who cannot read normal print, is published under the auspices of

THE ULVERSCROFT FOUNDATION